ALMOST
Submerged
IN SOMEONE

ALMOST
Submerged
IN SOMEONE

PREWI P. WILSON

PARTRIDGE
A Penguin Random House Company

ISBN: Hardcover   978-1-4828-3948-7
             Softcover   978-1-4828-3949-4
             eBook   978-1-4828-3947-0

To order additional copies of this book, contact
Partridge India
000 800 10062 62
orders.india@partridgepublishing.com

www.partridgepublishing.com/india

CONTENTS

I dedicate this book to my brother Prathyash.

A love story of Roshen Samuel & Jessie Joseph.

ACKNOWLEDGEMENTS

Writing a book and publishing was not my intension, but just a dream. If my book has reached in your hands, apart from me, there are lot many helpers beside me who supported a lot, that helped to experience the light of a published Author. I would like to thank those who were really with me, throughout my book project.

Foremost, I would like to thank God Almighty for making me what I am; by giving me various experience that made me feel good, bad, happy, sad, disappointed, and much more emotions which I finally could understand what all can be involved in life. Especially I would love to thank him, for giving me such a wonderful people, who are my parents, relatives, and friends.

I specially thank my parents, for supporting me for this opportunity and my publisher, Partridge India for giving me this opportunity.

I am thankful for all my friends who was been a family to me, since we began to be together. They were with me, so close, that made me feel missed whenever we were not together. Some of them who are involved in this book project were Shika Varma, Alka Rajchandran, Silpa Nandhakumar, Sruthi & Smrithi N, Karthika D T, Ashmi R, Shravan Pradeep, Adhin Louie, Kishore Narayan,

Adharsh Sasi, Abhinand Jyothiprakash, Gowtham Byju, Vishal Venugopal & Praveen Lakshman. I would also thank all my cousin brothers and sisters for helping me a lot and a lot, especially, Nidhil Paul, Tutu Babu, Akhil & Nikhil John.

Along with, I thank Amrutha Prakash, Naveen Narayan, Arun Sir, Dev Anand, Ann Mariya Jose, Bert Soliot and my sincere thanks to all my English teachers who taught me to read and write, right from pre-school to college.

For every work, there would be some inspiration. So I want to thank few Authors; Chetan Bhagat, Durjoy Datta, Nikita Sing, Ravinder Singh, Preeti Shenoy, Manisha Gupta & T D Ramakrishnan for showing "this is the way to go".

Aside from all these, a special thanks to you, for holding my book and for being an important part of my first book in my life.

"Without readers launching a book is of no use."

ON THE RAIL

I was at the railway station with my father who accompanied me to Thrissur. The train arrived and we moved to the front, searching for the A/c compartment. Though we found it, the train had not stopped. As it was moving slowly, anyone could easily jump in through the open doors on it. But my father won't allow me to do so as he remains completely against of entering into any moving vehicle.

My father was a retired Navy Officer from Indian Navy. After retiring, he worked as a tutor in a Navy Tutorial Collage in Chennai, which is India's fourth largest city. He was been waxed us into his Navy strictness. So I would always take care of myself without missing any chance of getting away from home. It complemented me for becoming a regular student in my school, even attending special classes.

After the failure of my first engineering entrance examination, my father asked me to repeat the entrance exam by attending the "Crash Course" which is being conducted at P.C.Thomas institute, Thrissur. I agreed even without having a second thought about it. Moving to somewhere away from home would give me a break from my parents continues advises and taunts. Moreover, I could remain peacefully from Manju's presence.

Yes, Manju; she was my girlfriend from my school; but now, no more my girlfriend anymore. I constantly ignored and avoided her whenever I see her but tries to find out one reason to get her back by forgetting what she did to me. Because, once upon a time I loved her that much that it killed me alive by what she did to me. So we have recently broke-up. But she partially believes that I still loves her blindly and hence, I never gave her a chance to meet me or talk to me. I did changed my mobile number immediately and instructed my friends who are also her friends, to not to give my new mobile number to her, at any cost.

The only thing that I was worried was leaving to a place where I haven't made any friends yet. Usually I am always sick without any friends. My father had told me that he would be arranging my accommodation in one of the private hostels, where I think there would be some freedom.

We entered into the compartment and occupied the single seat that was near to the window. It was cold inside, but not that freezing cold. Nothing was being heard from outside as it was closed with thick glasses. My father sat in front of me, pushing my bag, under the seat. That was the only luggage I was carrying with some of my cloths and some notebooks for namesake.

I settled comfortably in my seat. Through the gap of the closed curtains of my right side, I noticed a girl sitting with her mobile connected to an earphone. Her face was not clear as her untied hair almost covered her face. She was concentrating on her mobile; maybe in search of songs. She was the only passenger I could see near my seat.

There was a complete silence within the compartment and I don't remember when I fell asleep. My father woke me up when we reached the *Thrissur railway station*. My watch showed 4:30pm and I looked for her again. The berth was vacant, and the curtains were being moved aside. Do you remember the girl I saw before I slept? Yes, I was looking for her, but unfortunately, she had left. The compartment was almost empty. Even my father went out and he may be waiting for me. I pulled my bag and took it in my hand. While leaving I saw a black purse over the berth where she sat. I kept my bag down and took the Purse. I opened it and took something from it. No! It's not money that I took. It was an ID card of Donbosko Higher Secondary school, Thrissur. The card named "Jessie Joseph" and I looked at the photograph. I could hardly remember that face. 'Oh! It was the girl who was sitting here with her mobile.' I nodded myself.

She was beautiful in her ID card, even in her neatly tied up hair. I know girls look stunning when they keep their hair untied. It is beautiful to see them when their hair falls over their shoulders and some dancing along with the wind. I put the card back and put it in my bag.

When I boarded the platform, I could feel a sudden change in the atmosphere.

'What were you doing all this time?' my father asked me as soon as I came out. I hid about the Perce and didn't tell anything about it.

'Toilet' I said when he repeated the question.

'This much time?' he asked 'Where you cleaning it?'

I am sure that he was already angry with me. It's him, my Dad! Gets angry if the person along with him gets late. And always, I becomes his pray. Military people must calm down on acknowledging the white color shown to them, as it indicates *peace*. I, myself was wearing a complete white shirt; still he gets angry. "Shame shame puppy shame." I murmured silently in my mind, like a kid.

Silence while asking something; was something that could change him into a monster in human species. The anger he had could turn my *peaceful dream* into the real *rest-in-piece*. So before he beats me to death, I spoke something.

'No, I… just… freshen up myself.' I said when I was almost irritated.

Then we went to a tea stall and I followed him silently. He ordered a tea for both of us. While I was having my first sip of tea, I kept thinking – Why I was hiding the Purse from him. What would happen if I reveal about it to him? For all these questions, I decided a 'no' to myself. Because, if I give it to him, he may hand over it to someone, maybe to police, saying it is been got from the train. Why should the cops take the appreciation by giving it back to her? I do not want that and kept it with me for my chance. To be precise, there was money in the purse.

As I was thinking all these stuffs, I almost forgot to have my thing in my hand – *the tea glass*. My father had finished drinking his and paid the bill. Now he was staring at me.

'Make it fast. It's almost time.' he said.

After I finished, we moved forward, but I was still thinking. 'Oops' I forgot to take the Purse. I went back and took my bag, which was lying in front of the stall. When I took it, the man in the tea stall smiled at me. I also smiled back saying 'you will also forget something someday. Then I will smile.' I said it in my mind. The station was crowded. As we moved through it, I could see commuters waiting for their train, some talking to each other, some getting down and boarding into the train. Finally, we exited the station through a big hall and I saw many cars, autos, taxis, bikes, but no busses though there were some Lorries. There was a big parking lot outside the railway station. We called for an auto and entered into it. The driver signaled where to go?

'P.C.Thomas Institute' my father spelled very much correctly.

'Chaithanya College?' driver prodded

'Yes' my father confirmed.

He put the meter on as we moved. I rarely find auto drivers using their meters. If they use that means the passenger has a lucky day.

1ST DAY IN THE HOSTEL

I am here to stay until my Crash Course gets over. This private hostel didn't seem to be a hostel. In my mind, a hostel looks something like, having at least two-floored building in which there are many rooms with wooden doors and windows. But this is something like House-Made-Into-Hostel. The car porch was being closed and converted into an office.

Simple adjustments will lead to carry out a profitable business – *like hostels.* 'What a tricky people' I nodded and we entered into the office – *the car porch.* The office has two tables in different corners and the openings of the car porch were closed with curtains.

Would you believe if I say there was a complete silence in the hostel? Yes. It was as silent as a Silent Valley. The only sound that surrounded there was the sounds of vehicles, my father and the man so called *the warden.*

'The students went to the evening classes and will be back at 4 p.m.' warden informed. 'You have to attend both morning and evening classes and you will get a break in between to have lunch'

If there is no phenomenon like having food in the evening, then they might have utilized that time too. We moved into the hostel and he showed me a bed near to the door.

'This is your bed. You can use it during the nights.' He said. 'Only at nights' he stressed. 'And you should always keep in mind that you must wake up between 5 and 6 AM. But not beyond six.'

I simply nodded.

That room was a living room when it was a house and now it's a hostel. So everything simply changed. I kept my bag under the bed. There was another bed next to it. Both were kept near to each other. My eyes popped out as soon as I saw the huge red phone, that too next to my bed. (I forgot to take my mobile phone for the first time in my life.) This phone could be used by waiting for a long queue to talk for a whole one minute. Because the time allowed for calling someone using that phone was only half an hour. If I am not wrong, half an hour contains thirty-minutes and according to warden's statistics, there would be probably thirty to thirty-five students to use this phone on each day. The rest will manage with their mobiles.

There were two adjacent rooms next to the living room which were similarly filled with such beds. Both have attached bathrooms. Those rooms were once their bedrooms.

He called us to the terrace and showed the study place. The roof of the terrace was being closed with aluminum sheets and the back sides of the terrace were also closed with curtains. We came down to the bed so called my bed for the time being. My father was going to leave and while leaving he gave me a 500 rupees note. Then a 'U' smile stapled on my face as I remembered that someone's lost purse was with me. I went out of the hostel and called an auto for him.

'I will call you when I reach back home' my father said and got into the auto. I said nothing.

'Take care.' he said and left. I went back to my bed and the warden came inside with me. I was ignoring the warden and the hostel. I ignored everything as I hung myself here away from my home for the whole two months. I was not upset for being away from home. It was all about not yet having a companion here.

After writing the entrance examination, I waited for the results. But I was not eagerly waiting. The judgment day had arrived. The judgments for whether I could join any college soon or else still have to write again. When the results for my entrance exam were being published, there was a Hiroshima & Nagasaki effect in my home. I was the victim for that. My parents hit me that strong, with words and with what not!

When some of my classmates joined different colleges after cracking their entrance, I am writing it again. My father could easily give some donation and make me admit to some college. But entrance exam was his gateway and I was his gateman. So I have to write it and clear it, in order to open the gate of a good college.

'Do you like the place?' warden asked when I was thinking all these.

'Hm' I replied and it almost meant – *a fucked up place.*

I was alone in the hostel as soon as the warden left. I looked at my watch. Still, there was half an hour more for the students to be here. I pulled out my bag and kept it on the bed. I opened it and took out a bed sheet and the Perce. I opened the Perce and took the ID card. I read a Thrissur address on the ID card. As I don't know the places, I went to the next detail. It was a mobile number. I went out and looked out the surroundings to check out whether anyone is there, *especially the warden*, because this was not the time to use the phone. There was no one and I came back. I took the receiver of the phone. Then the screen displayed – "DIAL NUMBER". I dialed – "8006113456". It rings… and the ring stops after a while

'Hallo' there came a female voice.

I didn't respond.

'Hallo. Who is speaking?' she spoke again.

I still retained silence…

I disconnected the phone. I couldn't ask anything, as I didn't know what to say as I heard her voice. All I have is the ID card and the purse.

The phone rings again. I took it.

'Hello'

'I got a call from that number just now. May I know who this is?' again the same female voice.

'I am Roshen' I said

'Yes? May I help you?' she said

'Are you Jessie Joseph?' I said

'No' she said

'Do you know her' I said

'Of course. She is my daughter. Why? What's wrong with her?

'No...th....ing... actually I wish to meet her. Could you please help me?' I said. I don't know why, but I was shivering out of fear.

'For what?' she asked.

'Just to talk to her, I have something to give her.'

'What do you mean?' she was almost angry.

'At least can you please give the receiver to her? I will introduce myself to her.' I said.

'She is in India.' She said

'What? India?' I said.

'Why? Haven't you heard of that country before?' she said. What does she mean by that? Am I that bad whom didn't even know the place where I lives for a lifetime.

'Is your daughter here in India? S...o where are you? Abroad?' I am totally confused by now. Because I thought the owner of this number would be here in India, but she is saying something else which confuses me a lot.

'Whom do you want? My daughter or me?' She asked.

'Why should I want you? Old-stuff-lady.' I said by covering the receiver.

'Hello?' she said in a louder voice.

'Please let me know where you are from?' I became a little bit confused.

'This is America. I am Reethika. 39 years old and working here as an automobile engineer. Is this enough? Or if you want, more give me your e-mail ID. Then I will mail you my Bio-data.' She disconnected the phone.

'Hoi. You angry old bird, your daughter's ID card is with me!' Now it's only me on the phone.

I kept the receiver on the phone thinking what kind of a lady she is. I wondered how would be her daughter. If she is also like this lady, then she will be slapping me with her heals asking 'why did you steal it?' No, she won't be like that. I consoled myself. By the time, the student came after the P.C.Thomas classes. I was being ignored by the students, but I didn't bother as now my hangover is Jessie. How will she appear like? How will be her voice like? Will she be slim or too fat? Why can't ID cards use full size photos? Why did her mother talk like this or does she have any problem? How will be her father? Will he sounds good to me? I don't know when I slept by thinking all these.

THE SUNDAY

The big-red- phone rings.

'Hello' I said as I picked up the phone.

'Hi, I am Jessie. You haven't seen me yet. But I know you. Could you please meet me at the railway station? Girls are not allowed in your hostel. That's why. Will you promise me that you will be there at 5pm?' I was listening to her sweet voice.

'Sure. I will be there sharp at 5.' I said immediately she finished.

'So bye. See you and take care.' She said and disconnected.

I stepped into my new dress as soon as possible and rushed out of the hostel. I called for an auto. Luckily, I got it immediately.

'Railway station' I said to the driver.

He moved through the traffic.

Because of his high speed driving of the auto-driver, I felt to get down and walk through, in order to reach there on time.

'Please go fast' I said.

'Do you have to catch any train?' driver asked.

'Asshole, I want to catch a girl.' I didn't say though I wanted to.

'Hm' I replied.

He increases the speed, but there was no difference.

'I can't go on. Others won't permit. Please get down here.' He stopped the auto. I didn't understand what he meant. But it was clear that he wants me to get out. I looked at my watch. It showed 4:45pm. I was afraid that she might leave if I wouldn't reach on time. Now I have to cross the busy junction of Thrissur and walk a distance to reach the railway station. I paid him whatever he asked and rushed out of the auto. I moved forward on the road. I didn't even look about the vehicles passing by. I just signaled in front each of them to stop and moved on. I could hear the horns of the vehicles that were blowing around by different vehicles. I didn't bother to care them, as my intention was to reach the destination as soon as possible.

Suddenly I heard a loud sound of a single horn coming near to me. It was a Big-Red-Box *the K.S.R.T.C public transport bus.* I could see the driver close to me. Passengers at the front where popping their eyes out as if they have seen a film star in front. The bonnet of the bus was too close that I could feel the heat of the engine. It hit me. I realized that I was lying somewhere. When I opened my eyes, I could see the black road very close to my eyes. Then after some time I could see that, the black road turned into a brownish-red color and my vision was almost blared. I could see uncountable legs in front of my eyes. Everything around me was rotating. I fainted.

When again I opened my eyes, I saw lights passing downwards on the ceiling. I was confused whether the lights were moving or I am moving forward. I saw blood all over my body. I could feel myself wet and sticky. I saw a slim guy in white dress pushing me. I thought I was on a structure bed. I realized that I am in a hospital. Then I closed my eyes again. When I opened it again, I saw bright lights above me. Probably this may be the operation theater. When I was closing my eyes, someone patted on my shoulder. I tried to open my eyes but couldn't. Then I felt water falling on my face. I thought why there is rain inside the hospital too. This time I could open my eyes when I felt someone shaking my shoulders. I saw a big blared face with giant spectacles. But after a while, the vision was clear. 'Oh God!' It was the warden and I realize everything I saw before was just a dream. I smiled at him.

'Get lost you geek.' I wanted to say but didn't have enough strength to say it. I made it short and said a simple 'good morning' to him.

'Get up' I heard a voice from him.

I got up partially and perched my head on the pillow kneeled on the bed. My rear end was like the rear end of a Maruti Swift car. The warden came and kicked my ass.

'Get lost you dump' he said in an angry voice.

Actually, I wanted to say this to him, but I just said a *good morning*. I shouldn't have committed this sin. I hate people pulling out heavily from my sleep. This was an ass-fucking place with everything done on time, as if, if not the roof will collapse straight away with his head.

Yesterday I saw my home when I woke up, but today it's the hostel. Yesterday my mom woke me up, but unfortunately, there were no dreams. But today the warden broke my dream. If not I could see her in dreams. I wished to have a phone call from her just like in the dream, but every call was outgoing.

I took my toothbrush, bucket, soap, and dress. Then I went to the bathroom. I have to wait for a long queue.

'Move' a senior boy said in a firm voice and went ahead.

'Fuck your ass. It's been five minutes you went in. Aar you coming out or should I lock it?' the senior boy shouted to a boy who is inside the bathroom. I was there in the queue watching all this and I was a little bit afraid of those seniors.

'Hi, I am Suresh, your roommate. My bed is next to you. He told me and gave his hand to shake. 'There are three senior boys here. The other two senior boys are on the above floor.'

Anyway, Suresh was not like others because he is the only one of the other seniors who kept calm. He was a decent-looking-guy among the other seniors. The other seniors started raging, who all was entering to the bathroom. As I got the support of Suresh, I could escape from those ragging easily.

'It's common here...what your name is?' he said when I looked to the seniors who was ragging a guy in front of me and I was the next.

'Roshen.S.' I said.

'S stands for?'

'Samuel. Roshen Samuel that is my full name. You can call me Roshen.' I said and enter into the bathroom.

The bathroom was as good as the office outside. Anyway, at least it was clean. I have completed everything and came out in 15min. I had a fear of being raged. However, nothing happened except another senior boy entered with a bucket. When I was moving into my room, someone called me from behind. It was he, the senior who entered the bathroom with his bucket.

'Oi!' He called me. 'Go upstairs and get my underwear from Arun. Go.' He said

'Underwear? Me!' I asked.

'Ah!. Then who? Arun knows it. Go and get it fast.' He ordered in a rude voice, peeping his head out of the bathroom.

'Bloody gays' I murmured climbing up the stairs and searched for Arun like a Google search engine.

'Is there any guy named Arun here?' I asked the boy who was studying seriously.

'There he is. The one who is sitting there with an ear phone.' He pointed to a corner of the room.

I went there. 'Arun?'

He turned to me. 'Um?'

'Underwear' I said.

'What? You didn't have it?' he laughed at me.

'Not that. Your friend asked me to get his from you. He has forgotten to take it.' I said.

'Who Salim? Wait a minute.' He said.

'Ye lo' he gave me the underwear. I went down with it and gave it to him-Salim. He did not even thank me for bringing his junk. I went back to my bed. Suresh, my roommate was studying there as if he has an exam the next day.

'If the warden sees you, then he will kick your ass like he did in the morning' Suresh said as he saw me lying down on my bed as because I had nothing to do that day.

'I am getting bored here in this hostel. I feel to go out for some time.' I said.

'For that you must ask his permission.' He said.

'Ok, I will ask and we will go together' I said.

'If he permits.' He walked out and I followed him. We went out and stood at the gate. He climbed and sat on the boundary wall. I leaned on the gate and swing on the gate in back and forth motion.

'Will he come today?' I asked.

'Hey, don't worry. He will be here within sometime as usual with tea and snacks.' He said. 'You are here for Crash Course. Right?

'Hm. How is your class? Are you enjoying here?' I asked.

'I am enjoying in the hostel. That is all. Ones if we enter in the college it is full of classes and there is no leisure in between expect a break in the evening to have food.' He said. 'Don't worry; tomorrow you will be experiencing it.'

THE BREAKFAST

A white Maruti Omni car stood in front of the gate. The driver got down and he slides open the door, which was facing to the gate. There was a big steel filter and two big urns covered by the newspaper on the top. Many people use the newspaper for these covering purposes.

'Come and hold it.' He said to Suresh.

Suresh signaled me to help. I took the filter, which was being filled with hot tea. Suresh, and the driver took the urns. The driver went up stare with the food and entered to the terrace. Suresh and I followed him.

'Is he warden's driver?' I asked to Suresh.

'He is not a driver. His name is Alex. Warden's one and only son. His marriage was over in the previous week.' He said.

We reached on the terrace and students crowded around us with their plates and glasses. That time I realized that there were many students in the hostel. There were many tables and they kept their urns on a single table that was being placed apart from other tables. I lifted up my tea filter and kept it on the table with a jerk and the tea overflown on my hands. It was too hot. When I wiped my hands with my dress, Alex stared at me. 'Don't waste it' he said in a serious tone.

No one took anything from it, but the crowd was still in a queue. I went down to my bed and took my bag from underneath the caught. I opened the zip of my bag and took the plate and teacup. When I closed the zip, Suresh came and took his cup, which was being kept, beside the window.

'Are you not taking your plate?' I asked.

'I am eating from the hotel. Are you coming?' he asked.

I smiled and kept the plate and cup in the bag.

'Take your cup.' He said.

'Why? The hotel doesn't have any tea cups?' I asked with a fake smile.

'Common... we should at least have to take tea from here. Otherwise, it won't be good.' He said. 'Don't worry, here the tea is fine'

'Oh' I said and I followed him with my cup. We reached there and joined the queue. I was standing behind Suresh and I was the last one. I had the same feeling of a person standing at last in the queue of a ticket counter in a cinema theater. I thought that the tea filter would become empty by the time I reached there. I patted Suresh.

'How much will a tea cost?' I asked.

'It's free here' he said as if I do not know that.

'I asked about the hotel-rates...' I said.

'I don't know. I always drink from here.' He said.

'You always stand last in this queue' I said.

'Yeah, why?' he said.

'Nothing.' I said smiling. The queue was still moving forward and we are still far away from the tea.

Another boy joined us. He had an earphone in his ears. 'You came early!' I said to the boy who was standing behind me.

'Look forward and mind your own business.' He said.

I pulled myself a back from him and again patted Suresh. He turned to me.

'What?' he said.

I pointed to my back facing forward in such a manner that the fellow standing at my back will not see me pointing...

'Amal, when will you give my money that I have given you two days before?' Suresh asked to him.

'Fuck off… you ass hole. It's just the case of Rs. 350 and I will give it today evening' he said.

'If not you will get it from me.' Suresh said.

'Is he my senior?' I asked to Suresh.

'No. He is a freaky guy. One day I will bump him down.' He said.

'Why?' I said. 'For money'

'Not for money, but he is playing too much in the hostel' he said by looking forward.

By the time, we reached at the tea. Suresh gave his glass.

'Where is the plate?' Alex asked as he poured the tea in the glass.

'I am not taking breakfast' he said.

Alex gave the glass to him. Next was me. I gave my glass.

'You are also not taking?' he asked me pointing towards the breakfast.

'No' I said and took the glass from him, which was been filled with hot tea.

We went down with the tea glass. Suresh and I sat in my bed, and drank the tea. Though Suresh will never talk too much, whenever I accompanied him that feature is silent.

'Where is your home?' I asked.

'Tamil Nadu' he said.

'Oh, I stay in Palakkad. Where do you stay in Tamil Nadu?' I said.

'Coimbatore' he said.

'So you are my neighbor!' I said.

'Not a great thing' He smiled and stood up as his tea is over. He went to the washbasin underneath to the staircase. He is always precise and will never expand his replies. However, I was almost opposite to that nature, because I have to explain too much in order to convey my message. I have never yet learnt to be precise and I am sure that I will soon learn from him. My glass also became empty and went to the washbasin.

'I will be waiting at the gate' he said as I was washing my glass.

'Hi' a boy said who came outside the bathroom, which was adjacent to the basin. He came out after bathing. Today I discovered one more bathroom in the hostel.

I dressed up and went to the entrance gate and Suresh was waiting there for me.

'Girls will dress up faster than you' he said

We started walking on the road. As it was not a busy road there were no much vehicles. We reached the hotel beyond a house next to the hostel.

'Oops. We didn't ask to the warden.' I said

'I asked' he said.

'When?' I asked.

'I saw him just now, when you was grooming' he said.

'Grooming?' I asked.

'This is the hotel' he pointed to the building, ignoring me.

It was next to the house. We entered in the hotel. There were only limited tables in the hotel and occupied a table at the corner. The waiter came and stood near us.

'What do you want?' Suresh asked me.

'Sandwich.' I said.

'Two Sandwich' he said to the waiter.

'Tea?' waiter asked.

'No.' he said.

"Two Sandwich." The waiter said in the kitchen as he went from us.

We then didn't talked much. What Manju did to me was haunting me seriously. Wherever I am, the picture of Manju being with him comes to my mind again and again. Though he used to roam around with us in school, I never expected him to do that. Even by knowing well that Manju is my girl. Moreover, it was hard to believe that she voluntarily involved with him without any kind of reluctance. But reality is always meant to be believed. So I did. Even the gossips on Manju didn't made me believe anything bad about Manju. But when I saw it with my eyes, everything came to an end.

'Do you have a girlfriend?' I asked to Suresh.

'Not yet. Why?' he said.

'Nothing, just asked.' I said. I wanted to have a change. A change that will make me alright from the sadness in my mind about the way Manju boldly cheated me.

The waiter came with two plates of roast, but gave to the adjacent table. I stared at him, but he did not notice. I took a glass, which was being kept upside down on the table. I poured water in it from the jug.

'I want your help.' I said after I took a sip of water.

'Help? What kind of help?' he lifted up one of his eyebrows.

'I have got an ID card from the train' I said.

'Whose?' he said.

'ID card of a girl and her name is Jessie Joseph.' I said.

'Do you know her' he said.

'Yes, I met her from the train. When we reached here, she was left and her purse was forgotten on her seat.' I said.

'So you took it and just kept it with you.' He said.

'I searched for her at the station, but she left in the meanwhile.' I reasoned.

'How much was there in the purse?' he said.

'What?' I had a sharpened face.

'Money man. Was there money in that.' He said

'I didn't count.' I said.

'Anyway, you are not going to meet her. So why can't we have food in a better hotel tomorrow?' he said.

The waiter came with two plates in his right hand and kept each plate it in front of us.

'Anything more?' the waiter asked.

'Nothing' we said and he went.

'So what about the money?' he asked.

'Yes of course. Let's do something.' I said. 'I think she lives here only. It will be awesome if we could meet her.'

'I don't want to meet her. You are just fascinated with her. I am not.' He said and poured water into the glass from the jug.

'Her ID card has a Thrissur address. So it may be pretty simple to find her.' I said.

'Yeah, it's pretty simple' he said and drank water from the glass. 'You do one thing. Arrange a car and a mic. Then announce her name throughout the roads and streets. Or give an advertisement in the newspaper?' I listened curiously, as he said.

'It's not practical.' I said.

'Mr. Asshole. This is Thrissur city and not your house or colony to search someone in one goes.' He said and stood up as he finished his food. He went to wash and I have not yet finished. I made it fast and went to wash my hands. He was not there in the washroom. I opened the tap and the water did not come out of it. I opened another tap where there was water and washed my hands. Suresh came out from the toilet as I closed the tap.

'Now go and pay the bill.' He said.

'For both the plates?' I asked.

'So what? I am your senior and I am helping you. So you better pay it.' He said.

I went to the counter and paid the bill. We walked back to the hostel. Though he shows seniority to me, we became good friends. As we entered, I saw Amal sitting on my bed and tying his shoe lies.

'It's my bed' I said to Amal.

Then he stood up and turned around facing his back to me. He lifted his other leg and kept on my bed. As he tied his lays, Suresh pulled him and stood face to face.

'Evening 4 o'clock. That is, your dead line for paying my money back. Don't forget it you prick.' He said.

Amal went outside as he tied the other lays also. Our friendship gave me much strength to survive between these nasty creatures.

MY NEW FRIEND

I took the ID card from my bag and put it in my wallet. Suresh came down from the upstairs; there was a boy with him.

'You are here for what?' He asked.

'For repeating the entrance. And you?' I said.

'For the same. When did you come here?' Joyal asked.

'Yesterday.' I said.

'Oh, so you guys know each other. Anyway, I am going upstairs. Bye.' Suresh said and went.

'He is the only senior boy who studies almost all the time.' Joyal said as he moved away from us.

I smiled and put my right hand around his shoulders. Then we walked outside and stood near the gate. We have known each other for the past one year. He was the best friend of Kishore, one of my classmates. We three always get together whenever Joyal comes to his house. Gradually we became close friends who never miss out any opportunity to mess out in our locality.

'Is not your house nearby?' I said.

'Yeah. Are you coming? I am going there today.' he asked.

'Yeah, sure. I thought it would be so boring over here in the hostel without any of my friends. I didn't know you will be joining here.' I said.

I took the ID card from my wallet and gave it to him. He looked to the ID card red the address.

'Do you know her?' he asked.

'Nope' I said. Then I narrated the whole incident to him as I said to Suresh.

'What says.' I asked him as I put my hand in my pocket.

'You are mad like usual. And I know this address very well.' He said looking to the ID card.

'Can we go now?' I said with a smile.

'Sorry dude, we must rush to my home now and will be back at night.' he said.

'Hm…alright then.' I said.

He smiled and went in but I remained there. He turned around to me.

'However, I will be saying that you came with me to do combine studies. Agreed?' he said.

'But I haven't got any books.' I said.

'Not a big issue' he said 'I will get some for you. I will help you with one condition.'

'Condition?' I said.

'Don't say anything about me to anyone in my home. Especially to my sisters.' He said.

'Telling about what?' I said.

'About smoking, drinks, party, so on…' He said seriously.

'Oh, sure' I promised.

We went inside and gone to the upstairs and entered into the terrace. When we went there, there were some students who were studying and some talking on their mobile. There were many textbooks lying on the table. Students usually left their books on the tables after their studies at late nights. Joyal went near a table and took some books. He came to me and showed three books.

'Physics, mathematics and biology. What do you want?' he said.

'As if we are going to study these. Grab anything.' I said and took all the books from his hand.

Someone called us from behind and when we turned, it was Suresh who was sitting in an extreme corner. We went near him.

'Whose book is that?' he asked.

'Don't know' we shrugged our shoulders.

'Today he is coming to my home with me. Are you coming?' Joyal said.

'No, tomorrow I have a test.' He said.

'Then bye, let's see in the evening.' Joyal said.

We went down and dressed up. There we saw the warden. He gave us the permission and we went out. Joyal called an auto and we left soon.

IN JOYAL'S HOUSE

As the auto stopped in front of the house, we got down and he was paying the money to the driver. I walked to the gate. It was a white big two floored building. There was a vast area in front of the house with a big beautiful garden. My eyes captured a car in front of the house. It was a black Audi A4. From my childhood itself, I was very much crazy about the cars. Audi is one of my favorite cars in which I want to at least make a ride in it. I opened the gate. As soon as I stepped in, I heard a barking sound of a dog, as if I stepped on a buzzer, which produces a barking voice. My eyes rolled out of fear as I saw a huge dog came barking and running to me from a distance. I could not move immediately as it was unexpected. Before it jumped on me, someone pulled me back and closed the gate.

'Gone mad? Why you want to go to someone's house?' he said.

'So, is this not your home?' I said.

'This big strange house is not mine. See the dog. No one can get in except the family who lives here.' He said.

'So why you stopped here?' I said.

'Is that a problem? Come, let's go.' He said.

He entered into the house, which was next to the strange house. I followed him.

'This is my house.' He said with a welcoming smile.

Though it was not big as that house, it was a nice house and has a small garden compared to the other one. He rang the calling bell. A girl opened the door. She was a little fat and little taller than me.

'She is my cousin sister, Jincy.' He said. 'Come in'

We went inside. His mother came from the kitchen. 'Who is this Joyal?'

'He is my friend, Roshen. Mom, he is staying with me in the hostel.' He said.

'Oh, I see. Please sit.' She said. Joyal went to his room.

'Where is your house?' his mother asked.

'Palakkad.' I said.

'Mom he came to have combined study with me.' He said as.

Jincy laughed as soon as she heard it, and sat on the sofa near to me. He gave her a staring look and went to his room.

'How is your class?' she asked.

'I came yesterday and not yet attended any' I said

'I will take some tea for you.' His mother said.

Jincy also went with his mother.

'Your sister has a very good impression on you.' I said to Joyal as soon as she left.

'Not only her. Every one of my sisters has this attitude. Stupid girls. But sometimes she does rescue me from getting scolded from my mother.' he smirked.

'Oh, great.' I said. 'Do they stay here?'

'No, they will go to their home at Nehru Nagar. They will go there on next Sunday. Their grandparents are alone there.'

I had an Understood – nothing expression. 'Just 15 min journey from here to their home. So they will be here most of their leisure time.' He said.

'So where are their parents?' I said

'They are in U.S for the past 14 years.' He said.

'You could have stayed here instead of the hostel.' I said.

'My parents compelled me to stay there' He said.

'Why?' I said.

'First, they know that I won't study as long as my cousins are here. Second, they know that hostels are very strict and there we will not play too much. They think that full time we are with the books.' He said.

'Yeah, she is right. All are in front of the book almost all the time. That's what makes me sick' I said.

'Really? Today when you go there, go to the study room and see what is kept inside the book.' He said.

He took a long towel from the burrow and gave it to me. 'Take a bath and soon there will be a surprise for you.'

He showed me the bathroom, which has attached to the room, and he went out. I entered in and took off my cloths. I opened the shower, but water did not come from it. When I looked up the bunch of water droplets punched my face. I moved back and again I stood in its flowing water. Water was cold and I finished bathing as he called me from me. I wiped my body with the towel and dressed. I opened the door.

I threw the towel in the basket, which has placed in a corner of the room. It has many clothes in it, probably kept for washing.

'Come, let's have tea.' He said.

'Fine. Do you have a sister?' I said.

'Yes, why?' He said.

'I just asked.'

He went to the dining hall and I followed him. I entered the dining room through the curtains which divides from the living room. His mother told me to sit and pulled a chair. I obeyed with a gentle smiling face. Joyal sat near me. In front of me, she kept the teacup for me which was full of hot tea. Fumes were still coming from it. The table was full of snacks which taste from bitter to sweet. Everyone started drinking the tea and I started blowing slowly on its surface to reduce its heat.

'Are you a Christian?' Jincy said.

'Hm, yes.' I said.

'She is my own sister Arya' Joyal introduced his sister and she smiled to me.

A girl came and sat in front of me as I continued to blow on the hot tea. I lifted my head and looked into her face. GOD! It was Jessie. The girl I saw several times in the ID card. She is the one who I have dreamt all night. This is my first sight. I could not take my eyes off her. She is the real beauty queen. I have no guess why she is here. I was just admiring at her. Someone patted on my leg. It is he, Joyal. I suddenly kept the teacup on the table.

My hands were burning with the hot tea. He moved his eyebrow up and down to me.

'She is Jincy's sister Jessie' Joyal said to me.

Jessie smiled as I smiled at her. A special smile that has all its sweetness in it. I have the least patience compared to anyone. My mind was tempting to propose her immediately. Nevertheless, I did not.

'Hello, I am Roshen Samuel.' I said to her.

'Hi' she said.

I began to drink the tea now. I had the snacks when his mother compelled. As everyone finished the tea, we all got up and washed our hands. His mother and sisters cleaned the table. Joyal and I went to the terrace.

'How was the surprise?' he said.

'I have not yet recovered.' I said. 'So she is your sister!'

'She just came from Hyderabad.' He said.

'Yeah, I saw her' I said.

'When?' He asked

'On the train.' I said 'I already told you about the story.'

'Oh. Arya and Jessie is the best combination here.' He said.

'Will she always come here?' I said.

'Almost all the time And also put me in trouble. One day I smocked on my terrace when everyone went to church. Then she saw me smoking and she put me in a great trouble.' He said. 'On that day onwards I limited talking to her.'

'So she didn't went to church on that day?' I said.

'She went and came back here to take her purse. She used to forget it, always. And this time I put her in trouble when I came to know that her purse is missing, which is now with you.' He said and I felt sorry for her.

If I could see her on that day itself, then these thinks would never have happened. Arya came to the terrace, called us down, and went back immediately. She was a cute and smart girl.

'Now I am so happy. Jessie will be always in trouble till she gets her purse back. Dudes don't give it back. Ok? Let's have a nice time with that.'

'No yar, I am going to give it to her back.' I said as we stepped down the satires.

He giggled. 'Crap! Are you on my side or hers?' He said.

'It's not that.' I said and we continued walking down the stairs.

'We must have called Kishore too.' He said.

'I know him for the past three years. He won't come leaving behind his cricket matches.' I said.

'I took photos of your paintings and showed to Jessie once, she likes painting very much.' He said.

I was searching for a good topic to talk with. I felt quite comfortable when I heard *she likes paintings*. I had a great smile on my face.

'Does she know I did it?' I asked.

'No, I just want to show her the glass painting you did.' He said. 'Or I will tell her now. Jessie…' He went near her.

'Wait' I pulled him. We were standing outside.

'What happened?' she came and asked. Her hair was falling on her forehead. The moment she came out, Joyal got a phone call and went to terrace again.

'Nothing your purse was missing, right?' I said to her.

'Yes' she said and moved her hair behind her ears. 'How do you know?'

'I know.' I said

'How?' She asked. 'Oh, maybe Joyal told you.' She said.

'But I already knew before that' I smiled.

Again her strands of hair moved towards her face by the soft wind. I wanted to say not to tug her hair behind the ears when she did so. Because I liked her face that way.

'Will you please tell me. Why you too want to play pranks on me like he does. I got fired from my sister so much this time.' She said.

'So this is a usual practice?' I giggled.

'Yeah a sort of.' She said and moved a step forward. That was so close to me that made me feel to hold her. But that was not for which she came close. She wanted to say something to me. 'Don't join Joyal's company. You will get spoiled if you are not yet spoiled. Take my advice if you find it useful.' She said and turned around to leave.

'Em, Jessie' I called her.

'What?' she turned around in one go. Wow. You must see that scene. Huf, she is just beautiful. If I say more, then you will think that I am blabbering.

'Your –' Joyal pulled me away from her when I was about to tell her about her lost purse

'Don't tell her. At least this soon. Give me some more time, please. I can't lose this chance. Please' I partially agreed to his plea.

He talked about the class and examinations taken at the end of every day. Likewise the time passed to evening. We had food together and we all talked about our families and studies. Jincy actively participated in the topic of studies. Though Joyal tried to bring the topic of Jessie's-lost-purse, I interrupted and changed the topic. I thought she would smile at me when I rescued her. But she didn't even looked into my face.

Jessie was almost silent and she finished her food first. His mother made me eat too much. Mothers are always like that. They will always feed to the extreme. They manage to finish whatever they had prepared. Though I finished it late, we all got up together.

CBB2 BATCH

The warden called us as usual in the early morning. I woke up immediately as he patted me. I looked at the clock, hanging on the wall. It showed 5:35 AM. I got up slowly and got ready for going to the campus. P.C.Thomas collage is famous for the entrance coaching and there were numerous batches like, Crash Course, crash course, vacation batch, and still more. I walked alone all the way to the campus as everyone left before me, even Joyal went early. I had a bag that hanged on me throughout the whole way until I reached there. When I reached there, I saw no student outside. Then it was pretty clear that I was too late.

The gate was not yet closed. I went in through the gate. Just in front of the gate there lies the office. Thank God, that it was not like the stupid office in the hostel. It was well built purposefully for the office. Front side of the office was closed with cooling glasses, and was extremely good looking. There was a way beside the left side of the office, which led into all the classes. In addition, there was another building at the left side of the office. It was an old building with sloping roofs and was being separated in another plot, with a boundary wall. Besides that old building, long wild grasses were being spread all over the plot.

I was in a situation like, don't know where to go. It is like being a child left out all alone by its parents in an empty auditorium. There I found no one and I decided to step into the office. When I started moving, I saw a man coming through the way, beside the office. He was around 35 year old bearded man. His long legged trousers were the only cloth on his body which looks ironed.

'Where does the Engineering Entrance Crash course class conducted?' I asked him. He pointed to the old building.

'Should I be there?' I said, thinking myself being in that old building when there were well constructed buildings.

'Are you new to here?' he said.

'Yes joining here today.' I said.

'You are already late, go and sit there. That building is for temporary.' He said.

I went there and peeped inside the room, which even God might not know when it will collapse.

'Yes?' the professor said.

There was only one class in that building. The classes were handled by highly experienced professors.

'Yes? What do you want?' he asked again.

'May I come in sir?' I said. 'I joined here today'

'Sit down.' He said and continued his class. I turned around and spotted Suresh in the last bunch. I smiled at him and he did the same. I went and sat near him. There was only three raw in that class.

'Are you here?' Suresh asked.

'I guess. The bearded man guided me to this class.' I said

'But…show me that receipt' He whispered. 'Your class might be in the next block.' He said reading that slip.

'But I don't know where exactly it is.' I said.

'There is a way going inside to that block, next to the office. Take that way and you will see a corridor on the left side.' He explained to me.

'Silence.' The professor said.

'Give your ID card.' He whispered in my ears.

'What? I didn't get that stuff yet. I have an admission receipt with me. Do you want that?' I said.

'You are distracting the class. If this is being repeated one more time, both of you will be out.' He said staring us.

We couldn't exchange any word between us and so had to hear all the words he spelled out in the class. I was not able to understand anything, but he was saying some blah-blah thing from the study material in his hand continuously. Two things were sure that he was speaking English and of course, it was not an English class. I couldn't wait for long. I gave my admission receipt to Suresh and he read it.

'So enter the corridor and take the stares, and search for' he stopped as the professor looked him.

'For?' I said.

'CBB2 batch. Rush! you are late. Best of luck' he said and went inside the office.

Though I felt some trouble in his *best of luck,* I felt a little safe, as I was a new admission. The campus was little big as expected. I was thinking of how to get out from this class right now. Because I entered that class as if I am a student of that class.

He didn't note, my movement. The professor turned around to writing some kinds of stuff on his blackboard. It just looked like an address format, but it was some kind of formula. Whatever, I didn't bother. I moved from the bench and sat down on the floor to hide from his sight. At that time, if anyone saw me, they will assume that I am shitting on the floor. I looked above the bench to see the professor. He was completing his address, may be some formulas. Anyway, his artwork with the chalk piece doesn't bother me while quitting his class. I just went out of the class through the door as the professor was facing towards the blackboard. I guess he didn't see me.

THE SHIFT

I went through the corridor and saw a staircase on the left side and I climbed up. I found many teachers sitting in their staff room. Some reading something and others were writing. I went to the table. There was a teacher sitting with a bald head and professors' specially made spectacles.

'Excuse me sir' I said and gave my admission receipt to him. 'Could you please show me which classroom, I should go?' I said.

'There it is.' He pointed to a classroom.

'Thank you.' I said to him and moved towards it.

The room was being closed and I could hear a female voice from inside. I saw a girl, sorry, a lady teacher teaching in the classroom.

'Yes?' she said as I opened the door.

'I am a new student. I joined here today.' I said

'Come in' she said with a smile. 'Where is your ID card?' she asked when I went near.

'I didn't get that, but I have this one.' I gave that receipt.

I scanned her when she was verifying my receipt. She was a young teacher and had a cool voice. She had a long hair. She was wearing a *sari* as if her navel was clearly visible. She was too young that she looked like a college student. If possible, I would have asked for the exact number of break ups she had and which one did she like the most. I stopped staring as she spoke something to me.

'What's your name?' she said.

'Roshen S' I said.

'Sweet name, my name is Neetha and I am a newly joined teacher. Please take your seat somewhere here.' She said puzzled as all the seats were full.

I sat at the edge of a bench in the third row and it was crowded. Not only the bench, but the whole class was crowded with students. There are two rows and at least 10 benches at least with 5 students in each row.

'It's little congested but I hope you will adjust yourself soon.' She said seeing my discomfort. 'Hope you will enjoy my class.' She said. I smiled at her.

I took my notebook and kept it on the table. There was not much space for it but I have to adjust myself as she said.

'Hi, I am Sajan.' The boy sitting next to me said.

'Hi' I said to him and smiled.

'Your name is Roshen, right?' I nodded as he asked. 'Where do you stay?' he said.

'I stay in a private hostel. Its name is some Anu….. ma hostel or something like that. Do you know?' I said.

'It's not Anuma, its Anupama hostel. I stay there.' He said 'You came Saturday evening. Right?'

'Yes. But I didn't see you.' I said.

'I went to my friend's hostel.' He said. 'Who all you met in our hostel?'

'Suresh and Joyal. Which hostel you went? Ladies hostel?' I giggled.

'How did you know?' he said.

'I guessed' I said.

'Don't guess too much.' He said. 'Joyal and I smoke at night in the study room. Are you joining?'

'Let me think of it.' I said. 'I know Joyal before. We were already friends and we would enjoy whenever he comes to my place.' We started a conversation like that and talked much more things.

Neetha ma'am noted us talking. She came to us and stood near me. She was really a young sexy teacher there. She may be the only teacher in this campus in this appearance. She looks hotter in her untied hair and her *sari*.

'Can you please share the joke with us?' she said with a fake smile.

'Sorry, we just…' he said and she stopped him.

'See Mr. Sajan, I already said that I am newly joined in this campus and I am being friendly with you all because I have no experience in a big institute like this. Please understand me and don't do this again. And mind you, everything is being noted on the CC T.V in the office.' She said in a convincing way. We felt sorry for her and pretended silence for the rest of her class.

She looked a little tensed while taking the class. I felt her class interesting and so could understand everything.

Her explanations were so clear and everyone was free to ask doubts in the class. We all enjoyed the interaction in her class. She always used to walk between the two rows.

After some time, a lady came to the class. The lady said something to her, which was not audible to us.

'Roll number C5923' she called out.

Everyone looked at each other. She called out again and I stood up as I realized that it was mine. I went to her and she gave an ID card to me.

'You have to keep this always with you.' She said 'Give me your admission receipt.' I gave it to her.

'You are supposed to be in classroom number 14. So you must shift now.' She said and left the class.

'And now where the hell is that class?' I asked to Sajan as I returned to my seat.

'Climb the stairs again and you will find a class next to the stairs numbered 14, Bye.' He whispered slowly when I kept my book in the bag.

'See you in the hostel.' I said.

I went to the classroom 14. Here the door was not closed.

I went and stood at the door. There was as much as students in the previous class.

'May I come in sir?' I said.

He was standing near the blackboard and was busy in taking classes. As I interrupted, he came near and stood in front of me. I gave him my ID card and he asked me to sit in the 6th bench at the right side row of the class. I went there and faced the same condition. There was no space on the bench. Though I am slim, I had to work hard to fit myself my ass in. There were six students sitting in that bunch, including me. A lot of difference was being felt in that class as compared to this one. The teacher was strict, there was no one from my hostel, and no one talked to me in that bunch, the class was almost boring and I could only do was just counting the strength. The only similarity there was that, it was first period and it was the same chemistry class, but I was doing maths- *the counting*. My eyes popped out as I found out the result; there was hundred and ten students plus one myself in the classroom. There we have to take down our own notes while teaching. All the class went on as like the first period. I scribbled something as if they have dictated just to take down.

Every period went on like that. Many teachers came and went took the class seriously. I was busy in counting many things done by the professors in between their classes like, saying OK after every explanation, scratching their head, number of questions they asked, the number of times they used the blackboard, and still many. If they found us sitting idle without writing, they will fire us. Therefore, I tallied whatever I count. Finally, I found out that I had made a table of tally in different topics. Great! I appreciated myself. We went out as the first half was over. It was lunchtime and we have to go to another hostel for taking food. I saw Joyal when I was eating. He was standing in a queue to take food. He joined me after getting his plate filled. I narrated everything from visiting Suresh's class to the way I counted in the class time. We returned to our classes. Today there was no physics class as the professor was not present. Other subject teachers took it. Afternoon session also went on like in the morning. However, this time I was playing *Bingo* with my bench mate. Today's whole classes were over. They sent us out in a uniformed way like leaving one class one after another in a proper queue. We chucked out ourselves through the dark and crowded corridor.

SEE YOU THE NEXT SUNDAY

After the classes, Joyal, Suresh and I joined at the main entrance gate of the campus. Many students went back to the hostels and some hanged in the office. We stood still at the gate. I also waited there until the girls went out of the campus.

'I will come just now.' Joyal said and left.

He didn't give me the time to ask where he was going.

'Oh, he went to meet Avita. It will take time. Let's go.' He said and walked ahead.

'Who is she?' I followed him.

'The girl he is stalking for three days. He wants to propose her and she doesn't even want to talk to him.' He giggled. 'But both will have an eye contact with each other when she comes to that shop.' He pointed to a shop ahead.

The shop was so small and not much crowded. Hardly a few customers were standing over there. In that two were Joyal and the girl whom he was stalking. She spoke something to him for a moment and left.

'What she might have said to him? I said.

'For the past three days they do the same when she comes to that shop. He may say '*I love you*' to her and she will respond with a '*fuck off look*'. That's what I think.' We laughed.

'So sad. What does she have to buy all day?' I asked.

'Condom.' He murmured.

'What? Really?' I amused. 'So definitely she would be having a boyfriend.'

'Er...you prick. How do I know what she would be buying from that shop? I was just kidding.' He said.

'As if I believed you' I shot back.

'Now shut up and come with me. There he is.' He pulled my hands and led to Joyal. He ignored us and already started walking towards the hostel from the shop. We reached near him and Suresh put his hand over his shoulder.

'Dude, what happened?' Suresh asked.

'Nothing, today she responded.' Joyal said. He stared at Suresh.

'What did she say?' Suresh asked.

'If it is a yes, then we want a good party.' I said immediately.

'"*If you took three days to say just three words to me then how could you date with me?*" that's what she said.' He said and I started laughing like hell. After some time I controlled my laughter.

'What's there to laugh?' he grinned at me.

'Hey, do you get what she meant?' I asked.

'What?' he said.

'She graded you as not-a-man!' I said.

'What the fuck! She didn't, how could that mean like that?' he asked, looking at her walk a few steps ahead of us.

'Then what?' I laughed again. 'She told indirectly that you are not of her type.'

'Congrats! Buddy, let's try another.' Suresh left us after his compliment.

'Damn' Joyal was frustrated by now. 'I will see you in the hostel. Bye' he said.

At the same time, a white swift car stopped beside us. It was Joyal's mother. The car looked clean and white except its tiers.

'Hi Aunty' I greeted his mother as she smiled at me.

'How was the class Roshen?' She asked.

'It was great! Very interesting' I lied.

'Till when?' Joyal murmured from my back.

'We are going to Jessie's home. Her grandmother is sick and Jincy is alone there. So next Sunday stay in the hostel itself. Ok?' Joyals' mother said to him. 'And for God sake, please study something and-'

'I am fine' he interrupted her and moved on.

Jessie was sitting at the back. I could just smile at her when Joyal's mother talked to him. She peeped out of the window and looked at me when the car moved. She signaled that she would call me and waved her hand to me. At that time, the world's largest smile came on my face – *the smile of happiness.*

'She smiled at me!' I twitched him and said.

'I told her that you painted those pictures in the church.' He said.

'Thank you' I said to him and we reached the hostel.

We went inside and he went up to the study room. I kept my bag on my bed. Alex, the warden, brought tea and snacks and kept near the staircase. Everyone came and made a queue. I waited for Joyal and I joined the queue as soon as he came. We collected the tea and went out. As I stood near the gate he offered a cigarette to me. I refused and he slid it back into his pocket.

'Why can't you ask Suresh's help?' I said and sipped the tea.

'Once, when I was in tenth grade, I had asked help from my senior. I told him to tell the girl that I am in love with her. That bustard went and proposed her for him. Though she rejected his proposal, he told I asked to propose her.' He said and I finished my tea. 'From that day I stopped asking help for this.'

'So didn't you asked him about it?' I said.

'Yes, I did. He said that he became panic when she turn down his proposal. Then he accidentally blamed me to her for that.' He said. 'Then again, like a fool I tried to explain this to her. She might have felt me as a disturbance, and then she used that senior to beat me.'

'And what about that senior and the girl?' I asked.

'She flirted well with him and eventually ditched him after a few days.' He said. 'I want you to come with me to see Avita. Now.'

'For what?' I said.

'Just for a company, please' He said.

'Yeah, sure, you are my friend. How can I not help you.' I said.

'Does Jessie have any boyfriend?' I asked as I thought that this is my best chance to know it.

'No way, that she would even think about it.' He said. 'Roshen don't screw her. If her father come to know about anything like that, he would bury her alive. Then you.'

'I am not doing anything!' I rescued myself and we moved out to meet Avita.

'And do you know who this Avita is?' he asked me on the way.

'Yes of course! The girl whom you were stalking for three days.' I said like a genius.

'She was the girl whom I messed up with that senior in the past.' He smiled.

'Holly shit! Really? Then I certainly want to meet her.' I said

We went in and I noticed everyone sitting on my bed and having their tea. I wanted to burn their entire ass if one drop of tea has fallen on my bed sheet. Hostels are always like that. Everyone will be using others things if there is no security. As my bed is being kept in the living room, everyone sits on it for having tea, phone calls and so on.

Past Became Present

'But why?' he said.

'I am not ready for it. Who knows that you are making fun of me, like before?' she said.

'No, I am not! I really loved you and still I do.' He said.

Joyal started to explain everything that had happened. Avita were busy with their conversation for the whole three minutes! I felt it like three long hours. Because I can't participate in their conversation, I have no role to play in it, I had no mobile phone with me, and the best thing is that we were standing at the roadside near her hostel. I wanted Avita to agree with his proposal soon. Not because I am considering about their building-up-relationship. I just want to escape from this not-getting-over-sort-of-conversation by the two.

The whole situation is becoming sour for me. And at the same time I can't leave him alone and go. He is a good friend of mine, but this is too much to suffer. It's been fifteen minutes I am standing on a street, alone like a street-peddler who stands still on the roadside without knowing where to go next.

I even made signs for him to notice that I am making. I started scratching my head, kicking out the stones, and then finally settled myself by leaning on the wall behind by realizing that what all I did is of no use. Though we were near the ladies hostel, I couldn't see any girls from there. If Avita could bring some of her friends, then at least that would have passed the time.

'Give me the cigarette.' I asked him.

'Er...' He took it immediately and handed it over to me. Though I felt like avoiding me a little, I just ignored it as I know the situation well.

'You do smoke Joyal?' I heard her questioning him.

'Em...not really, but-' he struggled to explain

'But sometimes. Right?' she asked.

'Not like that Avi,' he said.

'Avi? Anyway, I like that name.' she smiled for the first time in their whole conversation. 'Em...I don't want you to smoke Joyal just because I stopped it some months before. I find it difficult to avoid and if you continue to smoke, then how can I stop it?'

That time Joyal was smiling, laughing and whatnot. He didn't grab her and kissed her as it was public. But he did everything, except that. He held her hand and started talking for the next half an hour.

This made me paranoid. I lit the cigarette and started smoking slowly and comfortably. They took their time and I took mine. They exchanged their present phone numbers and he came to me.

'Let's go' he smiled.

'Don't repeat this.' I said to him.

'Repeat what.' He asked.

'Joyal' She called from behind and we turned around in unison.

'I love you.' she said and left to the hostel.

'I will come right now.' He said and I caught his hand to stop him.

'I am not waiting anymore.' I said

'I will give one more cigarette' he said

'Don't bribe me. I am going back to the hostel. It's so boring yar. You won't understand!' I said

'Ok,' he thought for a moment. 'If warden or anyone asks about me, tell them that I went to buy some books and …that's it. Just books. That will be fine. Bye.' He instructed.

'Joyal but-' I tried to stop him. What to do now? He left without hearing anything from my side.

I went back to the hostel. Our hostel was very much punctual in certain things, especially time. That's why I tried to stop him.

Suresh and I were in the study room with our study materials. Joyal joined with us in the study room. We stopped our studies when Alex came with the food. No one took anything from it as he kept it on the table, but the crowd was assembled on the terrace and the warden came in. We formed a neat queue and took the food. We sat on a bench and started eating.

'The food is nice!' Suresh said and everyone nodded.

'What about the money? Did you get it from Amal?' I asked.

'Yes, he gave my money back when you left for Joyal's house.' He said.

We all finished our food and came to the washroom. Joyal went after washing and I stood behind Suresh for my chance. There the phone rings.

'Roshen it's for you.' Joyal shouted as he took the phone.

I washed before Suresh finished and rushed to the phone.

'Don't go crazy' Joyal handed over the receiver to me. I smiled and sat on my bed as he left.

'Hello.' I said into the receiver. There was no one in my room. Everyone was in the study room including Joyal and Suresh.

'Is it Roshen?' There came a female voice.

'Yes. Is it Manju?' I asked. I prayed, let it be someone else. Manju was my ex-girlfriend. And ex-girlfriend's phone call will always have a terrific feeling. So I had the same thing.

'I am Jessie, Joyal's cousin.' She said. 'Are you studying?'

'No, I just had food.' I said happily as my prayer got activated.

'Oh, can we meet someday?' she asked politely.

If I could travel through the telephone line, I would have been there right now in front of you.

'Sure. Let's meet somewhere at…anytime as you say.' I said.

'OK. Then let's meet next Sunday in the City center. What says?' she said in her sweet voice.

'I will be there at 10 AM.' I said.

'OK, then bye. See you the next Sunday' I said. 'So I won't be having any classes too.'

'See you then. Is Joyal there? I want to speak to him.' She said.

'He is in the study room. I will call him. Please hold.' I said and kept the receiver aside. I went up to call him. When I reached the staircase I turned back to the phone and thought for a moment. I took the receiver and put it on my ear.

'Hello' I said. 'Joyal went out just now. Should I say something to him?'

'No, just ask him to call me once he comes back.' she said.

I tell you. Her voice is so awesome! And will feel more and more wanted to hear her speaking. Always.

'Will you spare some time for me? Now.' I asked her. 'It's a little boring here, and if you don't mind, let's talk till Joyal comes back.'

'M...ok, but I don't have enough balance in my mobile.' She said.

'He will be back soon, Jessie' I said.

'No, sorry Roshen. Have to go and will see you the next Sunday. Bye.' She said and disconnected the phone call. I felt it like avoiding me. But while thinking on her side, she is right in what she did. Who am I to talk to her on the phone during the late nights? We were not *yet* dating. So...I left the chance with a hope that it will happen soon. I went back to the study room and met Joyal.

'Tomorrow we should go to the city center. My sister messaged me just now.' He said.

'Oh, I see. For what?' I asked as if I didn't know anything.

'How do I know? Anyway, thank you for taking her purse from the train. Thank you so much dude.'

'You are talking as if I stole it! Damn.' I protested.

'I didn't say that.' He shot back.

'Then what? Why you want to put her in trouble? It's so shame on you, idiot.' He dumbstruck as I said that.

'When did you become so concerned about her?' his question made me speechless.

We spent much more time on talking about the classes and other topics to pass the time. What all we did there will never include studies. We just enjoyed. Time passed and most of us in the study room went back to sleep. I came to my bed and I threw myself on it.

"But I am meeting her on the next Sunday! Wow! For her this may not be a date, but I already considered this as one" I slept of by thinking these.

IN THE CITY CENTER

'What should I do now?' I asked him.

Joyal was sleeping under his blanket. We have planned to be there at 10AM in the *city center*. I have been cornering Joyal from the moment I woke up from my bed. This is the first time I am going to propose a girl. Yes, I have decided to propose her, but I don't know, whether I will do it on today or not. Anyway, I will talk to her at least. I went to Joyal's room.

'Are you still sleeping? Get up you dumb!' I twitched him and went to the study room to take my book.

Yesterday I was pretending that I was studying too seriously to get today's permission for going out. I forgot the book on the table. I went down with it and kept it in my bag. Then took a bath perfumed myself and dressed as soon as possible. I looked at the time. It showed 7:16 PM. I went up again and he had not even lifted his ass off from the bed. I switched off the rotating fan, thinking he would get up easily.

'Is that your dad's property? On it you ass hole.' A voice came from the corner of the room.

Other seniors were being slept in his room - Joyal had said once. I immediately switched the fan on and shook Joyal constantly like a motor, till he opened his eyes. I

70

have no other way because; I don't know where the hell this *city center* is. I don't know the route to reach there. But he certainly knows it. So I have no other way other than to wake him up.

'Why the hell you are here man?' he said to me. 'Bhaiya…' he called a senior in his sleepy voice to evade me.

'Joyal, we have to go to the *city center*.' I shut his mouth tight.

'We are to be there only at 10AM. Why you want to go now? Do you have any security job there?' he said.

'Now it's 9'o clock already!' I pulled him.

Now there was a little sunlight in the room and some had already got up. He went to take a bath and got dressed. We got ready and searched for the warden to take the permission. The warden came with Alex carrying the food. As we saw them, we went in the other room to hide. Otherwise, we will be asked to carry it to the upstairs. The warden carried the tea filter and Alex carried the urn.

'Where are you going?' Warden asked as he entered with the tea filter. Alex went upstairs with the urn.

'We have to go to the church' Joyal said.

'Wait there and I will come now.' He said and went up.

'He will ask for the returning time. Then we should say that I will be going to my home after the church and you will be coming with me for the combine studies, like we did the last time.' Joyal explained and I nodded to him. Now we have the plan to stay long at the city center mall.

The warden came down the stairs and sat on my bed.

'Your mother called me.' He said to Joyal. 'They will not be at home, so you will be coming back here after the church. Right? Now you can go. Come soon.' He said and left the hostel with Alex.

That was an unexpected disaster that stroked us. That time we couldn't say anything other than nodding. We both left the hostel. We walked to the *city center* as it had a short distance from the hostel. It took only 5 min. to reach there. We stood at the entrance and waited for her. Joyal's phone beeped and he took it. He read the message and gave it to me. It was Jessie's message.

It reads: "I would be a little late. Please wait @ entrance."

I gave the mobile to him back and walked into the building.

'Where are you going?' He said and came behind me.

'I have to buy something.' I said and boarded the escalator.

I entered to a stall. I bought a white A4 paper, pencil, eraser and a sharpener. I had decided to make a picture in it and present it to her. But I don't know what to draw. There I didn't find any proper place to draw. Finally, I went to a tea stall and sat on a chair. I asked the waiter to clean the table and ordered two teas. Joyal sat in front of me. Every time he was admiring to what all I did. I was like a kid who don't know what to do, but does everything appropriately. A man came and cleaned our table. As he left, the waiter came with our tea. Joyal took his tea cup and started drinking it. But my cup was in a still when I was drawing a *beautiful angel with a pair of wings* in the paper. That was the only picture I had in my memory.

I started from her hair, nose, lips, and chin and then I completed her face. I gave her a beautiful eye, and then it looks alive. Then I continued with neck, hand, hip and I shaded it with a pencil to make it more beautiful. I drew the wings to fly along with Jessie. I completed the picture. It was a side view image and was a pencil drawing, as I had no color with me. I finished it with various shades, like dark, dim, light, heavy, and so on. Finally, I rolled it after writing an important note for her to read.

'Drink your tea, dude.' He said and smiled looking at my picture.

When I lifted my hand to take my cup, the paper flew and got stuck in the next table. A lady took it and gave it to me.

'You are an artist!' she said with a pleasant smile.

'Thank you' I said to her and smiled.

I drank the tea in one sip like water. We went to the counter to pay the bill. I asked Joyal to pay the bill and we went to the *city center* again. While walking someone called us from behind. We turned around. It was Suresh.

'Today I have no work. Let's solve your problem with Amal. Come on.' He said to Joyal.

'You go and meet her, let's see in the hostel.' He said.

'What's the matter?' I asked.

'He stole my cigarette' he announced and they left before I talked something.

I walked and waited at the entrance. She was late and it became 10:30 AM. Then I went around in the city center. It was a mall and was not much bigger. I didn't buy anything and I reserved the money to spend when she comes.

I TOUCHED HER!

There came an auto and she got down from it. She was wearing a navy blue *kurta* with a black pant. Her smile made me forget the whole time I waited. She was an inch shorter than me. However, her heels helped her to reach my height. I have always thought of how girl walks with heals, even with higher heels and even walks faster with that.

'Hello' she came near to me, gave her hand, and smiled.

Wow! This made the day perfect. The girl I got fascinated with, in my first sight itself; is now standing before me and giving her hand for a handshake with a smile that was the cutest ever I had seen.

'Hi.' I smiled and gave my hand. The bright sunny day made our first smiles brighter. I felt happy. Not because I met her. It's because we were alone.

According to the plan Joyal should also be there with us. Luckily due to certain reasons he had to leave with Suresh. That made Jessie alone with me in this not-that-big-mall. I hope she won't be having any problem.

When someone accompanies you whom you feel so wanted, then you will feel that you yourself are lost in them. If you are meeting for the first time, then you even may don't know what to do and speak in front of her.

'Sorry, I know you are waiting for a long time and I am late.' She bit her lower lip. As soon as she released her lip, she started explaining again. 'Actually, my grandparents are alone at my home. So I was waiting for my sister to come back. That's why I still became late. Sorry Roshen.' She had a pretty looking, sorry kind of face at that time.

Even I would have waited for a whole year for that face, may be more than that. I couldn't respond and I just stood still as like someone giving the tips for an IAS exam. 'I can't leave them alone because my grandma is sick now and grandpa cannot handle her alone.' I nodded as she continued. We walked in. Finally, a smile appeared on my face.

It is a little bit difficult for me to interrupt her in between whatever she says. Though I don't like long conversations, I always loved to hear her speaking. Her voice was so sweet that no one would ask her to stop talking.

'Are you angry with me?' she asked and I felt terrible.

'It's Ok. Joyal was with me until now. He left just five minutes before.' I spoke! After walking some steps with her I could at least speak something to her beyond admiring at her beauty. But still I didn't get any idea why I am here or why she asked me to meet her.

'You have not told me yet, why you want to meet me?' I asked her out of anxiety.

'What happen? You didn't like my company?' she asked, looking directly into my eyes.

'No, not that! I… I, actually…I just asked. That's all' I said. 'I just want to know today's plan.'

'Nothing, much. I though you will be free today, so I thought of calling you to accompany me for shopping.' She said. 'It's really boring to go with Joyal, and my sister won't come. So I didn't have a companion.'

'That's fine. I just wanted to know why you called me just like that.' I said.

'Actually, I wanted to ask you something.' She said silently.

'What?' I asked curiously.

'Joyal told that you are an artist. So, will you give me any one of your art pieces? I liked it a lot?' she said.

'Oh, yeah, sure!' I said and she smiled. I didn't give the picture I drew for her – right now. What if she just came here for an art piece from me? And if I give it this soon, she may return to home right now. I just don't want that. I decided to spend the time with her, and give the picture at last.

Anyway, I knew this may happen. That she would ask for my art work. Joyal once mentioned that she is such a type that she would get closer to anything she likes so much in her life. So I wanted to take nice glass paint or any one of art works from my home and give it to her. But this meeting became so soon that I couldn't get any time to my home. It merely may take six hours to reach my home from here.

We were just walking like that without having a word with each other. I wanted to tell her about the purse because I don't want her to get into troubles. I don't want her to get hurt. But I don't know how to start about it. Will she think I am purposefully done it.

'Today let's spend the time here inside this building.' She interrupted my thoughts. 'It's too hot outside' she then added.

'As you wish.' I said. She herself is much hotter than the hotness outside. So I didn't cared to notice how hot is outside. Now I did not want to mention about her purse, being with me. I just walked with her.

We entered into a shop through a small door. That moment her hand rubbed mine. She might not have noticed, but I looked at her face. The touch gave me a spark. Her hand was warm and her skin was smooth. Like…I don't know what it was like, but it was smooth.

She turned to me and a shiver passed on my spine, thinking whether she understood the spark I got just now by feeling her touch. I was thinking weather she was bothering about how I was feeling about her.

'I will only take a few minutes here. Promise.' She smiled and started looking for some deodorant sprays and so on 'I never wanted to go out in this hot sun. It's too hot outside and I hate sweating.' She said again as she took the nourishing day cream.

'Do you like nail polish?' she asked me.

'What?' I mocked. I don't use nail polish. I wanted to say but didn't.

'I was just kidding' she smiled again.

'What nail polish do you like?' The sales girl asked her.

'*Loreal Paris* – black.' She replied.

The sales girl stood with a sorry face after searching the small shelves besides her and said 'Sorry ma'am, it's not available. If you want I will definitely make it available in the next week.'

'Oh yeah, thank you.' She smiled at her and moved towards the billing area in that shop.

Once I used to go for shopping with Manju when I was dating her. She never used such costly things like Jessie buys. The more time Manju spends with her dresses than with me. Moreover, that she drags me to the *Girls Wear*, her favorite shop. There she spends hours for selecting a single dress by matching at least fifteen to twenty dresses. At the beginning I liked to spend the shopping time with her. But after, when she said those things to me, I felt discomfort with her for shopping, talking even to kiss those bloody lips which were once so sweet and chubby. But when I was with Jessie I felt quite comfortable and a lot of difference from my ex. Jessie was cute, quiet, calm and of course beautiful – than Manju; in all means.

She billed her purchases from that shop using a credit card and moved on. I followed her and walked side by side with a hope that we walk hand in hand in the next moment. We completed walking in the down floor without spelling a word to each other. May be because, the human brain can do one thing at once. But here talking with a girl and walking with her is not separate tasks; not even a task. It's something different. At down floor shed didn't even tend to scan any shops, but I was definitely scanning the models displayed in front of the shops. I could see her searching for something.

Now we stepped on the escalator that moved downwards. Again the thought of Manju started haunting me. I remembered the smart breakup we had once in the school. I started an affair with Manju Millen, the white-doll of the class. Our dating ended within a few months before the last academic year ended. I felt it so awesome and got relieved after I did the breakup without making any delay.

****

'What were you doing with him in the last bench, when we all went to the lab?' I asked Manju during the lunch break.

'What? Oh, that was nothing. Come, let's go. Today I brought Maggie Roshen. Your favorite!' She rubbed my hair with her hand.

I held her and said 'Don't act smart Manju. Explain that to me first. I am your BOYFRIEND and why you KISSED him damn it?'

'Don't raise your voice. And I know that you are my so-called-boyfriend.' She said.

'Then what the fuck was that?' I asked

'Roshen, try to understand me! There was nothing like you think. I love you and only you. ok?' She said.

'I am bloody asking about HIM' I shot back for her seductive talk.

'Ok, I was just flirting with him. We are not serious like us!' she said 'If you don't like this, I will never talk to him again. Simple'

'Simple! WOW! My girlfriend kisses someone and sees this simple. Ama...zing! Ok then, FUCK OFF and GOODBYE forever.' I pulled the ring from her finger that once I have gifted.

****

NOSTALGIAS

We reached the first floor of the mall. As soon as she saw a bookstall, she entered into it and so I.

'Roshen.' She turned again and called me as I stepped in. I felt it amazing to realize that I wasn't with Manju anymore. 'Do you read books?' She asked as I was smiling at Jessie. She looked so cute, and those eyes on her face – small, and dark, which can lock once eye into her.

'Huh? Yeah, once in a while.' I said. I don't know which books were she is referring to, probably may be the novels like she was holding. On the book it was written *"KING OF TORTS"*. I used to read only the books that were being used for my studies, like textbooks, and other materials. That doesn't mean I am a top scorer. Other than that, I haven't touched other books like she takes from the shelves; not even dictionaries. Everything in the textbooks is just by hearted. Anyway, textbooks are also books. That's why I nodded.

She kept that book back to the shelf and took a yellow book. Its author was a familiar one. It was J. K. Rowling's book. But it's not Harry potter. It named —*"The Casual Vacancy"*. I had only heard of other novels by this author other than, Harry Potter. As novels are not my taste I just looked into her face for almost five minutes. Finally, she looked back and smiled.

'If you are not busy, can I ask you something?' she nodded, looking back to the book she took. 'Why you like my company?'

I feel it's better to know why she likes my company. I want to decide whether to flirt with her or to keep her with me forever.

She kept the book back into the shelf and faced me.

'You are a friend of Joyal. I love to have some company for shopping. And you are so sweet.' She ran her fingers on the books searching for another *title*. 'I don't like to take Joyal for shopping. If he comes he won't allow me to take too much time, then he starts cursing me when he get bored.' Finally, she took both the books ("KING OF TORTS", and "The Casual Vacancy").

'You are not taking much time like he said.' I complimented and she smiled. I know how much time Manju takes for every silly shopping she does. As compared to her, the time Jessie takes are nothing.

'You know one thing?' She looked at me, once again with that small eyes. 'There was a guy who was stalking me in my school and Joyal came to know it. Then he said to my sister and she said to my father. I got into trouble.' She smiled. 'So I told his mother that he was smoking. From there stopped his company.'

'So, what about your sister? Will she not come?' I said.

'She is of no use! You know what, she is a bookworm. Since, Joyal is better.'

'So what do you think about me? That I am better than everyone in your family?' I said.

'I didn't say that. I just like you.' She blinked her eyes and smiled at me.

'As if?' I said.

'Huh?' she said.

'Hm…nothing.' I don't know what the heck I meant to ask her. It just came out of me. *"I don't know. I just like you"*. Did she really say it to me? If so, why can't she edit those words into "I just love you"? Or does she mean the word "love" instead of "like".

I shrugged all my thoughts and gave her my drawing. The paper was being rolled and had tied a ribbon over it. A note was being written on it -*"I love you. This is not just a proposal, I really do love you"*.

'This is for you.' I said and she took it.

She untied the ribbon and stretched the paper.

Though it was a kind of difficult to straighten it, she managed herself to look at it.

It's been an hour, the paper was been rolled and it could be stretched mostly with the help of paperweights. "I should have being bought some paper weights too." I thought myself.

'It's beautiful!' She exclaimed 'My mother had once told me that any drawings should not be folded or rolled like this. Then we cannot enjoy its real beauty.'

'Em…I drew it for you.' I said.

'You drew it for me? WOW! You are such an artist. I love it.' She said. 'My mother used to give me such drawings in my childhood. Now it's you who gave my memories back. Thank you Roshen.' I smiled, as I couldn't say anything.

'So, is your mother in US now?'

'There was an air crash in India years ago. In that accident my mother left me alone. I was studying in fifth grade. My mother had settled in the U.S. with my father for years after her marriage. She used to come here to visit her parents, once in a while. This crash happened in one of her journeys. Now I miss a lot Roshen.' Her voice started jerking. 'Her funeral was done here in India. When I stay here with her parents I feel my mother is here with me. I have been here since my mother's funeral. My father allowed me to remain here until my sister finishes her Chartered Accountancy course. After that, he will pull us back to the U.S. There, I would be happy, if she had not gone. But now, I don't want to go'

I noticed her eyes wet. Those small black eyes. Tears will jump out to her beautiful cheeks in the next second. I don't know what to say or do. I do not like anyone crying, especially her.

'My sister is another creature who always goes on studying and will never accompany me for anything. After, my mother's funeral, I always feel that I am alone.' Her eyes were still wet.

'You are not and you will never be alone as far as I am with you.' I could say that. She hugged me as soon as I wiped her endless tears.

Finally, it happened. As far as I am concerned, proposing means saying *"I love you"*. But in reality, it's all about the mutual reactions that come at that particular moment.

The shelf behind us is the only reason why no one noticed us. I could completely feel her warmth and at the same time, I could feel her tears falling on my neckline. Her phone rang. She directly gave the mobile to me. The screen displayed Joyal's name.

FIRST WARNING

'Will that Roshen really come back to hostel today?' Joyal asked as soon as I picked the phone.

'It's me, Roshen.' I said. 'And what for you are raising your voice to her? If there is something, then directly tell to me.'

'Dude, it's already 7:30pm. As per the rule everyone should be in the hostel at six and in study hall at seven. You have not yet reached.' He said.

'Did Mr. Warden say anything?' I asked.

'According to what I said to him, now you are in the bathroom.' He said.

'WHAT? Don't you get any other reason?' I interrupted.

'Do you know what will happen if he is caught? You will just be fired and moreover that he will inform your parents.' He said. 'He may go out of the hostel after some time. If you come at that time, you can escape from him. I will message you once he stepped out of the hostel. Bye.' He disconnected the phone.

'I have to go' I said and gave her mobile back.

'Hm… when will we meet again then? She said.

'Any time you wish.' I said and she smiled.

She went to the counter with both the books. I stood near to her. She opened her new purse for the payment.

Still, I wanted to inform her about the purse but couldn't. We waited outside the shop for Joyal's message.

'So, do you love me?' I asked as we sat there on a bench.

'Yeah, I told you. I like you. You are a very good person. You-' she said

'Jessie' I interrupted 'I didn't mean that. I want to be with you forever.'

Like usual, it all starts with a forever. Though the relationship with Manju failed, I hope this time it works. But I need to know a perfect answer from her.

'I didn't mean that way! I just said that I like you. That doesn't mean that I am in love with you.' She said

'I liked you not because you told me that you liked me. I had seen you in the train; the day before I came to Joyal's house. You were listening to some music in your mobile. You looked stunning!'

'Oh, I was going to my friend's house in Hyderabad every month. She-' she said. I thought she was diverting the topic.

'I didn't ask you where you went. I liked you the moment I saw you on the train, I started loving you when I talked with you in his house, and still more I really do love you more as I came to know more about you.' I said.

'Sympathy?' she asked with a betrayed smile.

'It's not! Whatever happened to you is possible to happen in anyone's life. Do you think I don't have problems? In my home, it's all like click-and-do-process. That strict is my father. And no excuse and reasons are allowed. Probably my problems are not as big as yours, but each person's problem is more important to them.' I was not being advising her actually.

I was just trying to explain that I love her. I know how Manju was and how difficult was for me to be with her. But she cheated me. I didn't hate her till I found Jessie. Instead, I loved her *forever* till we broke up and after that I missed her a lot. At the same time it was difficult for me to avoid her too.

Jessie was not like Manju. As I said she was so…I don't know. I really like her. Apart from Manju, she is different in her own ways and I want a girl like her whom could be trusted. Whatever happens, I want Jessie to be my girlfriend. She likes me, she smiles at me, talks to me, even cried in front of me and shared her problems.

'So is not my problem yours also?' She asked after sometimes thinking. I don't know what she thought or meant and didn't dare to ask it.

'Meaning?' I asked, though I understood what she meant. I wanted to hear it clearly from her. I tried for that 'Is it?'

She just smiled. 'What is click-and-do-process?'

'What is that?' I asked. By the time I was so happy and I just wanted her face to know whether her face will also be like those smooth warm hands of her.

'You only told that in your home, it's all like *click-and-do-process* when you was advising me just a moment ago.' She said.

'That was not an advise!' I snapped.

'Then what was it?' she giggled.

'Jessie, I was trying to make you understand something.' I explained.

'That's called advising!' she widened her eyes.

That was a brand new expression, I saw in her face till today.

'It was *not*!' I protested.

'Hmf, whatever.' She mocked.

That was our first small fight. I liked to do it with her. I love to do everything with her.

'Don't tell to Joyal about this. Please.' She pleaded.

'Don't plead. It hearts.' She smiled as I said it. 'And tell about what?' I asked though, I know it.

'I don't know about that.' she looked down.

'Why can't you tell that you can't say it directly?' I murmured.

We really had our first face to face talk. I enjoyed looking at her small black eyes. I love her so much. She has a baby face. So cute and may be smooth and soft like her hand. I still hadn't touched her face.

'So, how about your father, I mean being alone there for almost years. Doesn't he come here.' I asked.

'Hm...not really. He never used to mingle with us from our childhood. I found no emotions in him when my mother passed away. After my mother's funeral, my father married another lady - Elena. She is working in his firm in U.S.A. He married that lady and said to us "life has to go on". That day I stopped talking to my father and I don't like that lady. I can never see another lady in my mother's place and she always acts like my mother. And she goes on advising what to do, what not to do.

After a week, we shifted us from U.S to India. Thankfully, he allowed us to stay in my mother's home, which was a relief for me. He made my sister join for a CA coaching and me to a higher secondary school here in Thrissur. Though we are happy staying here, still there are problems. After my sister's course gets over, he takes us back to U.S.' she took a deep breath after telling the whole story.

'Are you going?' That was the only thing I asked.

'I really don't want to go Roshen.' She said.

'Ok, now don't think about it. I will call you by phone every day and-' I said and took her hand in mine.

'No. Don't call me. I will call you whenever my sister is not there at home.' She took her hand back.

'Why?' I said.

'It might not be good for me if my sister knows it.' She said. 'When will we meet again?'

'No idea. Anyway, Sundays cannot be missed and let me see there is any chance before Sunday.' I said. 'You know, hostels are a little bit strict'

'Will you come home next Sunday?'

'Why not?' I said.

Her mobile beeped and the screen displayed -"Jincy"

The message read; "I told I have to go to my friends for studies and where the hell are you now? Come home within 15min. or otherwise I will lock the door and leave."

'I have to leave now Roshen, bye.' She said.

'You haven't said it yet.'

'What?' she asked and I continuously looked at her eyes till she understood.

'Roshen, I already told you! I like your company. That's it and had I said anything when you took my hand.' She noted it!

'Yes, you took your hand back.' I also noted that.

'I didn't mean anything by that. I just told not to call me.' She said.

'Then say now, that you love me. *Or not*' I said

'I want to think.' She said and left.

I didn't get the time to say anything. She left so fast. I know her sister is so concerned about her studies. She likes me. And I feel great for that. Now I have someone to consider. It felt so alone in the hostel. Joyal got himself engaged with Avita. It's like he got his old girlfriend back. And for me, I got a better girlfriend than Manju.

I have no idea when to enter the hostel. There is no other option other than to reach hostel as soon as possible and face whatever happens.

Firstly, I am late, and firing from the warden is a surety. I exited the mall and walked to the hostel as fast as I can. While walking, I was thinking seriously about the reason to be said to my father as well as to the warden, if I am caught. The best thing to be done was to get into the study room with a book. I should be careful that the warden will not notice me.

Finally, I reached a place where the hostel could be seen clearly. For my bad luck, the warden was standing in front of the hostel and I can't get inside before the warden leaves the hostel. I was very confused about what to be done.

If I go directly when he is there, I will be caught. Then he will inform my parents and I will be in a deep trouble. So I started waiting thinking he would leave soon. But the reverse happened. He remained in the hostel itself. So I had no other option. Hence, I had to move towards its main gate. That means I had to enter the hostel in front of him. I will definitely be marked as a latecomer.

I reached the hostel. *CAUGHT!* The first thing I saw was the warden's red face.

No idea about what to do. It was better for me to come earlier. I shouldn't have waited for the warden to leave. The way he fired could be made into an episode of storytelling. May be because of the first time he warned me.

'If I gave a complaint, then you can't study anymore at the institute and no other hostels in this area will accommodate you.' Warden said and left the hostel.

Everyone in the study hall were admiring at me. Now they got my clear picture and I just walked towards Joyal and took a book from him. I didn't have a word to Joyal about what all happened and started studying. "Admiring into the book" is what exactly I did. I am afraid weather the warden will inform my parents. I had nothing to do other than *looking-into-the-book* business, until the food comes.

THE TREAT

Like always, the warden woke me up in the morning along others. All the dreams were about her. Also, when I woke up, she was the one whom I was all thinking about. It was as if she woke me up, and I felt the agitation as soon as I realized it was the warden.

When a girl enters into one's life, then the only person he wants with him will be her memories. Rust everything will always be a headache, especially at the initial stage of his or her romantic moments.

When I looked at the time, there was still half an hour for the class to start. As when compared to our meeting on the next day, there was still a lot of time left ahead. Every time I was only bothering about meeting her, because she has warned me not to call her. So we decided to date every Sunday. Tomorrow is a Sunday.

All these days' classes became a secondary subject for me. I dragged myself to the bathroom for a bath, and pushed me to the class myself. At home, there will be someone to be there behind me, and now surviving in the hostel was definitely a big task. It was totally boring thing to walk the whole way from hostel to campus alone is a self-rebelling thing. No one was there to talk with me, nothing to do while walking to the campus, other than walking. Moreover that, I had no mobile with me.

My father never bothered to buy a mobile phone for me. In today's world, when, even small kids plays around with a *mobile phone,* my father used to say to use call booths when I am out of my home. I tell you guys. In this 21st century, it's very difficult to find out a booth.

Finally, I reached inside the campus. "Huff". That's what I said when I understood that I was not late! I sat in the 3rd last bunch at the right hand side of the classroom. The seating arrangement was based on our performance in the examination. So you can imagine how I was.

The class had no difference, as teachers would come, blabber, throws questions to students and finally ends in shouting at him (Of course, only boys were there in my class. Boys and girls have separate classrooms). Luckily, no one has asked any questions to me yet! Actually, it was something to celebrate; though escaping from oral questions within the whole 110 students is not a big thing. At the same time, when some teacher asks any question and then standing without knowing a word about the answer in front of the same 110 is a nasty thing.

The bell rang. Lunch break was the only relief I had between the classes. I would always join with Joyal and Suresh at the lunch. Still, they are the only company I had there on that campus. As usual, I was waiting at the gate for Joyal.

'Let's go.' Suresh came and put his hand around my shoulder.

'Where is Joyal?' I said.

'He went to meet Avita.' Suresh said.

'So he will not be coming soon.' I said.

We stood in the mess with a long queue. There everything is been served. So we have to be so careful and unwanted items should be prohibited to the plate. Otherwise, we have to struggle to make it finish, as nothing should be wasted in hostels. We sat on a table and started eating.

'Oh damn, started without me?' Joyal came and joined us.

'I thought you will be bunking the whole afternoon classes with Avita. And we assumed that you will have dinner too with her.' I prodded.

Joyal gave me a sarcastic look.

'What I said is exactly being done by everyone.' I leaned towards him. 'Because, if we are dating with someone, then in order to avoid the boring classes, bunking and spending with them is the finest solution taken.' I said.

'I just went to have a word with Avita. Finally, I am dating with her.' He said. 'And the classes are not boring to me.'

'WOW!' we echoed.

Suresh and I finished our food and now we are waiting to ask a treat to him. After many days of following her, they started dating for the first time. Definitely, this is the time to get treat from him. I was waiting for Suresh to come back after washing his hand. He is the better option for making him give treat. Senior's words will have some value better than I will.

'Actually you are a cheat.' Joyal said to me.

'Huh? I didn't get you.' I said.

'You proposed Jessie?' he said.

'Who is Jessie?' Suresh asked.

'How do you know?' I interrupted Suresh. I have never told him about anything that happened between me and Jessie. I became a little terrified. What does Jessie think about me? I am sure that she would definitely misunderstand me. I had no idea what to tell her.

'She told me.' Joyal told.

'What?' I got stunned. 'What exactly had she said?' I twitched him.

'Yes, she told me that she liked you.' He said.

'How come that happens?' I asked. She only told me *"Don't tell to Joyal about this. Please."* And the one who said it had already said that to Joyal. I felt like a fool between this. Is she playing pranks on me? I don't think so, but still there was a chance. Otherwise why should she ask me to accompany her to the mall? Why she pulled her hand back when I held it? I felt humiliated. I must talk to her about this. If something is wrong I will not give her purse back to her.

'What are you thinking about? Lunch break is going to finish soon. Finish your food.' Suresh warned.

'By the way Joyal, who is Jessie? You didn't tell yet.' Suresh asked Joyal as he took his empty plate in his hand.

'It's my cousin sister.' Joyal introduced her to Suresh.

'Wow, that's cool.' Suresh said looking at me. 'There came a twist in the story…' He mocked at me and left to wash his hand.

Joyal hadn't said anything clearly about it yet.

'Joyal could you please tell me everything about it. Please.' I asked him politely.

He took a deep breath and looked at me. 'My uncle called me home at the late night. And I went there.'

'For what?' I said. I didn't noticed him leaving the hostel and I only saw him now, at the lunch break.

'Jessie leaves to U.S today evening. So I will be going to the airport soon after the afternoon classes.' He said. I wanted to meet her right now. I didn't want to lose her these soon. I decided to bunk the evening class.

'Then?' I asked.

'Yesterday when I went to her house, she was crying in her room. When I asked, she told that she liked you so much and loves you. She was already fascinated about your paintings. She was holding your gift as well.' He said and took a deep breath. 'That's what happened yesterday and I also told her about the purse.'

'Thanks Joyal. I was thinking how to tell her about it.' I said. I said and we went to the wash room

'It's ok. I will give it back to her. You just hand over to me when we go back to hostel.' He smiled.

I became nervous with the whole incident. Firstly I like her, and I do love her. Till now she hadn't told that she loves me. I have no idea about why she said that she had to think. The only idea I had is that she doesn't hates me and she likes me. And that need not mean she loves me. That was why I was been confused. Now it's clear that she too loves me, but why can't she say it directly?

Moreover that, she told me, that she is not going back to U.S. and then what happened? I definitely need to talk to her. I went to Joyal and asked him to call her for me.

'Hello, where is Jessie?' he called and her sister took the phone piece. I slicked my ear to his phone to know what was happening. I heard Jincy yelling her name. I snatched the phone from him and waited for her.

'Hello?' Jessie spoke.

'Hi Jessie, Roshen this side.' I said.

'Wow! Hi, I just thought about you Roshen' She said.

'What were you thinking?' I asked.

'Nothing, just like that. About our date, em… I mean the day we did the shopping in the mall.' She said.

'Could we please meet today?' I ignored the way she was speaking.

She loves me. She knows. I know it. Even Joyal knows! Still she talks everything indirectly. It was clear in the way she behaves. She had considered the day we went to the mall as a *"date"* but she acts as if it's just a meeting. Why she wants to tell Joyal that she loves me when I am alive? Who the hell is Joyal in between this? A mediator? A

"Why you want to take this much time to agree to meet me one more time?" Though I wanted to ask, I didn't. I don't want her to feel bad about me

'Roshen… I too want to meet you, but I am not sure whether they will leave me alone to go out.' She said 'And you have class today, right?'

'Yes.'

'Er…could you please accompany Joyal?'

'Why you want Joyal with-'

'Why? What happened?' she prodded

'No, nothing. I mean…let me ask him. We got class in the next ten minutes.'

'Ok, if he is there with you, then I could give an excuse at home easily. That's why.' She said convincingly.

'Let me see,'

'Roshen'

'What?'

'I am…leaving abroad. I mean, back with my father.'

'So what?' I faked my feelings to her. I had already decided that I won't show any emotions or anything unless she says that she love me. Like the same way I want it. At the same time I won't let her go just like that. I love her.

'Nothing, Bye.' She said. 'And I will text you in five minutes. Bye'

'Bye.' She disconnected first. Then I gave it to him. We bunged the afternoon class. Just many *"Bye"* brought our conversation to an end, and still I am not sure that I could meet her today. If can't I can never meet her again. Today I want to know her. And I will get her soon.

DON'T JUST LEAVE WITHOUT A REPLY

We sat on a bench, at the same venue. The *"City Center mall"*. She wore a pink Salwar with the same untied hair, which she was occasionally adjusting behind her ears. That's what made her gorgeous. For a few minutes we didn't talk to each other. Those small cute black eyes were looking at me constantly, saying; *"say something"*. But I don't know what to say. And we just sat there as if we were meeting each other for the first time. And when we met for the first time, we never have been like this.

'At what time is the flight?' I spoke first.

She was motionless for the entire time, since we are here. 'Afternoon'

'So, when are you leaving to the airport?' I still looked at her as she did the same.

'Don't know. Jincy asked me to get back soon.'

'Joyal is not with me. Then how did you come?' I thought her sister won't allow her to meet me alone just like that.

'I just came.'

'They didn't ask anything?'

'Ask what?' She moved the strands of hair behind her ears once again. And this is the fifth time she is doing that. And I like it whenever she does it.

'Are you going alone?'

She shook her head. 'My father will come to the airport to pick me.'

'So, this would be our last time in our life. And I know that you won't come back here.' I said and she looked somewhere else.

'Don't you have anything else to say?' she looked at me again. 'I just wanted to see you before leaving. That's why I came here. So, say something else which is... nice to hear and don't go on questioning me.' she gestured and smiled.

'I love you.' and once that smile has gone from her face. I held her hand. She didn't pull back. 'Just say that you don't love me back, if you are not.'

She didn't say anything.

'Jessie. Speak something! I don't like this. I am not a radio. Say something back. Please. And don't just leave without a reply.'

'Roshen, I already told you that I like you, and I am not sure about anything else. I just-' She laughed and said which I never liked before.

'Joyal told me the whole thing that you said to him.' I raised my voice. I tried not to but couldn't. 'Sorry' I said immediately.

She became silent and never looked at me after I raised my voice. The *sorry*, didn't help either. I waited for some more time. She didn't speak anything. Now why should I be here! That's what I thought.

I got up to leave. She didn't say anything. I looked at her, though she is looking down. 'I don't know what you think. But still I love you. Bye.'

I moved forward with the smallest footsteps possible. Partially dragging my foot on the floor, as I don't want to leave her soon. I thought she would call me back.

I noticed her from the corner of my eye. Still the same result. I felt angry about everything she did to me. I started walking faster. I reached at the exit of the mall. I felt that she stood behind me. I slowed down and wanted to turn around. But didn't. I expected her to call me. She didn't. I turned around just to find out that she was not there. I looked to the people. Not even anyone resembled her. She was nowhere. I felt exhausted and left. I walked back to the hostel. I felt it a waste to bunk the whole afternoon class just for her. And what she did was a humiliation. I can't think anything else.

She told Joyal that she loved me and I don't know what happened to her after that. Can't she just say that to me instead of telling that to Joyal? Moreover, why she needs time to say what's there in her mind. I ignored everything and lay down on the bed as soon as I reached the hostel. The entire time I acted sick. I woke up to have some tea when Joyal came back after the classes.

'She was with you right?' he said.

'Yes,' I said. 'What happened?'

'She hasn't reached home yet.'

'What?' I felt a shiver in my body. She should have gone back home by now. 'We were in the City Center. Had you gone there'

'No, my mother just called and told me that she hasn't reached home yet. And they are not able to call her.' He said.

'Have you tried?' I asked

'I didn't even dial her number.' He said

'Give your phone, I will call her.' I said.

He took the phone from his pocket and gave it to me. I typed *"Jessie"* in the search column and it showed no result.

'Where is her number?' I asked him

'Look for *"Jincy"*. It's her phone.' He said.

I took the number and called her. She took the phone after a few rings.

'Jessie' I said immediately.

'Don't you hate me?' she said.

'Where are you' I shot back

'The same place where we sat a few hours ago.' She said.

'What are you doing there Jessie?' I asked 'Everyone is waiting for you at home. And why haven't you picked up the calls? You-'

'Roshen, I want to talk to you.' She stopped me.

'Yeah, tell' I was still in the same hangover on what she did. I don't hate her, but I can't understand her.

'Come here. The same place where we sat. Please'

'A few hours ago, I was there. That time don't you have anything to say? I really wanted to hear what you said to Joyal.'

'Roshen, let's talk about it. Please come here.' She said 'Come fast.'

'Ok,' I said

'And don't bring Joyal.' She disconnected the phone.

'I will come now.' I said to Joyal, who were still having not finished his tea and ran outside to reach the mall soon. On the way, I took a lift on a motorbike with a stranger. He drove a little faster and dropped me near the building.

THOSE HAPPY MOMENTS

I hurried inside the mall to the spot where she asked to come. But I couldn't find her. I dialed her again. I hadn't given back Joyal's phone to him. Instead, I took it with me. After so many rings, I disconnected. I redialed her number. She didn't respond. I walked around the mall searching for her. The mobile beeped in my pocket. I took and looked into the screen. It displayed the name *"Jincy".* It was a message from Jessie.

"Sorry for not taking your call, come to the book stall. I will wait☺"

I dung the phone piece into my pocket and ran to the bookstall. I had a guess on why she was calling me to meet again. Either she will say that she loves me or she will have a man-made-excuse to evade me forever. Whatever it is I will become free minded after getting the result. The only time I didn't like is the time she took. It made me feel that she changed her mind after she said that to Joyal. Now, I could no. If she again takes the *time,* that's it. I will never talk to her. At the same time I was overexcited on thinking what she would be saying.

Yes, there she is. I spotted her again through the large glass pan of the book stall. The same Jessie I fell in love with. She is still cute and more beautiful now. I stepped in and stood there looking at her. She didn't notice me. She had a book in her hand. This time it was small in size. I was so happy and the happiness made me forget every bitterness on her in my mind. Once again, I love her. This time, even more.

'Jessie' I called her a loud enough to hear a ten-foot away.

She pulled her eyes from the book she held to look at me. One more time those black-cute-eyes made me melt. I went near her.

I sighed loudly 'Finally.' I smiled.

'Sh…' She too smiled back.

'This is not a library.' I informed.

'Whatever. Let's go?' she asked, holding that small book in her hand.

'Are you buying it?' I said as we reached the billing area.

'Hm, yes. Do you want?' she said, and the lady took the book and started billing it.

'Nope. What about the other books you bought that day?' I said

'I finished reading that' she said

'This soon!' I gulped

'That's how the people who read books. Why can't you buy one?' the lady said and handed over the book back to her.

'Hello, the library in which I am having membership has more books than you have.' I said.

'Sorry, I didn't know you were an avid reader.' The lady said. 'She is our regular customer. So I thought you will also be interested in buying one.' She smiled and pointed towards Jessie. We smiled back and moved out of the stall.

'What all types of books your library has?' She asked as if she met me again to ask these stuffs.

'I don't know'

'You said that you have a membership. You read a lot right?'

'I have a membership but I don't read. I was just kidding with that lady.' I said 'In my school, every student must have a membership card. So, that way I too had.'

'Oh, I see. I used to read many books and keep a collection of good ones in my room.' She said.

'You didn't say anything about that yet.' I said.

'Ow...that. Em...why can't you come home with Joyal?' She asked.

'Yeah, sure, I will come. But, before you have to tell what I was waiting for.' She looked at with those cute eyes.

We stood near the escalator, which run downwards. Before stepping into it, we stood still looking to each other. Today she was not wearing her heals. So, I had to face down a little to meet those cute eyes as she was an inch shorter than me. A few people walked beside us to take the escalator.

'Say something. Anything you feel like. Feel free to say if it is a *no*' I said softly, in a lower voice which she alone could hear. At the same time I begged to God not to make her say "no" in even lesser voice, which I could only hear. She went into her thoughts, without looking at me. May be thinking what I will feel if she says a no. Because I am half sure that she see me much smarter to accept my proposal, so easily.

'I always feel to be with you. But,' she said and paused.

'But' I wanted to know the rest.

'Em…but, I, you know. I… I will… I am going, back to U.S with my father. So, I didn't want you to… I mean I didn't want *us* to get apart in the future.' She looked at me deeply. I just want that look, for remaining alive in every sleepless night ahead. She was so beautiful and hot. I wanted to console her to agree to be with me for the time being she would be here.

'So, what you mean to say.' I asked 'You want this to be over?'

'I don't know'

'Jessie. This is what I don't understand.'

'I want to be with you, but at the same time I don't want to hurt you too'

'I don't understand what you are trying to tell. Can't you just say your decision?'

She kept silence. And spoke after sometime. 'You tell. What should we do? I definitely have to go to the states with my father. Or…let's put this to an end. What is the use of getting committed if both of us are in two different countries? That too far from each other,'

'So?'

'Let's close that chapter. We are just friends. Ok?' She smiled and put her hand forward for a handshake.

I don't understand what girls do mean by "just friends" agreement. That too when both like each other.

'Let's wait. I can't lose such a girl like you. Let's not end this so easily. Let's begin. Please.' I said 'Let's find our own way to be committed forever. I will never ever hurt you.'

'My father will not spare you if he comes to know about this.' She said.

'Let's not tell him.' I smiled.

'Stupid.' She laughed and punched me playfully.

'Still, you haven't said that' I said

'What? Em...,' she looked at me and she smiled 'I love you'

'Love you too' I said happily.

'I have to go now.' She said. 'Come home with Joyal'

'Yeah, definitely.' I said and held her hand 'Let's go,' we stepped onto the escalator and moved downwards. 'I will go to the hostel now. And I will come to your home along with Joyal.'

She just smiled at me.

We reached at the ground floor. I looked at those cute eyes one more time before leaving. 'I like your eyes, the most.' I said

'I got my mother's eyes' she said. 'Bye' she waved her hand and turned to leave.

'Jessie, call me when you reach home.'

She nodded 'I will.' She called for an auto.

THE PHONE RINGS...

'Please.' I said.

'No. I won't allow. How many times do you want me to say he same thing?' He questioned.

'Please. These will be the last time. And a friend of mine leaves today. So, please?' I said.

'No, you are not going anywhere. At what time will you come back?'

'Before... 8 PM.' I was not sure about it, but still I gave a time.

'In this hostel, if someone is going out, he must be back here before 7 PM. And that's the limit.' He said

'So, Joyal-' I said

'His parents called me and they want me to leave him to his house.' he said and took his leave.

I ran behind him and stopped him at the gate. I wanted to go with him and meet her before she leaves India. These are the last moments and can't lose the opportunity.

'I promise that I will be back before 8 PM. And it's not that late.' I argued

'Are YOU the warden or me?' he shot back. 'How can I trust you? First of all; now the time is twenty minutes past seven. How will I make sure that you will be back before eight?' he said and I wondered if he is teaching me time like "*now the time is twenty minutes past seven*" as if I don't know.

'I will. May I go, please?' I asked again politely before he was about to say something.

He moved an inch forward and stood near me. 'Did you ask my permission when you left today? Go to the study room, now.'

He left the hostel and I stood at the gate. I was disappointed. I sighed and turned around. Joyal was standing there looking at me.

'What happened?' He asked, coming near to me.

'M…hm, he won't allow. What if I came with you just like that?' I suggested

'That's risky,' he said 'not only for you. He will catch hold of me too.'

'What to do now? I want to meet her Joyal.'

'It's ok; I will ask her to call you.'

'Bye' I said and he also left.

I remained at the gate for a long time. This day I had no mood to study anything. So, I had not seen Suresh after the class.

I felt helpless for not being able to meet her. I waited for her call by standing at the gate alone by the roadside. But I felt that she was angry with me for not going there. I was making my own assumptions on how she will think. How long will it take for her to call me? I also thought about calling Joyal, but something stopped me from dialing his number.

It's time for food and they came in their white Omni car with the urns. The warden asked me to take one of the urns. I took the smallest and the lightest one from it. I stared at the warden for not allowing me to go, which he casually ignored. I moved to the upstairs with the urn in my hand and kept it on the table as soon as I reached there.

As usual, everyone formed a queue and today I stood in front of the queue. I took little food and sat on a bench in a corner. Suresh also joined me after some time.

'Where is Joyal?' he asked

'He left to his house' I said

'Didn't you go?'

'Huh?' I asked.

'Usually you would go to his house whenever he goes. That's why.' He said.

'Warden didn't permit' I looked at his face.

'Wonderful' he mocked.

'Asshole' I murmured. And I am sure that he would not have heard me. Because he didn't react.

'Jessie is not good for you. Why are you behind her?' he said

'Why?' By the time I had already finished my food.

'She doesn't even stay here anymore. And…I don't know it would work out.'

'I want her and I love her. That's enough.' I said 'I don't think anything else. By the way, you are saying this because you don't know my past.' I stood and left to get to my bed, after washing my hand.

rw .Wlo

I switched off the light and fell on my bed. I was thinking about her and the ways to contact her once she left. What Suresh said will never affect our relationship. Much that, I love her. That was the only reason why I decided to get committed to her even after knowing that she would go back to the U.S. anytime. But it's not forever. She will anyway come back again.

The phone rang…

As the phone was kept near my bed it was easy to get me faster. I would be the first one to pick up the calls, almost all the time. I even liked that. But for the first time, the call came in the late night. I looked at the time. My watch showed 11:45 PM. I was about to fall asleep when the call came. I stood from the bed and sat on it.

'Hello' I sang on to the receiver in a half-sleepy-voice.

'Hi, do you forget me?' She asked

'Why? You only told not to call you. Otherwise, I would have called you ten times till now.'

'Hm, why you didn't come?'

'Why you didn't go. Actually, you must have boarded the flight by now.'

'I asked first.'

'My warden didn't allow going out of the hostel. Do you know, I had many plans by coming there?'

'What plans?'

'Nothing much, just to be with you and to…by the way why you didn't leave?

'My father couldn't come and told me to come along with my sister. So I will be going only after her course gets completed.'

'Wow!' That was really exiting.

I lay down on the bed again facing to the ceiling while talking to her. I became so happy for her not going to U.S.A.

'I was feeling sad for not able to meet you today.' She said.

'Sorry, I told you about it.' I said

'What were you doing?' she said

'Sleeping, what else.' I moaned

'Ow…um…let's talk?' She too

'I feel sleepy,' I said. In between I was also falling into sleep, but wakes up soon. 'Feeling so tired'

'You didn't come today. Moreover can't just spare sometime' She said

'Jessie, I feel dizzy and have a head ache too'

'What happened?'

'I don't know. Where is your sister?'

'She is sleeping nicely on the sofa in the living room. And I am in my bedroom. I just too her phone to talk to you.'

'Hmm, call every day or I will call you.'

'No, don't call me. I will call you almost every day.'

'Do you sleep alone?'

'Em. Sometime Jincy will sleep in my room.'

'Hmm…'

'She may also call me early in the morning and asks to make coffee for her.'

'Hmm…'

'So, I will make coffee.'

'Hmm…'

'You must drink my coffee, it's really tasty.'

'Hmm…'

'STUPID.' She said a little louder. Louder means, in a feeble voice. 'Idiot! I am talking and you are humming over there?'

There was silence for; I think just for, say five seconds. Accidently I fell to sleep.

'Roshen! Have you slept?' I woke up when she became serious. 'Roshen…' She moaned 'Please Roshen, let's talk for some time. I am also feeling sleepy. See, I am talking to you. Then why can't you. I feel so happy that I am not going to the U.S. now, not leaving you, and guess what? We are going to meet again!'

'Hmm…ok, me too fells so excited to meet you again.'

'So sweet, love you…'

'Hmm…' Again I fell asleep and I think that I didn't say anything back except a hum.

'If I were there with you I would have bitten, your ears, and made it red.' She said

'Of course, with pleasure. And I will bite your lips with many love bites on your…neck, hand,'

'Wow, so my boyfriend is on now.'

'Hey, I mean it. When should I give it?'

'Um… next time, maybe.'

'I would have given you today if I could come there in the evening.'

'It's ok, now I am with you, near you'

'Hmm…'

'Started?'

'No! I just,'

'Good night.'

'Jessie, let's see tomorrow.'

'Ok, are you really tired?'

'GOD! Then what did I tell you?'

'Ow… It's ok, how are you now?'

'Em…feels better.'

'Bye,'

'I will see you tomorrow, bye'

'Bye.' She disconnected the phone and then I put down the receiver.

Rain Was Not
the Problem

'You should not give any fake promises, Roshen.' Suresh said to me.

'Huh? I didn't get you.' I said.

'You got a girlfriend and no treat! DUMBAS.' He said. 'Common, let's go somewhere.'

It was always nice to get parties from others and if the chance comes for us to offer a party, then the moments to get heart attaches begins. But this time there was no way to escape. I took a deep breath and let it out.

'I will give it today in the... evening. And this time I won't trick you.' I said. 'Don't look like this. Trust me. Let's go at 6pm to City Center.' they had such a look that can burn my head away.

When I said to Suresh about Jessie, he was behind me for the treat. I was skipping myself from him whenever he asked to treat. I only have a 500-rupee note that my father gave me on the first day of my joining here. Yesterday my father sent my ATM card that I left in my home. That is the only relief why I agreed to give treats to them. And this time I will make Joyal share the expense of the treat.

When you spend your money with your partner, you will know how much you had spent only when your bank balance becomes NIL.

'Em…actually Joyal also must give the treat. He too have a girlfriend.' I said to Suresh.

'Yeah, fine, I don't mind. Whatever it is, I must get it.' Suresh said.

'I will call Avita too.' Joyal said. 'That's too much.' He said as Suresh moved to the washroom.

We three together moved outside the hostel and joined in the evening classes. It had no difference from the morning hours. Only the topics changed. I was trying my maximum to run the time and concentrating on classes expect biology and physics everything is a kind of boring. And mathematics is another subject that always plays pranks with me. Whenever I try to solve a problem, the answer I get will be no where linked to the question. And the climax will be; folding my book for the rest of the day.

So I started counting *"how many OKs and SOs were spelled by the teachers"* as usual. That is the only way I could spend my time in the class.

As the time went, the classes got over and I started walking to the hostel with them. As this was not our hometown, we had no cycles or any other options other than to walk, in order to reach the hostel. Joyal had no cycle as if like he hates bicycles.

As usual, the warden started distributing the tea and snacks in our hostel. And after collecting the tea, most of them dumped their asses on my bed. Though I don't like it, I couldn't say anything to them. The only thing I did was just staring at them while drinking my tea.

I took the receiver of the *coin-phone* and inserted the coin inside to dial the number.

'Hi' she took the phone.

'Hm, hi. Will you come to the *city center*?'

'When?' She said on the phone.

I was speaking with her once again on the phone. I had a relief that she won't be saying any bad news like leaving to the U.S. with her father. I was relaxed when I was speaking to her.

Actually, I was not speaking, I was asking her to come to the same venue. The *City Center mall*. She agreed with one condition. She made me promise that I would leave her home on time. Everything was fixed and we disconnected the phone.

Suresh was the *odd-one-out* from us. I have never seen him dating with anyone or talking about any ex-girlfriends. Joyal and I were following Suresh as if we don't know the way. When we were about to reach the place, tinny spots of water droplets started appearing on the road. The numbers of drops were increasing and I felt water falling on me too. As it started to rain heavily, we rushed into the building. The sound of rain also increased as the thick line of water rushed downwards.

We entered into the ground floor. We three looked each other and partially laughed.

'Just escaped from the rain! Let's not just stand here. What if they came already?' Joyal said.

'They may be sitting somewhere inside.' I said.

'You go and search them. I will be there in the parking lot.' Suresh said and moved off.

'Parking lot?' we said in unison, but he already left.

I didn't understand what he would be doing in the parking lot. I was tracking, where Suresh was exactly going in this rain. By the time Joyal went inside the mall. While I was searching where Suresh went, my eyes hooked up when I saw Jessie coming through the way. She walked to me under her umbrella. She was wearing a purple top and a black pant. With the same untied hair as her trademark. I always like to see her that way.

'Hi.' She winked and folded her umbrella as soon as she reached near me.

'Let's go.' I said.

'Where is Joyal?' she asked and continuously folded and unfolded the umbrella. The water on it got sprinkled on the floor.

'He already went with his girlfriend.' I said.

'Girlfriend?' she said as we moved in.

'He didn't tell you?' She shook her head in a wide angle.

The door opened when the lift reached to the ground floor. We entered inside, together. As soon as I realized that there was no one in the lift, I groped her waist immediately, as the door closed.

I looked at her. Those small beautiful eyes and the admirable face with her untied hair made me feel lucky to have her as mine. She was gorgeous. I moved my other hand behind her neck and pulled her closer to me. So close that I could feel her breath and the warmth on her skin.

She looked at me quizzically into my eyes. I still felt the cuteness in her eyes. I was more tempted, just to kiss her at least once. I pressed her lips with mine. She closed her eyes. Her lips also remained closed. Then she too kissed me back. I started kissing more. She followed. I moved my tongue between her lips.

Suddenly she pushed me when the lift had already opened its doors. The screen showed "**4**". We reached the top floor. Luckily there was no one near the lift to see what we were doing. Otherwise, she might not have allowed me to do it with her again.

This floor was almost empty as compared to the other floors. There were many empty rooms, which were upcoming stores. We walked over five minutes away from the lift and she had not spelled a word to me yet. I was a little tensed that she was not feeling good about what happened moments ago. I was provoked to ask her about it, many times till now. But was not able to. What if she really feels bad about it?

'Roshen' she called me. Thank God, she finally started to mingle. The relaxation I felt then was really great and pleasant. So there was no issue with the kiss. I doubted that she hadn't liked me kissing her this soon. 'See that.' She was standing near to the edge of an escalator and I went near her. She pointed to Joyal and a girl near him. 'Is that the girl you were telling? What was her name, yeah Avita. I got it. Is it?'

'Yes, she is his girlfriend.'

'When did he hook up with that girl?'

'Oh, that's a long story. Any way you like stories. So, I will narrate it now. Once upon a time, when he was in school-' I started.

'Common Roshen, make it precise. I don't want to know everything. It's our date. Just tell about it quickly.' She interrupted me.

'Ok, Long ago Joyal was behind her, and he lost her due to some reasons. Now he again met her here within the campus and eventually.' I took a breath and let it out. 'Now he is dating with her.' I said it so quickly.

'DATING?' her eyebrows rose up.

'Why are you getting so emotional?' I asked. 'He let us do that and what if he says about our relationship to your sister.'

'It won't affect our relationship.' She said and took her mobile phone from her purse. 'And I have seen her with another boy in a coffee shop.'

'What you are doing?' I asked.

'Calling Mr. Joyal.' She said.

'Don't be her mother. Leave them alone and can't we just spare this time for us? As you said, *it's our date, Jessie.*' I took the mobile from her hand. She then just stared at me. By the way, I also don't know where they are. Suresh went to the parking lot as soon as we reached here and Joyal left as soon as he found Avita. Anyway, I was not bothered about finding them at this time. At the same time I don't want to spend my money to treat them.

'I saw her with another guy in *Cinema Theater.*' She grabbed her mobile back from me.

'That may be her brother or someone.' I said.

'They kissed like we did!' She said and I smiled. Wow! I liked what she just said. "They kissed like *we did*"

Her phone beeped. As I also looked to the screen, it showed Joyal's name. She opened the message. It red; *'com 2 d parking lot Urgent'*.

We looked and shrugged to each other. Suddenly I remembered Suresh leaving to the parking lot. But he would not be standing there till this time. It was a total confusion for me. We waited for the lift to come up to our floor.

'Now don't kiss me.' She said as soon as she found there was no one in the lift.

The lift dropped to the second floor and the doors slide to both the extreme sides. Jesters filled my face ones a load of people pushed into the lift. There was a child standing near to us. He was holding a bar of *dairy milk* in his hand and his mouth was pasted with creams of chocolate. The lift reached the ground floor. We were the last one to get out from the lift. She holds my hand as we walked through the people around.

Someone called my name from behind as soon as we stepped outside the lift. It was a familiar voice. I turned around to see Joyal with a girl right behind me. I figured her to be Avita. I am seeing her for the first time and she looks nice. I can't hide; she was sexier than my girl. Nevertheless, sexy looks are only there in her dress. Jessie is hotter, sexier, and the beauty queen in whatever dress she wears. And I am sure that she looks the same even if her dress is being peeled off. May be at a later date.

'Hi.' He said to Jessie and faced to me. 'This is Avita. My girlfriend.'

'Hi' Avita smiled and gave her hands to Jessie. They shook their hands and smiled. I can see Jessie' eyes asking many questions to her about the guy Avita was with, in the theater.

'Where have you gone?' I asked him.

'We were here only. Actually, you were missing and he was looking for you.' I was surprised to see Avita was talking to me as if we have known each other for ages.

'Oh, we went to the top.' I smiled to her.

'Do you know her before?' Jessie pulled my hand and whispered in my ears. I shrugged.

'Why you called us now?' Jessie asked to Joyal before I did.

'Suresh called me and asked us to come to the parking lot urgently.' He said to me.

UNEXPECTED

Though we reached the parking lot, we don't know where he was. So Joyal dialed his number.

'Where are you?' Joyal said on the phone. 'Ok, we are coming.' he said again after some minutes. I could not hear what Suresh said from the other end.

'Come, let's go.' He said after disconnecting the phone.

'To where?' Avita held his hand like a modest child.

Joyal pointed to a black Audi car being parked in a corner. We all followed him. Suresh was standing near the car and waving to us. "But how come he gets an Audi?", "Is this really his car or he took it in rent" or "he stole it". I was thinking seriously while walking with him.

'Who is he? Do you know him?' Jessie interrupted my thoughts.

'He is my roommate Jessie' I said. 'We all came here together.'

'I don't want everyone. I just want you with me.' She said.

I too didn't want this to happen. As planned we would be coming here together and will slit it their own business; though it all started in the name of a treat. But Suresh doesn't have any girlfriend yet. So we had no idea why he called us now. Though if he was having a girlfriend, then also we will not be knowing why he called us. That's Suresh acted devilishly that day.

As far as I knew about my girl till now, she was very different from other girls, I have ever seen. Beyond her beauty, there is something, which I sometimes don't like. First, she doesn't like Joyal and she wants me not to talk to him. Whenever I ask about it, she skips to another topic. *Seducing* is the best word to describe *another topic* here and says she will tell about it later whenever I compel her to.

'Hi.' Suresh said. 'This is Avita and you are Jessie. Right?' he pointed to each of them and said.

'You said it man!' Joyal applauded.

'He knows you guys and of course, girls will be holding their boyfriends' hand only. So investigator's head is not required to find this.' A giggling expression filled on Jessie's face.

'Oh, you seem quite serious.' Suresh said and smiled.

'She is always like this.' Joyal announced. 'And Suresh hasn't in a relationship with any one like you are in with Roshen.'

'Obviously I AM in a relationship with Roshen and dating with him, but not flirting like you.' She said.

God! She is coming to the point, which I said not to speak about to him. I could only stand there and could not say anything when she was talking to him in an agitated manner.

'Excuse me! Don't drag me into your bullshit talk.' Avita defended.

'Why not? You are the one I saw in the theater with a guy.' She said and I pulled her hand a back when I felt she was going too far.

'WHAT?' Joyal almost shouted.

'Joyal… he was just my friend!' Avita explained to Joyal.

Jessie shrugged her hand and made me release the hold I made in her hand. 'Yeah. Just-a-friend. That's why I used the word *"flirt"*. Kissing random guys after making them friends. If they are not willing to, then you will give them a promotion to boyfriend.' She moved forward.

'Bloody dick head. You are crossing the limits.' Joyal stood between Avita and Jessie.

'And a bitch like you is perfectly MADE FOR HER TYPES.' She said.

As he raised his voice on Jessie again, I was not able to stand aside, just like that. I pushed him and he leaned on to Avita, as the force was a little stronger. He came forward and held my shirt. 'Stay outside.'

'She is my own girl and just a cousin sister to you. And she doesn't even like you so the one who should be OUT is YOU.' I said and Suresh departed us aside.

'Time Out! Now don't fight and yell any more. People started watching.' At last, Suresh got some breath of life.

'I and Jessie had a deal for each other. Now she is making the hell out of here and ruling me.' Joyal said to me.

'What's that' I asked to Jessie. She ignored me from behind and again went into their own argument.

'The bloody deal was at home. And why you want to interfere in our own business?' She asked Joyal holding my hand, which I really liked; but I was still in the state of confusion about what was happening there.

Jessie never liked to dig up the past or the older things happened with her family members. She didn't like to narrate the bad fights or good things in her family like a story. So I had never insisted her to. Instead, we just mind our own business, and I was falling in love with her more deeply in every passing moment.

'Suresh. I am ready. Let's go.' A new female voice said from behind.

I turned back to see who was it. A girl came out of the rear seat of the car. She was fair, slim, and extremely hot. She closed the door and pulled her T-shirt down until it covered her navel. Her hair was being scribbled all over her head as if she had not seen a comb after her birth.

'Start the car. I am coming.' Suresh said to her.

He was seriously talking to Joyal for the past five minutes. I don't know what he was talking about with him. And I was having a look at all the three girls. If these three girls are compared between one another (Like the Audi, BMW, and Mercedes Benz are being compared.) my girlfriend will become the cutest of all the three.

She was simply staring at me when I was scanning the girls, especially who came out of the car. I smiled to Jessie when we met our eyes. Suresh and Joyal came to us and Avita in Joyal's' hand. I have no idea what's going to happen next!

'Warden wants to see you urgently. So we have to go now.' Suresh said.

'So are you leaving?' Jessie asked me. Her expression changed from *staring face* to a lost kid's face.

'Let's go after some time.' I said to Suresh ignoring Joyal completely.

'No issue. You can take your time. But if warden-' Joyal said and I cut him off.

'Who asked you? You are out of the play here after. And no more interruption. PLEASE. I am begging you.' I said and faced Suresh.

However, I was not willing to ignore Joyal when Jessie wanted me to cut off his company. But, what he did to her at the parking lot is unforgivable. That too, he shouted at her in my presence.

'Don't make the warden angry. Otherwise, you can't go out of the hostel again.' he said 'unfortunately we have to go now. No other way.' He then said it to Jessie and she nodded silently.

Suresh's girlfriend was blowing horn of the car (probably her car) for the third time. Every time when she did that, I felt like kicking off her for disturbing the conversation. By the time, Joyal and Avita came and joined us. I didn't even look at him. But definitely had a glance at Avita. No boy can avoid looking at her. That day she had exposed her cleavage!

'Jessie, we have to leave. And I will see you tomorrow! What says?' I raised one of my eyebrows, waiting for her reply. I didn't show her my disappointment though it hurts every time when we take a leave.

'I think it's not possible because…' she looked at Joyal and pulled me to the other side of the car. 'Roshen… my sister's friends are coming tomorrow. They will only leave after three-four weeks. She needs me at home because she may leave to go outside with her friend uninformed. My grandparents are alone at home, so-'

'No chance for us to meet soon.' I groped her. I loved to do that always, so I never missed any chance.

'Roshen'. She bit the corner of her lower lip and tilted her head aside.

I perched my palm behind her neck and she held my forearm to stop me from kissing. We stood closer. 'I will call you tonight.' I whispered in her ear.

'I told you not to call me…' She fondled.

She is saying this for the hundredth time; seventh time, or eighth time. I am not sure about that. But she says this repeatedly though we know that I know it. But still I want to keep in touch with her, always. Either to feel her warmth or to hear her beautiful-girly-voice.

The only mobile phone in her home is being used by her sister. So when my calls were picked up by her sister will not be good to her. On the other hand, I had not learned to restrict myself to call her. At the same time, I, keeping myself not talking to her in a day was more than like living a whole day without having food. So she always took care of solving that problem. She will call me.

I touched beneath her lower lip with my thumb when she started talking again. I dragged my thumb downwards. When it reached on her jaw, I leaned forward to kiss her and she leaned backward.

'No, not now. I will call you. Bye.' She smiled and waved her hand to me. 'Bye,' she said, looking at me, into my eyes with her cute black eyes, which I loved the most. She walked out of the parking lot and I moved near to Suresh watching her walking away.

'Yeah, let's go.' I said to Suresh when I lost her from my sight.

Every one of us, including Avita, started moving out of the lot; once Suresh's girlfriend started her car again.

'Should I drop you guys?' She offered when her car reached near us.

'No, thanks. We will walk.' Suresh said and she left immediately.

Joyal's phone rang which he disconnected continuously, whenever it rang again. I doubted it would be Jessie, but after the incident, I dare won't had the guts to ask him. Moreover, it's not my phone piece. Ugly phone.

VINCENT VAN GOGH
ESPRESSO VODKA

It's been two weeks after we have met each other. Though she calls me whenever she gets a chance, it was not enough for me. I really started missing her cute-black-eyes, those tempting lips and the way she moved her strands of hair that falls on her face occasionally. Every time, when I think about her I feel to meet her and grab her right at the moment to kiss those lips and to say that I missed her a lot.

"Because of her sister's friend's visit, I can't even see her. Stupid friends. Can't they just study from their home? Why should they all come to your sister like this for studies? As if your sister is the founder of the Chartered Accountancy. Bull shit." I would always tease her through phone like this whenever I am not in a romantic mood to talk to her.

Otherwise, when she calls me, I would ask her how much she loved me and I would explain how much I missed her. And occasionally that ends up in a quarrel which helped us from preventing to call each other for two days. It all starts only when I compel her to come for a date and the exact point of starting the quarrel was when I insist her to let myself visit her home.

'No way Roshen. Can't you just understand my situation? If at all you come, what will I say to my sister about who you are? And my grandparents won't understand if I bring a boy to my home, saying he is a friend of mine.' She would say.

'That's enough. Instead of saying not to come to your home, you need not want to say all these bullshits. Just understand one thing that I am not able to remain like this for a long time without seeing you at least once. Its two whole weeks Jessie. Do you realize that? And I want to know that-' I said and she immediately disconnected the call.

Now what does that mean? I just banged the receiver on that big-red-phone. And kicked on my caught out of frustration, which only resulted in lying myself on my bed with the pain on my toe. After a short time, which I already felt like an hour, the phone rang again. I took the receiver and I heard a female voice saying a sweet *hello*. Who else. It's my so called girlfriend, Jessie.

'Hm, hello.' I said with a rough voice in return.

'Sorry Roshen, I-' She began to reason.

'KEEP DISCONECTING MY CALL when I am saying something seriously to you. Don't you have any sense? Stupid.' I interrupted her angrily.

'Idiot! My sister came to my room to take her book. First of all, learn to hear completely what someone is saying, before barking like a STRAY DOG.' She snapped me back. That's how we began.

'Mad madam, instead of teaching me now, tells me a day which we can meet.' I shot back

'Not this week.' She calmed down.

'Then get lost. Bye.' But only she calmed down. Not me.

'Roshen, don't irritate! Can't you understand me?' She started her hot engine angrily.

'Can't you understand me!' I asked the same which I too wanted to know at that moment.

'OK. Wait for one more week to pass on.' She said. When I am in this condition, she had no choice to give a suggestion.

'Not possible' I declined enthusiastically.

'Then do whatever.' She put forward an option.

'Alright, I am going to make another girlfriend.' I picked one option professionally.

'Yeah, sure! Let she too be in trouble.' She said sarcastically.

'Asshole' I got irritated and disconnected the call. That was the climax of our last fight. It's been four days and five nights since she had called me. Though I always felt to call her and to face whatever happens next, my heart never allows me to hurt her. So I maintained patience which will expire at the end of this week, which is after two more days.

Joyal had never talked to me since after that incident. No. actually it was me, who never turned up. I never let him to interact with me. Suresh had left to his house as soon as we came back from the parking lot, that day. Eventually everything turned up like a hell for me. All the time it's the institution, books, class tests and hostel

Prewi P. Wilson

stuffs. After classes, I had never gone out with anyone, like before. I had no one to pass the time with. Always digging my eyes into the books, but nothing was entering into my head. But, anyway Maths was fine, because I am least bothered to learn it. The only thing I know in Maths is that, when expanded, it becomes Mathematics.

I decided to take a half-day leave. While walking towards the institute, I was thinking about a good reason for the leave, which should be said to the warden. The reason has to be strong that I should convince the warden. *Headache.* Wow! Headache is the finest and genuine reason. No one can easily find out that I don't have any ache. I reached the hostel. Though the door is open, there was no one around including the warden. I stepped in. The rooms are all vacant. I sat on my bed.

Every week at least once, we could meet each other. Now it's two weeks and still one more week is over after she called that day. I want to see her. I want to talk to her. I badly feel wanted. I became restless.

'Why you are here?' Suddenly Mr. Warden came inside. He became angry seeing me in the hostel. 'Don't you want bloody go to class? Idiot! Speak up.' He raised his voice.

'I am having a headache. That's why. I-'

'SHUT UP.' I stood up from the bed as he started shouting at me. 'You cannot take leave for these simple reasons. Headaches are all silly things. Who gave you this idea man?'

'No….no one' I said. I should have said some *fever* instead if I knew that this is a silly thing for him.

'If it is some fever, then anyone can find it out. And such aches cannot be found out by anyone. RIGHT?' he asked. Is he reading my mind? Is he-'what do you think? I am doing this hostel business for more than ten long years. Moreover, every year there will be many stupid like you as a headache for me.'

'Sorry. Actually, I was feeling dozed and the pain is severe. I don't have any medicines. And-' I explained but he again interrupted.

'Stop these bullshits. *One* more time if you are repeating, then YOU-ARE-OUT of this hostel. Finally, you will be terminated from this institute. Got it?' he asked and I shook my head. While he was leaving, he turned to me 'And no more SORRIES. Mind it!' he said and left the hostel.

'Hi' A boy was coming to me from the staircase. But I had already forgotten his name. We met each other in the class on my first day in the institute. We were bench mates. After that, I am seeing him now.

'Did he leave?' he said and peeped out of the door to have a look.

But how can I forget his name so easily! That too after himself introducing him to me. I again tried to remember his name. God! I am not able to remember. How can I ask his name? I felt it so bad.

'Hey, you ok?' he came and asked.

'Yeah. Why?' I said.

'Nothing, you look so dull. That's why.' He said. 'Half day leave?'

'Yes.' I said.

'You bunged it. Right?' I smiled as he asked the truth.

'Come.' He pulled my hand. 'Let's go upstairs. I have something for you. It will definitely push off your sadness.' I followed him. I was still in my own thoughts when I was climbing the steps. The thoughts that was not able to stop. I can meet her like before after one more week. But previous two weeks were so painful and thinking about when to meet her up still remains in me as a hangover.

'Sit.' He said, pulling a chair for me.

We reached the study room and sat in a corner of the room. He took a plastic cover from the bag, which was kept underneath his chair. He took a bottle from that cover and kept on the table. He didn't throw the plastic cover. Instead, he rolled it with something inside the cover, and kept aside.

'What's this?' I asked him. Definitely, I understood that it's liquor bottle. But I didn't get which brand it was.

'Do you need a drink?' he asked. For the first time he looked at my face, after we sat there. 'This vodka. My uncle brought this home, the last evening. I just took one of the four bottles, moments before coming back here from home.' He smiled.

'Vodka, nice. Normally girls use it.' I said.

'That doesn't mean this is only made for girls.' he replied in a firm voice. 'Have you tasted *vodka* before?' he continued.

'Only beer.' I said.

'Good. Come and give me company.' He said and took the bottle from the box. I didn't say anything. 'Man, there is no glass for you. Go and take some glass for you.' He said.

I didn't move from there. I was staring at him. First of all, I didn't like him commanding me. That, moreover, I was not in a mood to give a company to anyone.

'Stop staring and go man.' He raised his voice. I stood up from the chair. I saw the warden walking towards the hostel, reaching near the gate.

'Warden! He is coming.' his eyes popped out as I announced it.

'Run from here and lay down on your bed. And you will not point out that I am here.' He said and I just ran from there to reach my bed before the warden sees me.

Though I never liked the way he talks and his commanding behavior, I decided to accompany him for today. Anyway, I don't have any company here, and if I stay alone, I may go to her house. I didn't want that and that's the only reason why I stayed calm with him. As I reached down I heard the warden calling my name from the gate. Luckily he did not step inside. I went near him.

'I will not be available for the next three days. Don't go out anywhere. And if want anything, then, contact Alex. Tell this to everyone when others come back.' he said and gave me a big brown envelope. 'It's for you. Today morning your father came and gave this to me. And is there Sajan inside?' He asked.

'No' I prodded and he left.

When I looked I found my ATM card, a mobile phone and its earphone in it. There was a note kept in it, which was by my father. It red *"CALL ME WHEN YOU ARE NOT STUDYING"*. I switched on the mobile and dialed his number. But the call didn't go. The reason was that it had a *zero* balance. I called him in the *hostel phone*. I suddenly disconnected it as I remembered that I took a half-day leave for no reason. If I called him now, then I would have to answer many questions from my father.

I went back to the study room with my tea cup, which will serve the purpose. I sat in front of him and kept my cup in front of his glass. And beside our cup and glass there was the great vodka bottle standing like a brave pillar.

He was waiting for me to open the bottle. He poured into my cup at first and in his glass after. I took it and had my first sip when he finished half of his glass. Gulping by him and sipping by me carried on for the rest few minutes. It tasted like coffee and I felt a little better. He took a smoke from the plastic cover which he rolled ad kept beside earlier.

'This is coffee flavored vodka.' He announced.

'I got it.' I acknowledged.

'Usually Suresh accompanied me. But he is not here now, that's why I called you.' He smiled.

And that's how we started the conversation which ended up in girls and jumped to drugs. He told his old stories regarding how he and his ex-girlfriend used stuff at the weekends, together. He also revealed that they regularly made out after taking stuff and they broke up when she got caught at home.

But I didn't say anything about my dating with Jessie. That was not to reveal to anyone like his affair. We were damn serious about ourselves. That's why I am becoming restless when I miss her a lot.

A FRIEND IN NEED, IS A FRIEND INDEED

I recharged my mobile and decided to call her. But calling her directly will not be a good idea. I thought of making a call to any of my friends. I dialed Roopa's number because girls can help me better in this case. She is one of my best friends from the last four years.

'Hello. Who is this?' She asked as soon as she picked up the call. Because of not having a mobile phone, I had never made a call to any of my friends frequently. So no one understands my voice through phone immediately.

'Roopa…I am Roshen.' I sang on the receiver.

'ROSHEN!' she exclaimed. 'Are you drunk?'

'No yar…' I said.

'LIER.' She fought back immediately.

'Ok, Ok, Ok. I surrender in front of you as usual. Enough?' I asked. 'Do you smell me through the phone?' I have drunk the day I called Roopa. After the day, I spend with Sajan; drinking as much that he filled the rest of the vodka in a water bottle and gave it to me. When I feel to drink it, I finished the entire bottle before calling her.

'No' she laughed. Every time she used to find out anything, I hid inside. 'Where are you getting this from?' she asked.

'My hostel mate.' I answered genuinely. 'Now stop your bloody questioning. Have to tell a lot, madam. First of all agree that you will help me now.' I said. 'Now' I stressed.

'How can I do it before hearing what it is?' she said.

'O…I am not gona ask you to kiss me.' I said. Throughout these years with her I have never felt any love kind of a thing. If I hadn't found Jessie then probably Roopa will be the best one I will have.

'Ok, tell me.' she giggled. 'I am listening.'

'You must not interrupt in between.' I warned. She always had a habit of saying something in between.

'Still, you haven't said what I have to do…' she said.

'I am in love with a girl here. She lives near my hostel. Imagine! She is a cousin of my friend and he stays in my hostel. Above everything, she is mine now. She loves me Roopa and I too-'

'Roshen. What about Manju?' As expected. She interrupted.

'That's why I told you. Don't interrupt. We can talk about Manju later. I had already considered her as my ex-girlfriend. It's over.'

'When?' she was diverting from the topic.

'I am drunk now and don't make me call f-words.' I raised my voice. 'If you repeat this I will disconnect the phone.'

'Ok…k…k…cool down. Now don't get angry. I wasn't aware of your break up. That's why. I will not repeat it. Tell me please please …' she said.

'Even Manju doesn't know that I broke up with her.' I uttered.

'What?' She blushed

'Hm, yes. She thinks that she could easily get compromised with me.' I said 'Do you know, she had two break ups before our relationship started. So it won't hurt her either.' She laughed as I said it.

'Now will you listen to me?' I asked.

'Yes yes yes.' She said. I could feel her nodding her head.

Manju was a fair girl. I won't say that she was so nice. She was a girl who wants to do only what she likes and she had a kind of behavior that irritated me sometimes. Moreover, that she just wants to show off in front of her friends *with a boyfriend*. And that means she can still date with any boys of her type. Our relationship was not that intensive and sincere.

However, we had decided to have a short-term relationship, I had felt a little disturbed after knowing the old stories of her ex-boyfriends. That too from her friends. (She had never had told me anything about that) She never said everything to me. Not that Jessie would say everything, but Jessie never hides anything from me and she has her own innocence. Whenever I compelled Manju to tell about her past, she would explain it as if she was a great fan of break-up-procedure. But I haven't said these things to any of my friends yet. Even Roopa doesn't know it.

'You won't believe it. She is so cute and beautiful.' I was telling everything to Roopa and she became excited to hear more about my Jessie.

'Did you tell her about Manju?' she said.

'Err…don't shit in-between Roopa.' I grinded my teeth.

'See. That's why I told you. It will not be smooth to talk with you when you are drunk. Do you remember the havoc you created during the combine study, we did that day?' she said.

'Please, I want your help very urgently, that's why I am telling the whole story to you now.' I said calmly to her. 'I can't trust anyone else other than you at this moment. Because, no one has any hint about the clashes happened between, me and Manju. That's why I called only you.' I reasoned to her.

Though she doesn't know any realities of Manju, she had already known that there was something burning in-between us.

'WOW! So you trust me!' She said and I got angry with her this time 'All right. Now I won't say anything. You tell me everything about her. Everything.'

I started telling the whole story about me and Jessie that had happened. Whole story means…that won't include the first kiss and phone-talks at late nights. Luckily, she didn't interrupt any more.

'So are you planning to break-up with Manju?' she said.

'Not now,' I prodded 'Why the hell are you bringing Manju when I am talking about Jessie. And don't give my number to Manju. Mind it.'

'Are you flirting with Jessie? Or really serious about her.' she asked seriously.

'Err...' I sighed irritatingly.

Why she is not getting me after telling the whole thing. Does she not understand that I really love her? I only know how I am feeling each time when I think about her going back to U.S. Though I never showed my nervousness about it to her, still I am tensed about it. And secretly I pray to God to make some reason for make her not to go to U.S.

She is the first girl in my life who I loved this much! And I don't know how to make it understand to others. Lucky I am that Jessie understood how much I love her. That was the most important thing for me.

If we could get a solid reason, then she could defend her father and I could support her. I could stop her from going. But –

'Why you became silent? Did you get hurt? I am sorry. I-' she cut my thoughts.

'You will never understand me. You won't know my feeling to her. Can you dare help me? I am seeing her seriously yar.' I said softly and convincingly.

'Sorry, I didn't get that' she said.

'GET LOST' I shot back and disconnected the phone.

I don't know why I did it. But I...I don't know. There was some more ml of vodka in my Bislery water bottle. I finished it in a single sip and lay down on the bed facing the rotating fan. "Who invented this particular fan? I am not getting any air from it, though it is rotating" That was what I thought the moment I saw the fan.

My phone beeped. I didn't look into as it was just a message. It beeped again. I raised my hand up to see the screen of the phone. It showed two messages from Roopa.

Message 1: I am sorry :p

Message 2: I am gona call you. Don't get angry…plz.

I pressed "reply" and started typing the message. "It's ok. Call me. No more bal with me" before pressing "send" she called me. I took it.

'Hi' I shied.

'Hm…leave it. You told that you need some help. What was that?' she asked.

'Oh yeah! I will give Jessie's number. You call her. And her sister may pick up the call. Then get her on the line and divert the call to me.' I explained. 'Please.'

'Hm. ok. What if her sister asks who I am?' she asked.

'You know how to handle it. Please do it for me yar. It's been so long that I had talked to her.'

'Alright. How is your hostel and couching going on?' she asked.

'It's going fine, Roopa.' I said

'You will crack the entrance na,' she said

I was not in a mood to explain it to her. 'Ew. Make the call first. I will call you some other time. Bye.' I said.

I was not bothered about anything at present, other than to have a talk with Jessie. I was missing her a lot and now I am going to talk to her again. Hearing her voice was something fantastic.

'Ok, Bye.' She said and disconnected the call.

I started waiting for her call. I felt that the time was running slower than usual. I felt she might have not started calling. I felt to call her and find out whether she is calling or not. But I realized that it will be a bad idea. So I just took the empty Bislery bottle of Vodka and just stared at it. As it was night, firstly; no one would notice if I am drunk. Moreover, after serving today's supper, the warden left to his house.

DIVERTED CALL

Finally, the call came which I was waiting for.

Roopa had dialed Jessie's number and diverted the call to me. So that I can talk to her without letting Jessie into trouble.

'Hello, who is it?' she asked casually just like anyone. Like always there was sweetness in her voice. I always loved to hear that again and again.

At the same time she was a little puzzled. Roopa might not have told that I made her to call Jessie.

'I love you.' I just said it to her. Partially my intention was to make her feel weird hearing that immediately from a not-understood-voice. It's been so long since I had talked to her. When I said it, the relief I felt was so great. I felt so happy, to hear her again.

'What? Who is this?' Her tone changed. I found no more sweetness in it. I thought she would recognize my voice if I say what I just said. Because who else will say it to her other than me?

'Hey dear! I am Roshen.' I said before she disconnects the phone out of strangeness.

'You! How come you call me? And who was the one who talked before and which number is this? Or have you gone home.' Though she shot with a number of questions, it was really nice to hear her. So I let her to question whatever she wants. 'Say something' she said after a small break to her questions.

'Which one should I answer first?' I giggled. 'I thought you would be happy to hear me after such a long time. Instead, you are questioning me, though it was a tricky kind of call I made.' I said.

'Yes Roshen, I am so…happy to hear you. I was really surprised to hear you because my sister told me that, some of my classmate is on the phone. That's why I-' she said 'By the way, what do you think? I was not at all comfortable without seeing you all these days. That's why, at least I phone you whenever possible. But these days, all the time, mobile was with my sister. Can you guess how I felt? I was eagerly waiting for her friends to leave. So that I could meet you know.'

'Jessie…' I stopped her. 'What if I come there? To your home.' I asked.

She inhaled aloud 'No. Her friends are here Roshen. We must wait till they go.' She said. 'But I want to meet you. As soon as possible.'

'What happened? Anything serious?' I said.

'Yes. I will tell you,' her voice became low. 'But latter. Now tell me something… Which number is this?'

'He hey, forgot to tell you. I got a mobile. My dad sent me one.'

'Wow! That's awesome dear!' She said.

'What is your sister doing there? Is she there near you?' I asked.

'No, she is in the other room. They will be always studying and I have no one here to talk with.' She said. 'Don't you have anything to ask about me?' she stressed the "me" with an extra effort.

'Hm…ok, tell me what are you wearing now?' I asked as I don't have anything special to ask, though we haven't talked for days together. Oh, NO. This is also special for me. *Only for me.*

'Why?' she asked innocently and I repeated the same question without answering her.

'Most of the time I will be in my skirts at home. Are you gona buy some dress for me?' she asked hopefully. She doesn't know that I don't have enough money to go for a shopping with her.

'Only skirts?' I asked. I had a different motive in my mind which she won't be expecting.

'Naturally I will be wearing something above it. Why this senseless questions? Stupid.' She said childishly.

'I am asking what exactly you are wearing today. Now.' I said. My sound was waving a little bit as I was drunk.

'Oow…ok.' She said 'A white top and a maroon skirt that ends at my knees. Enough?'

'Then? Continue…' I said.

'Are you going to strip me through the phone?' she asked. How come she knew it? I was thinking it myself. 'Is it?' she interrupted my thoughts.

'May be, no' I said.

'Yes, how can you not? Roshen…' She said my name. Now she too will become sexy and then into the mood, which I am in. WOW! I got her into the track. I celebrated but, things changed a bit.

'Have you drunk?' She asked instead of asking how beautiful she would be looking in her dress she wore tonight. Then I could explain her that romantically.

'No baby. I feel a little sleepy. That's it.' I said and luckily it worked. This is the first time I am talking to her after myself getting boozed. 'Are you smiling now?' I asked.

'Yes, how can I not? You always make me smile and never let me down like my mother.' She said.

Oh GOD! Now she is bringing back her good-old memories. It's always been the same. Now I will tell you what's going to happen.

She will speak about her loneliness at her home, how she felt when she lost her mother, how her father responded when her mother died, about his second marriage, how she hated her step-mom and so on. When she says all these tears will fill her eyes. That moment she will look down and strands of her hair will fall over her face. Then she will move it with her beautiful fingers.

Then it's me who was always consoled her. Not that I could do it successfully, but at least I kept on trying till she smiles. To be frank, I was not comfortable with this practice of bringing her past by herself and myself taking the strain of making her happy again. Not that I don't want to forget her past, because it's her mother, who brought her up caringly and the one who she loved so much in her life. However, I can't afford to see her being sad. So as usual, I shifted to another topic.

'So what about your holiday plans? Let's enjoy and freak out. What says, huh? And please don't bother about my vacation classes. Because I myself don't bother much. Let's be together, always.' I laughed, but only I did.

Whenever I changed the topic in the situations like this, she would become alright, even it takes some time. Then we start our good, funny talks, which will last in our good-time-memories till we will meet the next time. And the next-time's-funny-talks will also join the good-time-memories. It was a real enjoyment with her, even if it's just talking through the phone. We know that we missed each other every time, whenever we are not together. And each time when we return to our own places, the feeling of separateness increases our love to each other. The bond made me realize that I can't miss her. Ever. I need her throughout my life. I love her. Like she always does.

'Roshen...I love you and I don't want this to happen. But I am gona miss you for sure. And we can promise each other that you won't let ourselves miss each other. Ok?' She said. Her voice was in the same tone. Still, she was sad. And the drastic change on her emotion made me too nervous 'Roshen, I don't want to be in this, but I have no other option.' Her voice started shaking. I changed the topic, just to hear her happy. But now she is crying. And I am getting no idea on what she was panicking about, and the promise she was told to make.

'Tell me whatever it is.' I said softly to make her relax.

'Love you Roshen. And I don't want to go anywhere away from you.' She was weeping at the other end of the phone.

'Will you please tell what happened? For God's sake!' I already lost my temper and can't wait any more. I got the idea what she was about to say. But I want to hear it from her and make it clear weather this is going to happen for real.

'I am going with my father, and will be there for the rest of my life. He told that he would be coming here to take me and Jincy there. So…' She said.

'What the fu-' what she said was so clear that I heard it right. I can't believe it or I don't want to. There was an occurred silence in between us. Whenever I wanted her more she was going away from me. She was the one whom I always wanted to be serious about, in my life. I can't be comfortable even without seeing her at least in a week. She was the one whom I would think about.

If something could be done, it should be done by her. She must say her decision to her father that she wants to be here only. I wanted to enjoy each and every moment with her. And I would make sure that I am not going to waste any happy moments with her.

'When?' I asked.

'As early as possible.' She wept again. 'That's what my father says.'

I walked to and fro of the room. Now I had no idea about what to say. *"As early as possible."* When she said it, I felt that I have absolutely lost her. Soon. And why she wanted to be *"as early"*? Can't she go after -

'Do you want to go?' I myself interrupted my thought and asked her. I don't want to leave her either. I want her to be here forever. Near me. And not far away from me. I don't want to leave her across the oceans.

'Do you think so?' she said.

'Then why this hell with me? Can't you inform me about it before or do you want us to break-up now?' I became a little bit angry with her. I didn't wanted to be angry to her, but accidently I did. I only realized what I did, only after shouting at her.

'Roshen?' I felt sorry for being angry with her. 'I don't know about this. What happen to you? I never even thought about what you just said. Then why you are talking about the break-up and all? If I wanted to leave you just like that, I would never let you kiss me ever. I am not such a girl to flirt with you and walk away. And what about the phone calls we did at late nights Roshen. I will never regret about all those in my life, because I love you. I really do love you idiot!' She paused and I too kept silent because I don't have anything to say.

I know I deserve what all she just said. Though I got angry, it was an accident. I should not do that, because we both know that one day she might have to go. But now, I lost myself and moreover, that the frustration of not able to see her, the vodka in me, and the way I and Joyal ignore each other. Everything already gave a pain in me. When I called her even without calling my father (He had told me to call, the moment I get my mobile);

She just said that she was about to leave me. So I couldn't do nothing else but react.

'Why can't you just say "no" to your father?' I lowered my anger.

'I can't! He won't agree to it.' She said.

'Whyyyy?' I asked.

'Can you say NO to any government policy?' she asked. I became lost. We were talking about *us* and where does this government come from?

'How is the government involved here?' I asked surprisingly. 'I just asked you that can you say "no" to your father about going back to U.S.'

'It's like that Roshen. No one of us can say NO to my father's decisions.' She said.

'Ok, leave it and let's assume that it's over.' I said.

'Roshen...' she said.

'Then what else can be done? If anything has to be done from my side, tell me.' I said.

I again became angry by now. I was not able to lower it either. Maybe because of the liquor inside me. I can't show my anger to her or to others in the hostel. I was the only one who was not sleeping there and I tried my level best to dump my anger inside myself. There was silence, both in the phone and hostel. I checked the screen to confirm whether it got disconnected or not. What the fuck. She is still on the line. Then why this silence. "Don't test my patience". I kept on chanting myself, but still it was the same. SILENCE. Don't know whether she was angry, sad or whatever. No one spoke.

'SPEAK UP.' I shouted. That was all I could do suddenly. I thought someone would wake up in my voice. But no one did. If though someone would, I don't care. That's why I shouted. If I had counted the time taken by the silence it would be approximately ten minutes. Ten Minutes! In ten minutes I could give and receive more than ten kisses and what not. I was making this call in lots of risks. Then how can I not get angry for wasting time and being silent. At least she could speak some rubbish like she brought the government for an example. It will always be better than keeping mum. Still she is not moving her tongue! Damn. I was about to take the phone off from my ear to disconnect it.

'*I Love You*' she said without making it any delay. I had never heard her saying this in such a sweet tone. This time I felt like….she was…what should I say? I realized that she was crying all the time she remained silent. Her voice was like that. The feeble voice that we will have after crying continuously for some time. I regret for not considering. The first time when she mentioned it to me, I felt happy. But this time when she really said it, I melted in one go. This time I became speechless. I sat on the bed.

After some time I felt something crawling on my face. I moved my hand over it. It was water. Tears! Am I crying? How come it happened? For the first time I am experiencing it. I was casual, bold, and never cried for anything. But this time, even tears jumped out of my eyes even before me realizing that I was crying.

'Jessie…I am so sorry. I badly want to see you.' I finally spoke after a long time. This time it took more than before. I can't help it. 'What about the next Sunday?' I asked softly.

'I don't know really. I think my sister and her friends are leaving on that day.' She wept and said.

'What all happened till now just happened and now onwards we are going to enjoy the time you are here and will never make you sad from now.' I said. 'Let it go Jessie and will see what will happen to our future. I will be there for you, always.' I tried to console her. Luckily it worked this time. Though it was a little critical than before. 'Jessie, I Love You.' This time I said it from my heart.

'I am smiling now.' She said.

'Wow! I am so happy my dear.' I said. 'And I promise you that I will never, ever become angry with you.'

'Thank you,' she laughed 'Roshen I think my sister is coming down from the upstairs. Let me go, please.' I felt like requesting.

'Don't plead to me. Go before she catches you, talking to me. Bye, good night.' I said.

'Hm, Bye.' She said and disconnected the phone.

*123# -ALWAYS SHOWS LESS BALANCE

Though mobiles were not allowed in the campus, I took it. It was a little raining outside. I dressed as soon as possible and went out of the hostel to have food from the restaurant nearby as usual. Every day since I joined here, this was the regular place where I had breakfast. I entered into the restaurant and ordered for the same usual thing – sandwich and tea. For all these past days I was consuming the same thing from the same restaurant. Still the waiter comes and stands in front of me to take the order. I said the same thing to him. (Sandwich and tea). I checked the time. I was always regular in my things. So again, I am late for the class like that's one of the regular things I do. After I get finished what I had ordered and rushed to the washroom.

My phone beeped. I took it and it was a text message from Jessie.

Message: I love you.

I smiled as soon as I read it. It beeped again.

Message: Call me if you are not in class yet….

I dialed "*123#" to check my mobile balance. This time I was not surprised like always when it showed

Rs.0.13 (came down from Rs. 100 which I specially recharged when I got delivered my mobile. That too, by withdrawing the amount from the bank, particularly for recharging.). I called Jessie.

'HYE ROSHEN' she picked up the phone and spelled in my ears.

'Hi, what's up?' I was puzzled.

'Nothing much. My sister goes to Chennai with her friends for some project work. And this mobile will be with me always from now! How is it?' she said.

'Hm…So I could call you always.' I said and unfortunately the phone got disconnected as my balance got over. But soon she called me back.

'Sorry, my balance got over.' I said.

'It's ok. Where are you?' she said.

'In a restaurant. Came to have some breakfast. I am late today.' I said and got up and went to the toilet. I kept the phone tightly in between my shoulder and ear. So that I could keep talking. And I kept on talking.

'What's that splashing sound there?' She asked.

'Em…I am pissing here. That's why.' I said and pulled up my zip.

'Had your breakfast?' She said.

'I already had it Jessie.' I said.

'What you had?'

'Sandwich and tea'

'Today also! Don't you feel to have some change?'

'Nothing else here are of my taste my taste.'

'Come home. I will take care of your breakfast, and having hotel food daily is not healthy. Mind it.'

'So sweet, and I love to have it from you. And promise me that you will be feeding me with your hands. When will you gift those pleasurable moments Jessie?'

'Very soon, my dear.'

Someone knocked on the door. Actually, it was a sound of banging on the door. I asked her to hold for a moment and stepped out of the toilet. A bald headed man was waiting there for me to come out. He might have figured that I am talking to my girlfriend.

"Girlfriends make other people to wait" He whispered before entering into the toilet.

I walked back to the place where I was sitting. I took my bag and walked to the counter. I took the wallet and pulled a 50 rupee note from it. I gave it and he returned the balance. I bought a *Kit-Kat* and put the balance in my pockets without counting it. I striped the chocolate and started eating it. I was really busy in talking with her on the phone. We don't even know about what we are talking about. But we talked about everything and anything that came across our mind.

Talking, eating-chocolate and walking to the institute went on at the same time without affecting each other. I was happy, she was happy and we were enjoying the talk. And finally I reached the gate of the campus.

'Jessie, I reached here in the campus. Bye.' I said as we had already decided to talk only till I reach the institution gate. Actually, it was her decision.

'Bye.' She said. 'See you soon. And I love you'

'Love you too' I said.

I entered inside as soon as I disconnected the phone. I was the only one there outside the building. As I walked forward, a bearded man came to verify my ID card as usual. Every student was allowed to let in only after the verification of our ID card. He asked for the reason of becoming late and like always I blabbered something to him. He nodded as if I said what exactly had happened.

Luckily, today also, I reached just before the teacher entered the classroom. I sat at the extreme back bench of the class room at the right-hand-side. That was my usual place for two reasons. Firstly, I won't be noted by the camera so easily and the way I score in the exams won't let me go to the front.

The teacher came and stood on the platform of the class. He took the chalk piece and wrote "GRAVITAION" on the blackboard.

'Does anyone have an idea about gravitation?' He turned around to face us. And there came a mass answer from the class, excluding last benchers. I really felt the topic, so boring that I felt to sleep. If Newton hadn't seen that falling apple, then probably she won't be irritating me like this.

When most of the students in the class were concentrating on what he was told further. I, for the first time took my mobile out of my pocket and switched on its vibration mode. Now I opened the menu and gone to the message and selected *"write message"*. I started typing in it.

Message- "Hey lets chat in FB. Come online. NOW!"

And I hit the *"send"* option as soon as I finished typing. The screen showed a list of contacts. Soon the message was sent to my sweet girlfriend *Jessie J.* And I waited for her reply. It's taking so long.

For the moment I lifted my head to look up what the teacher was exactly doing. He was busy in teaching something. I peeped to look my neighbor's mobile to see what he was doing in his. He was watching porn as I was expected.

'Which site?' I asked.

'Sh…' he pushed me and put the video in landscape. Then he watched it more comfortably.

I ignored him as my mobile beeped. I took it. There it was. Her reply came. I opened it, and it red;

Message- "Ok, I will come in 15 min."

Logging in into one's account need not take even a minute. Then why she needed it? I was eagerly waiting for her to ask this first. I opened my FB account and waited for another 15 min. She came exactly she was told. I always liked her punctuality and I hope she also likes my punctuality for not being punctual. She used to warn for being late and I used to be like the same.

"Hi" – Jessie J

"What took you so long?" – Roshen Samuel

"Was tying my hair" – Jessie J

"You look beautiful in an untied hair." – Roshen Samuel

"1 sec." – Jessie J

I waited for her. I felt so happy and excited to chat with her again after a long time. At the same time I felt her happiness. She is so sweet in all means.

"Untied ;)" – Jessie J

"<3" – Roshen Samuel

"Where are you now?" – Jessie J

"Still in class baby" – Roshen Samuel

"What? So no one is there to catch you for using phone?"-

Jessie J

"Why? You want to see me caught" – Roshen Samuel

"No yar. I just asked" – Jessie J

"So where are you now? Home?" – Roshen Samuel

"Yeah. Where else? Safe in my bedroom." – Jessie J

"Hey! You are in your skirts, right?" – Roshen Samuel

"No, I am in my blue tracks." – Jessie J

"Hm? What happened? You told that you will be always in

your skirts." – Roshen Samuel

"Morning I went for jogging and didn't change my dress yet.

Went asleep soon I came." – Jessie J

"What happened? Not feeling well?" – Roshen Samuel

"Nothing, A little lazy to take a bath in the cold water." – Jessie J

"Eww… not took a bath yet!" – Roshen Samuel

"Hmf. Then bye. I am going to take bath." – Jessie J

"Stay for some more time. Where were you when I talked in

the morning…"- Roshen Samuel

"Was on the way back home" – Jessie J

"Hm…What else" – Roshen Samuel

"Nothing much. I didn't have food" – Jessie J

"Why? Aren't you hungry?" – Roshen Samuel

"Of course I am." – Jessie J

"So go and have something from the kitchen." – Roshen Samuel

"But today I am too lazy to do everything. Feels sleepy" –

Jessie J

"So? Staying with an empty stomach?" – Roshen Samuel

"No, just waiting for my sister to finish her studies. So that she will serve for me and we will eat together." – Jessie J

"LAZY CREATURE" – Roshen Samuel

"But not like you. I am lazy only at times :p" – Jessie J

"O-Ow…" – Roshen Samuel.

"Today do you have anything important to do?" – Jessie J

"No, why?" – Roshen Samuel

"Come home" – Jessie J

"What?" – Roshen Samuel.

I read it twice to make sure what I read was right. Usually she never even mentioned her house for our date. Neither my hostel. It's always been the *City Center*. Though I felt shocked, when she asked me to come home, a huge smile took its place on my face.

"Today @ 5. I will talk to Joyal." – Jessie J

"Joyal? You stopped talking to him that day" Roshen Samuel

"Brother – Sister relationship na. Can fight and compromise at any time." – Jessie J

"Unfortunately, I too stopped talking with him that day" – Roshen Samuel

"Who told you to stop talking with him? Boy! We need him☺" – Jessie J

"Hm, nice sister you are." – Roshen Samuel

"Don't worry too much, dear. Just come with him. I will take care of the rest." – Jessie J

"Hm…What else." – Roshen Samuel

"Nothing much. Ok, see you @ evening. My sister came. Going to have dinner." – Jessie J

"Ok, bye bye." – Roshen Samuel.

"Bye. I love you & kisses." – Jessie J

"I will give it, once I am there. Bye, love you too" – Roshen Samuel

She signed out immediately. But I stayed till the classes are over. What else to do! I told you, it's boring today. Do you want evidence for it? Then, here it is. See, my neighbor slept off already. Then what could I do?

CONFESSION

As soon as I entered my hostel, I put my bag on my bed and went to the bathroom for taking a very-quick bath. After fifteen minutes, I got out of the bathroom. I came to the main room where the snacks and tea distributed. But all the snacks were already getting finished and thankfully some tea was left. So I went to take the tea and when I asked about my share of snack, the boy near to me said that the extra snacks had already consumed by Suresh and other seniors. I felt it a little disgusting about it, but at that time, it was not important for me.

So I moved to my bed and took the bag of dresses, from underneath the bed. I took my fresh dress from it and went to the bathroom again. I entered into those fresh dresses, which was a body-fit black shirt and a blue jeans. I came back to my bed and put those old dresses in the other bag, which was kept for giving to the laundry which will be given twice a week.

I sat on my bed for a while, thinking about the days I spend missing her, a lot. Though we would communicate to each other through phone, calls, Facebook, or some time naughty texts from her. In each message she would warn not to reply, and there comes my frustrations for restricting myself without replying. So I just log in to FB, but she won't be coming online.

The last text message was the most provoking text from her, that made more wanted and I logged in to the FB, but she didn't turn up. I still remember the morning message from her which was long and unusual, because almost all the morning she text a simple good morning and says that she do love me and miss me. The last morning message were so tempting and it read:

"Today, you were in my dreams. We were kissing each other, cuddling and rolling over the bed and what not, that too in our nakedness. In between that beautiful dream my sister woke me up and left. But I still lay down on the bed: p and you know what! Then I badly wanted to kiss you like anything."

I don't want to call her, because I know what will happen to her if her sister comes to know me, then our relationship. So the very next day I called her through Roopa.

It's been weeks, since we had a date. Now I got thrilled and excited about getting the chance to meet her again. Only that, I was thinking about how to approach Joyal to know how and when we are planning to go to her house. I have never gone to her house. I know that her house is somewhere near to Joyal's house. Other than that, I know nothing regarding where exactly it is located, or nothing, about the root to reach there.

So I definitely have to approach Joyal. Whatever had happened between us, he is still my friend and I had a hope that he would help me in this situation.

I had never talked to him since that day. I haven't even bothered to notice him, for any reason. In this situation, meeting him was not that comfortable. Though Jessie told that she would talk to him regarding this, I was still feeling uncomfortable to face him.

I wished him to meet me, for some reason. So that I could tell him what I wanted. But nothing took place, like that as always. All our wishes will never happen, unless we at least approach it. So I made up my mind and went to the study room to see him. I didn't see him there. I walked forward and yes. There he was. Sitting with some study materials and a notebook, in which he was penning down seriously, from those materials. I lost my confidence in him accompanying me for today's plan.

'Hi' I approached him.

'I will drop you there at 5:30' He said without looking at me.

'Sorry' I said for the previous incident that happened in the parking lot.

'Jessie called me and asked to drop you there at 5:30. She might have already told you. Right?' He ignored the sorry and looked at me.

'Not that. I was talking about the parking lot incident' This time I made it clear for him.

'Roshen, I have to complete this whole stuff today. Please leave me alone.' He said and went back to his work when I just pulled a chair from behind and sat on his table.

'Hey, you guys doing something seriously?' Suresh came to us with his mobile phone in one hand and some books in the other. He too sat in the table we had occupied.

'Hm' That's the only thing what Joyal said where I kept silent, thinking how to compromise with him.

'WOW! Roshen, I thought you eloped with your girlfriend.

What was her name? huh, yeah I remember. Jessie, right?' Suresh broke the silence immediately.

'Yeah. No. I mean...I was hear only.' I said

'He hey! What happened, you guys are so serious now a day?' Suresh said, while doing something in his mobile. 'Where were you?' he looked at me.

'Huh?' I was in some other world seriously thinking on what will happen to the date today. If I know the way, I could have gone without anyone's help. 'I thought you were not here in the hostel.'

'That's what I asked just now.' His mobile phone ringed and he left the place keeping his books on the table.

'Joyal, why are you ignoring me all the time? What did I do?' I asked for a reply, but he pretended to be busy.

I sat silently staring at him for a while, when I heard him murmuring. 'You and you girlfriend keeps on using me.'

'We were not using you Joyal' I said.

Though Jessie told me that we need him, I had another perspective on him and our friendship. I wanted to solve the entire problems going on between them. But, I didn't understand why he was saying that we were using him. I never did that, neither her. I felt that it was better to understand what he meant by that, before trying to solve the problem.

'Joyal, I never did anything to hurt you. And why you want to show this distance to me. Please do respect our friendship and say what's there in your mind. Let's resolve it man.' I said

'Wow! You did nothing? Kishore always says you are smart and don't show it to me.' he said and I pulled his hand when he got up to leave. I didn't want this conversation to end like this. I wished to know what's in between them.

'Let's finish our fight with this conversation' I said

'If we did or not, I will accompany you to her house. Enough?' He said

'What do you think of me, Joyal? Haven't I come with you to talk with your Avita that day? You know what? It was so boring for me to be there, when you both were talking and making your pleasurable moments. Did I say anything to you against it?' I said, though it had no impact in him.

He just sat there silently, without responding anything. Suresh came near to the table. Before he sat down, he got another call. As soon as he looked into the screen, he left the place swiftly.

'Do you know what Jessie is doing to me?' Joyal spoke as soon as Suresh left the table.

'If I know it already, will I ask you what's happening within you?' I replied and had a glance at my watch. It showed 4:45PM. So still there was time, to meet 5; if he tells it quickly and precisely.

'She knows everything about me, like I do consume alcohol, I do smoke, and drugs for the first time in a month before. And you know what she did? She said that to my sister and you can imagine what would happen next. My mother stopped giving me pocket money; she took my mobile phone and locked it inside her bureau. Moreover that, she closed the internet and cable connection in my home. Now, somehow I convinced my mother and took the mobile from her' He said.

'Ow, that's why you are not coming online now a days na' I said.

'That's not the point. Now Jessie knows everything about me and she threatens me to do that and this for you. Otherwise she does mention all my habits to my screwing sister, and then reaches my mother. Ultimately my dad's role to -' he said

'Ok, I will manage it.' I understood what was going on between them and I didn't felt it as a serious issue. *Brother-sister relationship na*, as Jessie said. But still I will do my part. Because we need him, and he is my friend. I looked at the time, and made my mind to get sweet scolding from her for becoming late.

'By the way, why you where overreacting on that day, at the parking lot?' He asked once he recovered from his own trauma.

'Common man! It was over, and no more thinking over it. Let's go.' I said and got up to move.

I had already got ready before meeting him, so I don't have to spend another time searching where my cloths have kept. I went down and took my mobile phone. There were seven missed calls and a message from Jessie. I opened the message and it red;

"Come before 5:30, or I will go
for shopping with my friends"
                    AND THEN I REPLYED
"Baby, I will be there in two minutes."

I waited for two minutes for Joyal to arrive downstairs, but I had to shout his name in order to make him come down. As I tied the lace of my converse shoes, he ramped down the stairs folding his sleeves of his full-sleeve shirt. As soon as we reached out of the hostel, we started searching for the auto. Luckily, we got one immediately and left the hostel. In these situations, no one cared to acknowledge the warden.

AFTER WEEKS, SINCE THE LAST TIME WE MET

Jessie Joseph, the sweetest girl I ever have seen in my life. I feel so lucky to have her, and the ways she loves me, the way we miss each other and the excitement we had when we meet each other, make me trust her than anyone else whom I have trusted in my life before. She completes my life like any other sincere girlfriends. I started loving her more and more. The more I loved her, the more is the panic in me, when I think about her leaving to U.S. in any coming days.

When we reached in front of her flat, Joyal prepared to leave to meet some of his friends in the locality; saying he is not interested in coming inside. He informed that her apartment is on the third floor, 3B and also asked me to convince her in the problems in between them. He doesn't stay much time there.

I opened the big gate of the flat and went inside the building. I walked towards the lift, and pressed the button installed on the wall adjacent to its doors. When the door slid open in the opposite directions, I entered into it and turned around simultaneously to press the floor number. I pressed the button numbered *3* with my fingertip. Seeing the doors of the lift closing, I remembered our first kiss, which happened in the lift. But the only difference is that it was at the *City Center*. Now, I am in the lift of her flat which will take me to her corridor and I could walk to her apartment for the first time in my life.

I was all alone in the lift, thinking of our first kiss that happened earlier. A month was over by now and the depth of our relationship was more than anyone could imagine. We bonded together that made me believe that we would always be together in our life. Her black cute eyes, which I admire on all the time I see her, the fragrance of her body, the lips and the kiss that makes the perfect combination of our love. Now I am going to feel all these once again.

Can you guess where I am standing now! Right in front of her apartment. I was then thinking whether to text her up that I am here, or just ring the bell to make someone open the door. Options always confuse me. So casually, I lifted my hand to reach the calling bell. I pressed the switch once, twice and thrice. Still, the door remained closed. I feared that she might have left for shopping like she texted me before. I pulled my phone, from the pocket and took her name. I went to the options on the screen to opt "write message" and texted her;

"Where are you? Open the door baby. I am here!"

I even did not get a reply. So I got tensed and started calling her.

By the time, I was sure that she had already left with her friends. Though I said two minutes, I reached here after twenty minutes. Still, she could have waited for me.

We are meeting each other after a long gap and why she wants to go with her friends. After many rings, she didn't pick up my calls. Then I dialed again. This time I peeped in through the window that was partially opened while my phone was still in my ears hearing her phone ringing.

Through the open window, I saw her living room, where there was a television, a teapoy, four couches, which were neatly arranged around the teapoy. It was so tidy and I know Jessie would be behind this neatness. However, I could not see anything beyond that room because of the curtains. She was not picking up the calls of mine. I got partially angry and partially disappointed by losing a date.

I kept the phone back in my pocket. Meanwhile the door in front of me opened. I saw her standing in front of me, smiling cutely like always. I cannot resist mine. I too smiled.

'Hi' she said first, then I.

'Hm. Hi. What took you so long to open this door?' I asked.

'I was waiting for you so long. When you became late, I just took a bath.' She held my hand and pulled me in. 'Guess what! No one is here to disturb our privacy.' She winked at me.

'Where have they all gone?' I asked and sat on the couch. She stood near me. So I pulled her hand to make her sit. Just next to me.

'My sister went with her friends, and my grandparents might be in Joyal's house.' She put the strands of her hair behind her ears. 'They visit there every time they go for their regular checkup. So I guess they should be there. And don't worry. Usually they come late. So I guess today also it will be the same.' She said.

'Today, you are guessing too much.' I said and she smiled. 'So do they go every week?' I asked.

'No, it's monthly checkup.' She said.

I looked at her. Actually, I admired her in the skirt and top she wore. I have never seen her in this dress, so this time she looked different. And of course beautiful too. Whenever I saw her, she will be in her Salwar, or some jeans and top, sometimes Kurti. This time she looks stunning. And I noticed something odd.

'You look beautiful, but you are wearing your top inside-out.' I smirked.

'Ups, One minute.' She said and left in her room moving the curtains aside. The moment I remembered the first time I saw her in the train. I had never told her about that. That's just because I never cared about telling her. But today I had her, lost purse in the pocket of my jeans. Joyal told me not to give it to her, but I had already decided to give her the purse. I was only looking for an appropriate moment to give it.

I felt so relaxed by sitting there on the couch comfortably in her house. And the most exciting thing is that there was no one there. Not even her grandparents. A very rare chance we got within this whole month. That means we were surrounded by many unwanted things like the thoughts about getting ourselves separated which we don't want or the fear that someone who knows her in person like, relatives, friends of her family members, would notice us being together always at the city center. Because the way we held our hands, the way we sit closer, could make anyone understand that we are dating. Or in their eyes, they will acknowledge that something bad is going on. This will definitely create a very bad impact in her home. That is what made her restless, so do I. However, whatever it is, we cannot remain ourselves without meeting each other or at least having a word to each other in a day. It would be a frustration, when it happens.

'So, tell me.' She came out of her room wearing her top properly. She looked stunning like usual. She was admirable, every time she appears before me. It seems that she made me forget the outside world around me, when she is around.

'How are you, my dear?' She asked me sweetly.

'I missed you a lot in the past days.' I said.

'Really?' she prodded.

'Yeah, I think so' I teased her.

'I too missed you every moment you were not with me.' She said seriously.

I put my arm around her shoulder. 'Don't be silly. I am here no? Just put a smile on your face. It looks beautiful.' I said and she smiled.

'By the way do you want to drink something?' She asked, keeping her palm on my cheeks. I felt it cold.

'Mm hmm. No just sit here, with me.' I said and held her palms in mine. I griped it and she looked at it. It's been so long since we sat so close like this.

She looked at me so intensely. 'I badly missed you Roshen.' She said and put her arms around my waist laying her head on my shoulder. I know she needs me, so do I. Because we just love each other. Just one month of relationship made us realize that we cannot apart ourselves from each other.

'Sometime I even felt to come to your hostel or to ask you to come to the City Center, like always.' I could feel her jaw moving to my neck while she spoke. I loved this moment with her. It was so peaceful as we were alone together once again. There was no interference from anyone. Even our mobile phones didn't disturbed us. We were so happy to be like that. If the, world became stuck at that moment, we would be the happiest couple to celebrate it.

'When will your sister come back?' I asked her. I wanted to know whether I would be missing her again like this. So that we can at least prepare for it; like making some solution for being together and taking care of meeting at least once in a week.

'I don't know' She responded feebly after a while. We were still hugging. I feel great to keep her close to me for a long time like this.

'Your grandparents?' I asked the next important thing. Now I want to know when the oldies of the family will come back home. Just to know that how long I can hold her like this sit with her comfortably on the couch.

'Jessie.' She moaned as I called her. 'I asked you something' I reminded.

'What' She adjusted herself without moving her face, which was dug into my neck. Now she has settled relaxingly and leaning on my body.

'When will your oldies come back?' I asked her.

'Why?' she chuckled, lifting her head to face me.

'Your eyes are still beautiful. I am falling in love again with that' I smiled. She too smiled hearing that and leaned on me again.

I don't know whether is it because of us being together after weeks, or because of the privacy in her home, that we are enjoying. I felt this moment, so different and special. Something that I haven't experienced before. Even when I was dating Manju.

'Don't worry. They will only come later.' She smiled.

'Wow, that's wonderful.' I said and bit her ears softly. She tilted her head to the opposite side. 'I want to kiss you' I murmured in her ear.

NOW THAT IT'S MORE THAN A KISS

Though, she warned me not to remove her clothes, now we already undressed each other partially and laid sticking to each other, under a single blanket, on the bed, in her bedroom. She was happy once I agreed with her that I won't remove her clothes, unless she wants to. Now I am more than happy, that she could understand what I exactly wanted from her. So, she was the one who lifted her top first. I followed by unbuckling my pant and removed it. She helped me to take away my shirt and I slide her skirt down slowly as she lifted her hip, a little. Once I removed it, she rolled over me to the other side and kissed everywhere on my face, finally settling her lips on mine. We kissed and kissed for a long time.

I could see her eyelids so close to me, but I missed the beauty of her eyes this time. She never opens her eyes while kissing. But I was the opposite. While kissing, I never closed my eyes and of course mouth too. I felt so cute of her. Just like a small cute puppy, or sometimes as a beautiful angel from heaven. I hugged my angel tightly, and she kissed me more passionately with her tongue. At the same time, I moved my hands everywhere on her body. I felt a little terrified as she stopped kissing me, all of a sudden when I kept trying to unhook her bra for the past few minutes. But every time I fail to unhook it. I also sensed that I crossed the limit, when she looked at me. She got up from my body and sat on the bed turning around.

'What happened?' I asked politely, expecting something nasty to happen.

'This might be easy' she whispered back facing me and winked.

I held her waist as I got up and sat on the bed. I leaned forward and kissed on her cheek. She smiled and motioned to unhook it. I budged my hand from her waist to her back and did it. As she said, it was easier to do now. Once I did it, she turned around and pushed me to the bed, making me lie down again. As she climbed over my chest, I could see her cleavage much more magnificent. Earlier, we had left some undergarments on our body and now all those lies somewhere in the room. She laid over me and pulled the blanket over us.

It's been so long since we were lying on the bed, cuddled upon each other without bothering to wear our dress back. We are not even sure about where have we thrown our clothes. We certainly have to fetch for it. We are still glued to each other and lying there relaxingly.

It's been a long time since I am in her apartment. It might have become dark outside. Who bothers about it? When you are experiencing the happiest moment, then you will never care about what happens around you. I was looking at the rotating fan on the ceiling of the room.

She was resting her head on my chest. Occasionally, the strand of her hair flies and tickles my face. Then I move it with my hand and caress her cheeks. She was half-asleep beside me, after the on-the-bed-fun we had for more than an hour. Sometime I could sense the opening and closing of her eye-lid on my bare chest.

'Jessie' I whispered in her ears.

'Hmm,' She moaned.

'What will we do?'

'hm?'

'I mean…..about you. Don't go to U.S.'

She stood up and sat on the bed, covering herself with the blanket. She looked at me constantly. 'I don't know,' She said

'What does that mean?' I asked.

She faced downward. 'I already told you about that. I don't know what I should do for this.' She said in a feeble voice and looked at me. 'Though I want to stay here, I really don't have any idea about it!'

'Ok, I just asked. That's all. Don't get hyper.' I said.

'I am not getting hyper.' She said.

'Can we talk about this to Joyal? What if he gets some solution.' I said

'Why you want to bring Joyal in between?' she said. 'Then we will get into more trouble. I am sure about it.'

'Hm, whatever.' I said and got out of the bed, while she remained there.

I got down and took my dress. I wore everything but couldn't find my shirt anywhere. I looked here and there and finally I saw a small part of my shirt, which was visible from underneath the blanket that Jessie was covering herself. I pulled it, but it was stuck. I thought she might be sitting over my shirt and so, I lifted the blanket. She tapped my palm and looked at me. She had an incredible face with that look too. I wanted to grab her face and kiss it once again. But this was not the right moment, as I smelled something wrong with her.

'I think my baby is thinking about something.' I sat at the edge of the bed near her and placed my rested my hands on her thighs. 'What is it? Tell me.' I said and stroked her hair with one hand.

'I think, in the future, I have to regret about the sex we had now.' She said looking at me.

'What' I took my hands from her. 'What made you say this Jessie' I asked. I totally didn't get an idea on what she was saying about regretting in the future.

She didn't responded. She just sat idle on the bed.

'Jessie, you know that I love you and please trust me. I am not playing bloody playing fun with you.' I said. 'And I don't understand why you want to regret about this?' I got terrified of what she said. 'I am hurt Jessie. I didn't expect this from you too.' I said. I thought I will no more get humiliated anymore.

I pulled my shirt much more strongly and wore it as far as possible. I was preparing myself to go from there as far as possible and already decided not to come back again.

'Bye' I said and she hugged me much more tightly. So I also hugged her. I can't leave her just like that. All the more, she is my girl.

'I am sorry Roshen.' She said and kissed me, everywhere on my face like a small kid. 'Sorry' She kept on reciting it in my ears.

'It's enough Jessie.' I kissed on her forehead. 'You are all mine. A simple *bye* cannot bring this to an end. I won't leave you ever. Promise' I said and grabbed her face in my palms. She had tears in her eyes. I smiled and winked at her. She too smiled.

She held my hands. 'Don't you want to go?' She asked. I took my mobile. It already got switched off. It's battery got over and I couldn't switch it on again.

'My mobile has no more charge in it.' I said to her.

'My God!' She said 'What if someone had called you from the hostel?'

'Owch! I didn't think that.' I said. I could see the tension on her face. 'Jessie, don't worry. Nothing would happen to me there. Give your mobile.'

She clenched her blanket with one hand on her chest and leaned forward to take her mobile from beside the pillow. Her bare shoulder was seducing me again. I looked at her seductively. But it didn't worked. Now, the only thing that remained on her face was a whole lot of tension.

'Here is it.' She handed over the mobile to me. I took it and gave a peck on her lips. She smiled and I got out of the bed.

I took Joyal's number from it and called him. As I heard the ring, I walked towards the window and stood there. From the corner of my eyes, I could see her, collecting her cloths from the bed. Some from under the bed sheet, some from the floor. One whole ring was over. He didn't picked up my call. I re-dialed it again. The ring goes on, but he was not picking up.

Though she collected every piece of cloth of hers, still my girl was searching for something. I think she lost her earring or something. I disconnected the call and went to help her.

'I will also search. Is it your earring?' I asked.

'Earring? Nope, it's my bra!' She said seriously adjusting her hair behind the ears as she bends down to look under the bed. But it was clean there and there was nothing.

'Whew!!! Really?' I mocked.

'Idiot!' She snapped back. 'Did you get Joyal on the line?' She asked.

'No. How did you know I was calling Joyal?' I scratched my head, dialing him again.

'Who else will you call?' she asked, raising her eyebrows 'That too from my phone.' She giggled.

'Got your thing?' I asked still trying to dialing Joyal instantly.

'No, it's not seeing anywhere here. Have you taken it?

'Why should I?' I blushed and thrown the phone carefully on the bed itself. 'He is not picking up my.' I said.

'He might have gone somewhere fetching his Avita.' She said

'Jessie, but-' I tried to say something but she interfered and the moment I forgot what I was about to say.

'Ah, Roshen. Do you remember where you put my bra after removing it?' She asked and sat on the bed exhausted, covering herself with the same blanket.

'I removed it?' I asked, thinking what I wanted to say earlier.

'Then who?' she looked at me, with her puppy eyes that and her messed up hair. Still, she looked beautiful. Soon I gave up myself and stopped recollecting what I had forgotten to say.

'I remember removing it but I don't know where I put it.' I said sitting near her.

'You did it and you don't know where it is. Stupid.' She miffed

'Er...Jessie, let it go. Buy another. Simple' I joked.

'Are you not tensed Roshen? It's 8 PM! What will you say to the warden? Hey, call me once you reached there. Ok?' she put her hand around my shoulder.

'Anyway the warden is not there in the hostel. He has gone somewhere and now, his son is in charge there. So no need to worry' I said.

'It's not that. I feel afraid. Must call me soon you reach the hostel. Ok?' she asked.

Her phone rang in my hand. I picked it up so soon, as I was trying to get Joyal for so long and finally he called me back!

'Hello, Joyal where the hell were you? Can't you just pick up your phone when someone calls you? It was so fucking urgent yar!' I shot many things in one go without letting him say a simple "hello" first. Jessie came some more nearer and pressed her ear on the phone. He didn't replied to anything. I took a deep breath and started again. 'Where your phone being dug into the soil? Speak up ass hole!! It's been so long since I am here trying to reach you. Moreover, my phone got switched. I know I am late. So please help me to get into the hostel yar. Tell me. What should I do?'

After talking to him so much I felt a little relieved. Because, though I acted cool in front of Jessie, I was really scared thinking about, how to get inside the hostel.

What I have to say to the warden if I am caught? And thoughts like that really frightened me, since she revealed the time. Now I feel comfortable as he called me. So that, now I could know the current situation in the hostel and how to proceed there.

'Hello?' After sometime, for the first time in this phone call, he spoke. But, the voice. It sounds a little different. Something like a girls voice.

'Does he not sound different?' I asked Jessie and she looked at me shrinking her eyebrows. She leaned more and rested all her upper body on my shoulder. Then she pressed her ear on the phone more intensively.

"Oh My God! Is he still with Avita? WOW! I got company." I thought myself and smiled out of Joy.

'Who is it? Is it not Jessie?' She asked from the other end. The moment Jessie grabbed the phone from me and walked away to the other room.

Meanwhile, I switched on the lights in the bedroom and prepared myself to go. I took my dead mobile, stuffed into my pocket, and waited there for her to come back. I sat on the bed and looked around her room. Now only I got the time to look around. She really does care about the surroundings to arrange the things neatly and to maintain it. I was the other extreme of it. I didn't even remembers where my things are being kept.

Well, she was an avid reader and it shows in her bookshelf. It's all stuffed with numerous books neatly. I also noticed the book she purchased on that day we went to the City Center. All of a sudden, my jaw dropped as I saw the wall opposite to the window. The wall was not the thing surprised me. It was my picture that hung on the wall, which I presented to her on our first date. (However, that was a date only for me. For her it has been just a meeting. Whatever it is, now she is all mine.) It was neatly framed and suspended on the wall safely, like a costly painting. She was really my sweet heart.

She came and sat near me.

'Who was it?' I asked

'My sister' she butted exhaustedly.

'Anything serious?' I asked.

She nodded 'She doubted me. She asked who picked up the call and I had to say it was Joyal.'

'Oh, my. It's ok. I will manage him and will let you know.' I said and she nodded again.

'Don't get tensed. Everything will be fine, Jessie. I will call you once I reach there. Ok?' I said and left her apartment.

WAS WITH JESSIE EVEN IN HOSTEL

After walking for a long time, finally, I reached in front of the hostel. There was no one in front of the hostel. I opened the gate and went ahead to open the door. I entered inside the hostel. Still it felt empty space. Only the silence remained there. I took some book from my bag and the charger of my mobile. I pulled my mobile out of my pocket and plugged it for charging. Then I immediately rushed to the study room with the book I took from the bag, before someone noticing me. As I reached up stares, I saw some studying and many tables became already empty. That shows many have already slept. I couldn't locate Joyal, but I saw Suresh sitting at the same corner table, which he usually takes to study. So I headed there and smiled as he saw me.

'Hi' I said. I pulled the chair and sat there with my book.

'I didn't see you for the whole day. So I thought you might have already left

'Oh my God! Don't say bull shit man! I will get afraid hearing all that.' I said. 'Did the warden came here anytime?' I added.

'Yep. He came here when we were having food.' He said writing down some notes.

'Said something?' I asked.

'What,' he looked at me.

'Like…' I didn't wanted to reveal about it to him. What if he asked me to elaborate everything happened. Though he is my friend, he was also my senior, and I may not able to escape from him. 'Em…I mean…nothing. Leave that. Where is Joyal?' I asked instead.

'He already slept.' He said.

'I see, Ok, bye. See you in the morning.' I said and left the table, taking my book in my hand.

Before going down, I entered into Joyal's room. I wanted to know whether her sister called him. I saw him on his bed being shrunk under the blanket. I flicked him and pulled out his blanket.

'Joyal. One second. Please come out of the room. Please' I said as soon as he opened his eyes, covering his mouth. Otherwise he would shout and woke up others in his room. That too seniors. I didn't wanted them to kick me out. Though he hesitated completely, I begged him to come out of the bed. Because the need was mine.

'What?' He rubbed his eyes and asked me as soon as we came out of the room.

'I just want to know one thing.' I said 'Did Jessie's sister called you?'

'I don't know.' He said half asleep.

'So, do you so my missed calls?'

'No, why.'

'Because I called you a hundred times man! Why you didn't picked up?'

'One sec.' He said and left to his room. He came back with his phone. 'Sorry yar. It was in silence and I didn't noticed.'

'It's ok. Just check weather Jessie's sister called you.'

'Emm…Yeah seven missed calls from you, two missed calls from Jincy and a message from Avita!' he said and red her message. He started texting her back.

'Joyal please. Just one moment. I want to know something yar.' I pleaded.

'Just sending a *good night* yar.' He pleaded back. 'Ok, tell me.'

'Em, yeah. So you must call Jincy back in the morning and tell her that…em…tell her that, we went to the D C Books and you bought some books which she wanted.' I explained.

'Ok.' He said.

'Did the warden came?' I asked the very next important thing.

'Ah! I forgot to tell you that. He came and asked many things about you. Actually he was questioning me. Man just be careful. Ok?' he warned and I felt terrified when I heard about that.

'What all he asked?'

'Like where all you go, who all you talks with, how is your behavior, even he asked me weather you smokes, drinks all that.'

'What you said?'

'What else? I said everything in favor of you only.'

'Say exactly what you said dude. I am shivering out of fear.'

'Ow, I said that always we went together to the City Center Mall, restaurant, and to my home. And I told that I have never seen you smoking or drinking.'

'Is everything fine?'

'Yeah I think he is convinced. I am not that sure.'

'Hm, see you then. Good night.' I left tensed.

'Don't worry man! I am there with you.' He said.

Whatever it is I consoled myself and prepared to pretend, as everything was fine here in the hostel. Because I have to call Jessie soon. Although she was tensed, as I became late to come to the hostel. I took my phone and lied down on the bed. She took the call for the first ring itself.

'Is everything fine Roshen?' she asked as soon as she picked up the phone.

'Yes my dear. I told you, already that there will not be any problem.' I consoled her. I know how sensitive she is. Especially to her loved ones. So I lied.

'Hm. Now I am relaxed.' She said in her sweet voice.

'Ah one more thing. Joyal couldn't pick up your sister's call. So, everything might be fine there too. Right?' I asked.

'Yeah. Here there is no problem as such. She doubted me at first. But now everything is fine.' She said.

'What are you doing?'

'I was just watching TV. I was curiously waiting for your call.'

'Are you Ok?'

'Yeah I am fine. And you?'

'I came to hostel and plugged my phone into the charger to call you and went to the study room to see whether the warden is there. Luckily he was not there. Then I went to your brother and woke him up to find out whether your sweet sister called him. After knowing that he didn't pick up her call I became tension free. I rushed down, took my phone and lied down on the bed. Then I dialed your number. Now I have already narrated the whole thing to my sweet heart.' I took a long breath. 'Have you slept baby?' I asked

'It's really nice to hear you Roshen. It seems to be so long.' She said feebly.

'I just came from there na.' I said

'Yeah. But I am missing you.' She said.

'I am here. Very much near to you.' I said.

'Hey, someone has come. Just hold on.' She said.

I got up from my bed, switched off the light in my room, and switched on the ceiling fan. I took the earphone from my bag and flopped back to the bed. I lied relaxingly by covering the blanket over me; after plugging in the earphone. I was waiting for her to pick the phone. The hold was getting too long.

'Hey' finally she came back.

'Who was it?' I chided.

'That was my oldies.' She said. 'Oh my God. They are calling me. Please Roshen, don't angry. Just one second.' She said

'Again!'

'I will be back within a moment. Promise.'

I waited again. Except me, everyone at the down stares already slept. There was complete silence like always. And the silence was adding the atmosphere so romantic, but my girlfriend was missing at the other end. I could not hear any sound from the background of the other end. I hope it was silence there too.

'I am sorry.' She said as soon as she came back.

'Where you went now?' I asked

'I went to lock the doors there.' She said. 'What were you doing.'

'I was waiting for you. What else.' I said

'Have you slept baby?' She asked.

'No dear. I love you.' I said. Her sweet voice got my frustrations drained out.

'I love you too.' She said

'I miss the warmth of your body.'

'Now I am lying on my bed. Are you coming?'

'Don't provoke. I may come there now.'

'Let's just talk then.'

'The whole night?'

'The whole night.'

'Hey what did your sister said to you exactly?'

'She drives me mad sometimes. Leave it'

'Asked about me?

'Why? No she just asked who took the call. That's it.'

'What did you say then?'

'I just said it was Joyal.'

'Had she asked why he came?'

'She never asks such things. Why?'

'I told that she called Joyal know. So I asked him to say that I and Joyal went there together to give some books to you. In case if your sister asks him.'

'Oww…I see.'

'I see…' I mocked.

'When you went there, was there warden in hostel?'

'I told you na. There was no one here. So nothing to worry about it.'

'Ah…yeah yeah. I remember'

'Hey! Is there the love bites I gave still on you?'

'Idiot! My grandma saw the one you gave me on my neck.'

'Wow! It's exclusively for you, baby.'

'Stupid.' She chuckled and I laughed to that harder.

'Then what happened?' I asked

'What else. She asked me what's that the red mark on my neck.' She said

'What did you say?' I giggled

'I said some insect crawled over my neck. And that is why the red mark came.' She said 'You know? At the beginning, I didn't get what to say. I really got afraid. I can't even guess what will happen if it was my sister. Any way my grandma got convinced.'

'Bravo!' I said. 'And did she say something?'

'Yes of course! She said the most funniest thing. Guess what?'

'How do I know? You tell me.'

'Ok, She asked,' she laughed in between and continued 'that do I want to meet up a doctor.'

'You should have gone, then. It would be more fun.' I teased her.

'Blah' she said dejected.

'Hey! I was just kidding yar.' I tried to console her.

'Not that. I was just thinking what if my sister saw that.' She said

'Oh God. Don't be a kid Jessie. It will fade away in one or two days. Trust me.' I said 'However it's just one, and every other similar marks will go under your dress. So be cool.'

'Yeah I know that.' She said

'Then what' I said.

'Mmhm, nothing, I love you.' She said and I smiled. 'Did you have food?'

'Nope'

'Why?'

'Em…the food served in my hostel got over before I came.'

'So didn't had food?'

'Mm Hm. It's ok. Anyway I don't feel hungry.'

'But still…'

'You had?'

'No, I feel sleepy and doesn't feel to have food.'

'Why?'

'Just like that. Can we go to the City Center? That was our regular dating place no. Can we go there tomorrow?'

'Yeah sure. Me too want to kiss you in the escalator like I did that day.'

'Don't you have anything else to do?'

'Do you remember that day?'

'How can I forget our first kiss.'

'Actually it was not *ours*. It is mine.'

'Why?'

'Because you never kissed me back that day. You didn't even open your mouth when I kissed you.'

'Yes I did!'

'No you didn't'

'Whatever, but I kissed you several time later.'

'But not in that lift of that mall.'

'Hmf! You and your fascinations.'

'He hey! It's not fascination. It's because I love you dear.'

'Whatev-'

'No no no. If you agree to kiss me there in the lift, then only I will come.'

'Ok done.'

'WOW. So let's fix the date.'

'Yeah, let's fix it.'

'At what time did you want me to come there?'

'At the usual time.'

'Hm..ok. Will you wear the same dress you wore on the first day you came to meet me.'

'Yeah sure. Do you remember what I wore on that day?'

'You wore a navy blue *kurta* with a black pant.'

'Ah…ok, I will see to it.'

'If you want to sleep, then don't stay long talking to me.' Occasionally I could hear her yawning in the middle of her talking.

'It's ok. Let's talk please.'

'Hm. Whatever.'

I curled on the bed and we continuously talked for hours. Whenever I spent the time with her I never bothered about anything else. So as of now I was not at all bothering about the late hours, tomorrows class, or any other activities other than ours. I turned the other side as I saw Suresh coming towards his bed, which was very next to mine. I got an approximate time when I saw him. I knew now it would have become midnight. Because I know that Suresh would sleep at midnights after finishing his studies. And today is the first time I am seeing him. And today is the first time in this hostel I am awake. That too for talking with my girlfriend. Now days I am only considering and caring about her. Not even about me or the things that are responsible for me. Like exams, studies, engineering entrance, moreover that it's been so long, since I have called my parents. But I never missed a day calling her. If I do it becomes late night to sleep.

But today, though I came from her house it's still bothers me to talk to her for a long time. I am getting nervous thinking about what to say to the warden. So this was the better thing to do. Just talk to her. I was feeling good by doing that. And she made me feel good for the whole night.

TERMINATED

I t was a common routine in the hostel, to wake up early and the warden was damn strict on that. He never allowed anyone to sleep beyond 6 AM. By now everyone knew that. If someone violated this will not be hanged, but definitely be fired by the warden. And the day will become the worst day of the month. A few has already experienced it entirely. But some has narrowly escape from the warden and I was one among them. The rest was ideal kids of the hostel. They were the one who was apt to watch-and-learn. According to the warden, they were the role models of the hostel.

At present, I was sure that I would become one of the few who had experienced *the worst day of the month*. However, still I can stay as one-of-the-some who have narrowly escaped from the warden. But this time, I am not that confident because previously when I escaped it was only five or ten minutes delayed from six. Today it was not at all like that. Because, when I woke up, the clock showed 9:15 AM, which was beyond late. I can't even think of an excuse to be said to the warden. But when the warden had a glance at me, he didn't even stared or showed an angry face to me. I just pushed off from there to take a speedy bath. A bath that water just flown over my body.

Now the time was almost ten and I just dressed up. Now I have to take my bag and get to the campus, atleast before the lunch hour starts. I put on my bag over my shoulder and moved out of my room quickly. As I stepped out, I saw the warden standing near the hostel office. I got very much scared as the only existed student in the hostel, to be left to the institute was I.

'Where are you going?' he asked firmly. What I question! Definitely not to the bar. He knows. Still have to ask this? I thought.

'Class.' I said. *"As if you don't know"* I murmured without him noticing.

'Why can't you take a leave today?' he asked.

'Today, an exam will be held there.' I said.

'Really! I see… Then you must certainly take leave today. Skip it. Doesn't matter in your case.' He said sarcastically.

'But-'

'Roshen. Keep your bag inside and wait there. Your parents will come here in any time soon.' He said and smiled.

After the first day of my joining here, today only I saw that smile on his face. I silently went into my room and threw my bag to the bed. I had no idea what was going to happen next. So I simply sat on my bed staring at the floor. Anyway, whatever it is, it will not be good for me. I was preparing myself to accept the worst.

When I slept at late night, the bloody time was running like hell. And now! I am so tensed and don't know what exactly is going to happen, the time hardly drags the needle from one point to the other! It was terrific. I felt so alone then, except me and the warden outside in the office.

If I could call and talk to Jessie, it would be a great relief. But she would know that I have a problem and she would then defiantly compel me to tell her, what's going on here. Now I don't want her to know that I am caught because while talking, eventually if I tell her about what Joyal said to me; then she will ask why I didn't tell her about that yesterday itself. So I decided not to talk to her for now. At the same time, I am also confused about how to handle this when my parents comes here. Especially, when I think about answering my father's question.

I took my phone from my pocket and dialed the home landline. I wanted to check up weather my mother also was coming with my father. If so, things would be easy. The phone ringed for so long. But no one picked it up. I dialed again. Still no one picked up. I got relaxed. But that was not enough. My fancy thoughts was haunting me badly. Usually these thoughts comes into me in two situations. When I get crazy or bored and when I am depressed or tensed. I breathed faster but building of tensions in me was even faster.

I heard the sound of opening the gate. I jumped from the bed and peeped out of the window. It was his son; the junior warden. FUCK! He too there to screw me! Can't he just fuck his new wife and be at home? I thought.

Then came the second sound. But it was not from the gate. It was my mobile. It beeps. It was a message from

Jessie. It looked a bit occurred for receiving during this situation. It red;

"I will wear the same navy blue kurta with a black pant for tomorrow. What says? MUST REPLY. I KNOW YOU ARE NOT LISTNING THE CLASS."

"Sure baby, you look great then! Exam's going on now, will text you after words. Ok?" I texted her back. I know, otherwise she would continuously messages and ends up in twelve-fifteen unread messages.

As soon as I sat down on the bed after sending the message, I saw the warden entering into the hostel, followed by my father and mother walked in along with him. Behind them, Alex, the junior warden came inside and placed perfect number of chairs. (Junior warden ignored me. He didn't even told me to sit at least on the bed nearby me.) I lost all my hope. As they came in, I stood up and stood at a corner silently watching them taking their seats. I had no particular role to play there, but just to stand like a pillar supporting the wall nearby.

They settled facing to each other were I was cornered.

'So, I told briefly about what happened. I wanted you to come here to talk in detail, so that you can make your son to come on the right track. I mean, we want him to stay here, by obeying the rules of this hostel.' The warden stared explaining and I stopped watching them.

From the corner of my eyes, I noticed my father looking at me. But I didn't.

'So, though Roshen attends every class he is intolerant for us. Because he never comes back to the hostel on time, he never gets ready on time, moreover teacher's complaints on the other side. One of the previous days I caught him drinking alcohol with another guy. I warned him. But in Roshen's case I already gave enough warning in many things. What should we do now?' he asked to my father.

I could sense fireballs burning inside my father's head and definitely, he is going to spit it on me once after the show.

'Not only that sir,' Mr. Junior warden interfered 'on the other day, I found him smoking cigarette along with his companions, while coming back from the institute.' He switched another complain.

Does he not ashamed of complaining like a small kid? I thought while I constantly stared on the floor. But my mother's eye was always on me like how the eyes of a thief would be on queen's crown kept in the museum.

'Did you?' The first time my father spoke to ask this to me.

'No,' I lied knowing that he will not surrender with it. Still I tried.

'Ah ha! See how frankly he lies,' he said to my father.

Thankfully, my father didn't intrigued anything to it. My eyes were still on the floor. Staring on the floor didn't went waste. I discovered the ants moving to a corner in a well and disciplined manner. How peaceful their life would be. No hostel, no entrance. Therefore, no tensions. While thinking theses I heard another bomb been dropped by the warden. It was on mobile.

'All the time his mobile would be glued to his ears. And thus, he has no time to take the books. That's why he constantly remains as a backbencher in the class.' The warden take a break to get some breath. And continues 'Please advise him well before you return. Otherwise this time too…I don't think he will crack the coming entrance, if he won't change his rebel character.'

I didn't find any link in what he just said. I never got a chance to rebel. The only thing I always violated was just coming late to the hostel. Other than that… The warden is wrong. I never had been a rebel.

My father got up. So my mother.

'I am taking him home.' My father said to the warden

'So, what about the entrance then?' he asked

'Let him right without any couching.' He said

'Are you sure? I just wanted to point out how your son is doing here, so that he may become alright.'

'How will we trust him? And I am not ready to spend this much money for his nonsense and enjoyments.' He said.

'But-' he said

'I have already decided' my father said sternly.

No one asked my opinion. They went out. I kept on shivering. I was still standing inside the hostel at the corner; without knowing what to do next. All the ants left. The floor is clean and I was the only living body remained on that floor. The warden, Alex (Junior Warden), and my parents. All went out. I could hear them discussing seriously. While I stayed in – Stupefied.

Immediately I remained the date at the City Center in the evening with Jessie. By now I was sure about one thing. This was my last moment in this hostel and in the Thrissur district. So there was no doubt that I can't go there at City Center in the evening. I wanted to inform her that. Otherwise, she would wait there for me for hours until I come. (She very well knows that I will never appear on time.) I took my phone out of my pocket. I can't call her in the presence of my parents. So I started texting her. My fingers were shivering in a rhythm as I press the buttons on my mobile.

"Jessie, I got problem here. My parents came. Don't call me or text me now. I will explain everything later. Just don't come to the mall in the evening. I won't be coming."

After typing I was about to hit the send button. Before I could press the respective button; my father called out my name from the doorsteps.

'Ha!' I responded and my phone slipped down from my hands, simultaneously.

It landed at the floor safely. The battery, lid that covered the battery and the phone piece rested on the floor peacefully. The phone got switched off and hence I lost all the contents that I just typed. I bent down and took the three dismantled parts of the phone, and fixed it quickly. Before switching it on, I rushed to my father before he calls my name again.

'What you had to do in the phone now?' the very first thing he asked as soon as I approached him.

'Um…nothing, I –'

'Whatever, we are going to the office now, to discontinue your course.'

'But, I –

'No need to tell anything. I already received the form from the warden. There is no need for your justification.' He snapped 'Give your phone' he said and snatched my phone from my hand and they left at once.

The heaviest tension was that I couldn't inform Jessie. I had no idea what to tell her. She will now definitely wait there and what if she thinks I fooled her. No she may not. She knows me well. But I wanted to inform her. I should have done something about it.

IT'S ALL OVER

We were now in the train, returning to my home with my parents. I got chucked out of the hostel and eventually my father went to the institute to stop my course even before completing it. I didn't even got the opportunity to explain. I was just a spectator of the whole play.

Our train moved slowly from the station. But for me, everything was getting over so quickly. By then I was all thinking about Jessie. I was missing her a lot. And no more dates. I feel lost and decided to call her. I can't take the phone and speak to her in my parents presence. They were sitting right in front of me. I was thinking hardly what to do for calling her. I can't climb up on the upper-birth and talk to her. If my mother sees me talking on the phone for a longer time, then she wants to know to whom I was talking with, how do I know the person, and much more things. Gradually the situation turns into a havoc.

So I decided to move out from my seat.

'Where are you going?' my mother asked immediately I stood from my seat.

'I want to move out from here and get some fresh air.' I said

'You are not going anywhere.' She said.

'Mom! I am not a prisoner. I will come back soon.' I said and moved out. She just stared at me when I walked away. I just had to convince my mother alone, as my father already slept when the train moved.

I walked out of the cabin and stood outside, near to the toilet in the compartment. I could hear the hard sound of the moving train. When I saw outside through the door, I realized how fast I am leaving her behind. Once I got annoyed with her when she said that she had to go with her father soon. We also fought on that issue. Ultimately she agreed to find some solution to stay here itself for excusing herself for not moving with her father. But, now I even left from there even without telling her a word about it. I couldn't even text her. I feel guilty about that as I remember saying

"I am here. Very much near to you." I remember me saying this to her in our last phone call when she said that she misses me. Now I feel guilty about what I said to her and what I am doing to her right now. I immediately picked up my phone and called her. Normally, during the train journey, there will be lack of mobile range. So calling someone will be successful only by chance. Now luckily the ring goes fine and she picked up the call within no time.

'Hey! Aren't you in the class now?' she asked 'Or bunged the class to meet me?' she said.

'I didn't go to the class today' I said

'Good…then common get ready and call me once you are ready. Meanwhile, I will get out of the home.'

'Em…' I wanted to stop her for being this much exited but she interfered me soon.

'Remember what you said? That you want to kiss me in the escalator. This time I won't stop you. Let's not care about whoever enters into the escalator and lets not stop even if the doors opens. Let us go on kissing wild till we find ourselves breathless.' This time it feels like she was excited. 'What says, huh?'

'Sounds great, but-' I tried to tell her.

'What happen to my Rosen? You sound sick. Are you ok?' She interpreted me sweetly.

'Nope' That's what I could only say to her.

'Don't worry. Come over here. I will make you fine baby.'

In the moment I sunk into tears, but resisted it myself soon. I should have told her before leaving thrissur.

'Hello?' she spoke as I didn't said anything on the phone. I became too gloomy to talk to her by now. 'Are you ok?' She asked

'Yeah, I am alright.' I could only lie to her all of a sudden. She sounded too happy. Maybe because of our yesterdays night, or because I called her again. Whatever it was I don't want to turn down her happiness. So I acted all right.

'He hey. You are not. It's ok, I will be at the City Center mall in an hour and I will meet you there. And don't get too delayed.' She said.

I felt like she caught me. I don't want to extend this so long. I decided to tell what all happened now. If I hide something from her then it means I trust no one in the world. Because she was the one and only person in my life whom I would love to share every bit of everything in my life.

'Say something! Now you are keeping mum. If I do that you would have killed me.' She said. 'I was just kidding. Talk something na. Or I will say. Em...yeah. In the next apartment of mine, there is a small kid. His name is Ajmal. He is so sweet Roshen! You must talk to him. Yesterday when you left -'

'Jessie.' I stopped her.

'What' She asked me sweetly.' Her voice made me feel like board another train which goes back to Thrissur, from the very next station.

'I am sorry.' I said

'For what?' she asked innocently

'I can't come to City Center again.'

'Do you want to go to some other place? But only malls are safe for me. That's why. But don't worry. There are many more malls here.'

'Not that. I can't come to any place with you here after. I am going back to Palakkad.'

'Hm.'

'I stopped my course from there.'

'Hm.'

'Warden thrown me out from the hostel.'

'Hm.'

'Jessie, don't you feel anything?'

'Yes of course. I felt shocked when I got to knew it first. Then I felt sad. You know? I even cried whenever I thought about us. No more dates, no more kisses, no more nothing. And my grandma continuously asks me for what I am crying. I just ignores her all the time when she asks me that. Can I say "Oh…my boyfriend is leaving me. I can no more see him often." Can I say that to her? You know…there was no one to console me. You know how I felt? It was not because you are leaving. You could have said a word to me Roshen.' She burst out all of a sudden.

'It's not like that baby. I wanted to, but-'

'But what?' she didn't allowed me to say anything. I deserved this, so I heard everything 'Do you remember how you shouted at me when I just said that I will be going to America with my dad. Now you please tell me how should *I* react to what you have done today. You just forgot me. You didn't even without let me know what was happening there. You told everything is alright in the hostel and nothing was there to wory.'

'I am sorry. I know you are angry with me. But the situation was like that. I couldn't even take my phone from my pocket. Just imagine. And please don't compare me with Roshen. He may be able to inform you because he was not the one who was in that situation. I was the one who got fired. And that was the worst moment in my life. Please understand that. I already got enough shouting from everyone. Warden, mom, dad, everyone. Now it's you who is remaining. So carry on. I am here to hear you.' I slightly got raised. Though the fault was from my side, I was calling her expecting some sweet talk. But, as I didn't got any mercy from anyone, I lost my temper.

'Do you memorize calling me after reaching the hostel? Had I asked you whether everything is fine. How many times did I asked you weather warden said something about you. Do I. Did you tell me anything? You lied.' She said. 'Roshen. Joyal called me, minutes after you left from my flat. He told me everything that the warden told about you. I thought you would tell me everything and I could keep you calm and relaxed. So I told Joyal not to tell you about telling this to you. But you never mentioned anything about this. How many hours we talked Roshen? Can't you just say it?' She sighed out.

'I am sorry Jessie. Please don't hate me for this.' I said. I know she won't. but still I feared weather she had thought about break-up. Because I already ignored her for a moment that too when something serious like this happened.

'What?' she blushed on to the phone. 'You are the one whom I love the most Roshen. I can't hate you for any reason. Even if you ditch me sometime. I love you Roshen. Don't you get that yet? What all we did? What all we dreamt? I ever got laid for you last night. Still you didn't get how much I trust you? That's the only reason why I loves you like anything.'

'Hm..' I said and I saw my mother walking towards me from her seat. 'Jessie. I will call you after sometime. My mother is coming. Bye.'

'Bye. Roshen I love you.'

'I love you too. And I am sorry.'

'I don't need your sorry. Just don't avoid me.'

'Don't say that! I am not even planning to think about ditching you.'

'Ok bye.'

'Bye.'

I disconnected the call. By the time I pushed my phone into my pocket my mother stood beside me.

'Enough of standing here. Go now.' She instructed and I did just like she said.

I tailed my mother towards the seat. My phone beeped in my pocket and silently took it. It was from my girl.

"WRNINIG: if you ditch me, I will Kill you ;)"

I didn't understood what she actually meant by this text. So my mind urged to call her.

'Mom! I forgot to wash my hand.' I said to my mother.

'Chee…Are you out of your sense Roshen? Can't you remember the basic things that you have to do?' she said and left again soon. My intention was not to wash my hand. I dialed her again.

'What was that message? I didn't get it.' I said as soon as she picked up the call.

'Which message?' that was the reply. I realized that it was not her.

Guessing that it would be her sister, I asked 'Is it Manju?'

'Sorry wrong number.' She said and I disconnected the call before she did and went to my seat.

My parents were sitting silently in front of me. So do I too sat silently. My mobile beeped again. I took it and again it was her message.

"What? My sister came back. So be careful. I will call you in five minutes."

I smiled reading that and my parents saw me smiling.

'See he is too happy for whatever happened today' immediately my mother whispered to my dad, by waking him up.

'Let him be.' He said to her disgustingly and my mother stared at me.

I got up from my seat and climbed up on to one of the upper birth that was vacant. I didn't even looked at them. As she said, she called me.

'Hey, don't call me here after. Ok?' she said 'Did my sister asked you something?'

'No, I just asked what did that message means. When she asked which message, I was sure that it was not you. Then immediately I asked whether it is Manju and disconnected the call saying it was a wrong number.' I narrated everything to her. I did not want her to feel ignored again. When she feels like that, I feel like I am all alone.

'Bravo my boy! Bravo!' she mocked.

'No need for imitating me.' I said.

'Hm…' frequently she had been repeating the same thing.

'Can you please stop this moaning?' I got dejected.

'Hmm.' She did more of that this time.

'You never made this sound much when we made out erotically last night!' I teased her

'What?' she blushed.

'Em...I mean...' The kind of "what" she said made me confused whether she felt bad about what I did or felt bad on me saying what I did last night on her.

'Ow that! I did moaned! How can I not?' her sweet voice interrupted my thought.

'And the way you-'

'Hey listen! Do you know Ajmal?' She cut me off. I wanted to bring her to our at-times-phone-sex. It was really exciting. And it used to be, always. That was something she commented every time we doses off to sleep after the call.

'What now?' I asked annoyingly.

'Do you know Ajmal or not.' She asked excited.

'Yeah I know.' I said.

'You only told about a small kid near to your apartment.'

'Ah...yeah, I did.'

'Now what happened to that kid?'

'You must talk to him, da! You know, yesterday when you left from here, I saw him playing with the ball on the corridor. He was so funny. Though there was nothing much funny about him, still you will admire at him. That cute he is.'

I had no other way, other than listening her. This time, I was the culprit who made her disappointed. So I am responsible for hearing all these bullshit. Hearing all kind of this silly this make me feel to pull her hair. But she was my baby. So how can I do that too. I can't hurt her. So I had to hear her talking about the small kid all

217

the time. Latter she shifted the topic and reached to the kid's family. She was talking Ajmal's family like someone talking about their precious assets. And as far as I am her boyfriend, I was responsible to hear all those nonsense. When you expect something from your girl, that makes you horny; even the next days' exam become nonsense.

And it made me quite confident in talking her openly. But at times, she definitely shuts me up. "You boys always want the same all the time?" she asks the same thing whenever she ignores me while saying dirty thing with her. But still she goes ahead of me whenever she had a good frame of mind. I lusted her more for that. But I love her like anything when she was dull and unhappy. It became my pleasure to make her

THE MESSAGE

We reached home by noon. I locked myself in my own room, trying to do something that could give me a change of mind. I wanted to forget everything that happened today. The hostel experience, parent's hot words and my hot girls' phone call. Beyond her hotness there was something intangible in her which made her sweet and that was what made me fall in love with her. And when I did, she made me forget about Manju. Now I am in my home, at my place; remembering again Manju when I saw the old ring which I pulled out from her hand once. This time was missing Jessie a lot that I felt sprint out from home to reach the railway station and catch the next train to there. But as of now, it was not possible. So I did what was possible.

She picked up my call.

'Jessie.' I said

'Reached home?' she replied

'Don't you miss me?' I asked

'Hm, but we are not too far. We still could have some dates. Can't we?' she said.

'Why not baby? And we make out too...' I said and she laughed. 'Let's make sure that we would call each other every day. At least once.'

'Of course.' She said.

'I love you.' I said

'Love you too' she said. 'Don't ignore me, please.'

'Ow…Jessie, I told you already. I have not avoided you. I told what had happened…'

'Yeah, I understand. But still, just take care of it. Please. It do hurts.'

'I hate to hurt you. So understand that it was not my intention.'

'I know. I just said it.'

'I never want you to get hurt. So if at all you got hurt, I am there to make you all right. Trust me.'

'I do.'

'Feels exhausted after coming here.'

'Then go and take some rest. Go.'

'Should I? let's talk.'

'No, not now. Go and settle up yourself. Let's talk in the night.'

'Already I am! I am alright Jessie. Lets talk. That's only what I want now.'

'But you need some rest. You haven't slept last night too. Instead we kept on talking.'

'It's ok, baby,'

'No…baby' she mocked. 'Don't you feel guilt on what happened to you in the hostel?'

'I feels guilt for the only thing that you felt ignored. And you became sad, that too because of me.'

'Don't be empathetic. Let's forget that.'

'Yeah…ok,'

'I will call you at night.'

'Hm…bye'

'Bye.'

I kept my phone on my table and walked to the living room. There was no one and I heard noise in the kitchen. So I went there to find my mother there preparing for the lunch by herself. I found my dad nowhere around in the house.

'Where is dad?' I asked her.

'Does that matter anymore to you?' She snapped back

'Why?' I asked her softly.

'You and your life, that's all what it matters to you. Have you ever thought about us? We sent you there to study. We thought it would make you easier to clear your entrance exams.'

'I did nothing! Just came late once. That's it.' I tried to convince her but she gave me a deadly look after all.

'Yes. Why you want to go out? Can't you just sit in the hostel and study whatever you have to?' she said

'I do my studies regularly'

'And the warden said this was not the first time.'

'But mom, I-'

'Roshen! Grow up! For God sake! Please.'

'I am hungry' I said dejected and left from kitchen.

I did not felt to remain there anymore. Hence, I called up my friend Kishore and found out whether he was at home to head there. He told me to be at my home and he will reach here in sometime. I logged into my facebook account and found that there was 1 friend request, 3 unread messages and 2 notifications.

The notifications were from Roopa who liked my post and the other one was shocking for me. It was Manju. I had never talked to her ever after our break-up. Neither, un-friend her on facebook. But she used to hit like on each and every status of mine, that I post. And constantly I ignored that. Had Jessie never came into my life, I may have forgiven Manju. But who knows whether she already got committed with some other guy. According to me, I still believe that she would be dating some other fellow soon after our break-up. I even never bothered, if she had or had not got a new boyfriend.

I accepted the friend request. I was in a great passion of creating more and more friends on facebook and it was quiet interesting for me. Chatting with random people and it gets more excited to chit chat with some girls. When I were in school, Roopa always advices me to accept the friend request only to the ones who was known to me. But who cares when there was a tight competition between some of my friends to increase the friends list on facebook. Next was the unread message that I give least importance to read. Because, I very well knows that it may be some *"hi"* from some common friends. And I have never noticed any important messages in my chat box. The only chat that made me feel important and wanted was when I was chatting with my girlfriend. First was Manju, but when she left my life, Jessie came into me. She was someone most important for me in my life. I had never felt my life so occupied with love and affection. Even Manju was a waste of time for me.

I hit the message and there was two *"hi"* as I expected and one was literally message from Manju. After chatting with Jessie that day in the class, I had never opened me facebook account. Still there are only three messages from two friends and one unwanted person in my life out of 102 friends, which I managed to create in just two years.

This was the first time that Manju was sending me a message in facebook after months. What maximum she does was to hit like on all my status. So her first message very well tempted me to read. It red;

"Roshen I know what I did, but give me one more chance to explain what had happened that day. I don't argue that what I did was right. But what happened that day was an accident and I was afraid to talk to you after that incident. And it really felt terrible when you pulled away that ring from me. I don't mind, but please try to understand me to forgive me. Please take me back as your old Manju and let's have good moments in the coming future. Still I love you and more than that, I am missing you a lot. I won't force you, but sometime please care to talk to me"

I don't care to call you anymore. I said in my mind. Our relationship was once broken. Getting committed again in a broken relationship was just like sticking up a broken stick. It still looks weird. That was why I always doesn't even care to care how Manju cares me anymore.

The very first thing that I did after breaking up with Manju was deleting her contact number from my mobile. And I too changed my number within a week. But I didn't felt to un-friend her from my facebook. Neither would I chat with her. The only motive was to check up her updated post and regularly notices weather she had got new boyfriend. If so she would definitely change her status from *single* to *in a relationship*. When we were dating, she changed it from single. I still remember, once she borrowed my phone and changed her status, when we were in McDonalds'. That was our usual dating place.

There was an urge to reply her but I didn't want her to think that I had a change of mind. Instead, I left a message for Jessie, "I love you".

Having a girlfriend was fine, but dealing with the ex-girlfriend at the same time was tougher. I was sure that I have to deal with Manju soon in order to avoid problems with Jessie.

I went in front of my house as soon as I heard the honking of his bike. I smiled at him and he too smiled back. He put his bike on the side stand near my boundary wall and came near to the gate removing his helmet, while I stood at the door.

'You prick! Can't you call me from there? At least a message!' He said opening the gate and held the helmet in the other hand. I still stood there smiling. 'Even Joyal calls occasionally and also told that you had a girlfriend there.' He stood beside me.

'You won't understand my situation. There is lot to tell. Come.' I said and we rushed directly into my room.

My mother was still in the kitchen and I made him get into my room. Otherwise there was a chance for another disaster that could put me in torture. When she sees any of my close friends, then she would narrate every complaint about me. Kishore would only stand there and nod his head to everything but Roopa was a good companion for this to my mother. She not only hears everything but also supports to her scolding and even advises me when she gets me alone. Especially this happens during the parent teachers meeting in my school and every time Manju would rescue me from Roopa. So that I could at least escape from her, boring advises. I never called Roopa home much. If anything was there I would either call her up or meet her somewhere outside.

'Hey! Roopa told that your course was for two months?' he said as soon as we settled in my room.

'Yeah it was, but the warden forbidden me from my hostel. So my father stopped the course from the institute. Thereby my course shrunk to one month.' I said casually.

'What happened?' he blushed.

'Will tell you, before that let us get out of here.' I said and went to the kitchen to have a word with my mother.

McDonalds'

'This was your usual place no,' he said taking the glass of coke in his hand.

I knew he was referring to Manju.

'Sort of' I said fiddling with my phone. I was expecting Jessie to come online. I didn't logged out from the Facebook.

'Huh?' he said

'She used to come to my house too, in the name of group project. Roopa have came once with her.' I said.

Kishore was asking about Manju so I too talking about her. But not at all was thinking about her while talking, because I never missed Manju, any time before. I don't want to care. All I admired, even in my thoughts was Jessie. She already became family. She was something like, more than a girlfriend to me. So certainly, I missed her whenever she was not around. "Just leave a message in facebook. I will call you as soon as possible." She used to chant ever time in those three weeks while we couldn't meet up each other. Those three weeks were like a hell to us. We would adjust ourselves by texting, calling each other. So now, I understood there was something more than hell could do. Every time it was frustrating and furious for me without talking to Jessie. As Jessie's sister was at home, I cannot call her. So, have to wait until she calls me. Each time when I think about her, I was bothering her too much. And when he tells about Manju, the memories of Jessie haunts me too much.

'What are you thinking about?' he startled me with his leg from underneath out table.

'Hm. Nothing.' I said.

'Missing Manju' he mocked silently.

'Ew. Why should I?' I snapped

'Got paranoid?' he asked

'Let's not talk about her. And I never missed her. Manju is no more anyone to me.'

'Really?'

'What you mean!'

'What I said. Like you don't miss her?'

'No'

'Then, she does.'

'So what I am supposed to do?'

'Can't you just talk to her at least?'

'Not really.'

'Call her please.'

'But I am committed with-'

'Jessie' he interrupted me

'Hm. So you know it already.'

'Roopa told. I called Joyal.'

'To search whom I am dating with?'

'No, to know whether you are alive!'

'Wow. You must have called me instead.'

'What's your new number? Have you ever called any one of us to inform that your number had changed?'

'I called Roopa. Didn't she tell you?'

'No,' he stood up to leave 'Any way please call Manju. She had been trying to get you for the whole month.'

I followed him out of the McDonalds'. Reaching outside, he turned around facing me. 'She is sick without you Roshen. I know you won't b having her phone number. I will me forward it to you. Remember to call her. Don't let you regret later for this.' He said and sat on his bike. I said nothing. 'Do you want me to drop you?' he asked and started his bike.

'Nope.' I said.

He hanged the helmet on his hand and drove on to the road. I walked to the nearby bus stop. I took my phone. Still there were no messages from Jessie. I wondered why Manju want to contact me. The bus came in the meanwhile, and I stepped into it. There was no seat to sit. I stood in the middle of the crowded bus. The conductor gave the ticket and I gripped to the bar above.

I pulled my mobile from my pocket by the other hand, as it beeped. Soon it ringed. The screen displayed *"Jessie calling"*. I attended the call before checking up the message I got.

'Hey sweetheart.' I prodded as soon as I took it, without realizing where I was. The young man standing beside me gave me a look with a fake smile. I ignored him and lowered my voice. 'I was waiting for your call baby' I was sure that this time no one would heard that except to the one whom I am talking to.

'How are you?' She asked in a woozy voice.

'What happen to you?' I asked as I figure that there was something wrong with her. 'Are you not feeling well? Or is you dad coming to take you soon?'

'Not that. I want to ask you something. And don't get angry please.' She said

'Just tell me. And don't be upset. I can't hurt you.' I said.

'I know that. But still… don't shout, let us talk about what I am going to say. Ok?' she said.

'Ok…Don't go on like this. Be straight to me. I won't let you down.' I assured her.

'You are so…sweet. Now listen.' She took a breath and continued. 'Do you remember Nivya?'

'Yeah, your friend in Hyderabad. Right?'

'Wow you remember! Great, and now she wants me to stay with her for some days. She was telling that she can't be with me after me leaving to U.S. So-'

'But you are not leaving no.'

'Of course I am not. I told her that. But she knows my dad well. And she was not believing when I said that I am not going.'

'What does that mean'

'It means nothing! As we decided I will be staying here itself. The thing is that I am not able to convince her. You know that she is my ever-best friend from my childhood. So she asked me to spend some days with her in Hyderabad with her. I already talked to my sister and I wanted to tell you too.'

I kept silent. I wanted to go to Thrissur for meeting her the next week. When she said this, I felt so unsettled.

I even wanted to stop her, but I don't know whether she would agree to that.

'Roshen, are you ok? If you don't want me to go, then I will tell her that.' She said, breaking up my thoughts.

'No, it's ok. I was planning to come over there in the next week.' I said

'Wow that's nice. So…ok I will postpone this. And must tell me exactly when you are coming here. Ok?'

'Yeah sure.'

'If possible we all will halt in Joyal's house on the day you are planning to come. And you will be coming to Joyal's house only no?'

'No, to your house.'

'What? No no no, not my house. It won't be a good idea.'

'He hey! Cool down, I was just kidding. I will only be coming to Joyal's house as you said.'

'Huf' She sighed.

'So tell me. What's up? Met all your friends?'

'Hmm. What are you doing there?

'Nothing. Just thinking about you. My sister went to bath. So I called you.'

'Call me like this. Two-three times a day. It feels good when you talk.'

'I will…'

'Or if you want I will call you'

'I will call you.'

'Fine…and call me tonight too.'

'Em...I will try. But be online. If I can't call you, certainly I will be coming online on facebook. Promise.'

'Hmm...'

'Are you outside.'

'Yeah, why?'

'It's too noisy.'

'I am in a bus.'

'Where you went to?'

'McDonalds, with Kishore.'

'Ow....I see. Ok, Roshen, bye. Have to go now. Bye bye. Will catch you tonight.'

'Bye.'

'I miss you.'

'Call me whenever you miss me.'

'That's why I called you more than once today.'

'I love you'

'Love you too.'

'Ok, bye. I reached my stop. Have to get down the bus. Bye.'

'Bye bye.' She muttered.

I disconnected the phone and got down from the bus. I had to walk a few distance in order to reach my home. I remembered the message I got on my phone before attending Jessie's call. I took the pending messages to be red. There was only one message pending to read, and that was from Kishore. I opened the message. As expected, he sent me Manju's number. I saved the number and put my phone in my pocket. Yet, I haven't decided to call Manju.

AFTER REVEALING, I GOT RELIEVED

"I need not do this," my mind kept on chanting each time I hear the ring. It had been three days I kept on fiddling with my phone, thinking weather to call Manju or to ignore it. I even deleted the number once, but again I restored it to my contacts from my inbox. Each time when I think on whether to call her, there would be either a call or a message from my sweetheart. Otherwise, I will be thinking about calling her when I am online and have no one to chat on facebook. Suddenly Jessie sends me her pictures showing her facial expression to indicate her mood. Sometime she will be angry with me for not picking up her calls, or replying to her messages. Then I would chat with her until she compromises with me. Sometimes she becomes sad, and I have to beg her for a video call to see her face on the screen to see her smiling. Otherwise, she would give some fake response to console me. When she feels sleepy, she calls me until she dozed off.

Meanwhile, calling Manju becomes a burden. So till this day, as a matter of fact, talking to Manju is only a night mare. Because I was not able to see her neither as an old friend nor as an acquaintance who asked me to call. She was my old girlfriend. So talking again with ex-girlfriend was like digging up the past. And, I fell like betraying Jessie by talking to Manju again, when Jessie do cares me a lot. This feeling was not because I am talking to just another girl, but it was only because once Manju was someone in the place of Jessie. And I have never mentioned about her to Jessie.

And I fell so much disturbed when thinking, why she wanted to talk to me. Be seeing her message in the facebook, I even got afraid that, she wanted to sort out everything between us. And the message that Kishore sent me yesterday shook me as well.

"If you don't bother to talk to her soon, then you will regret on what you are doing to her so much. Don't avoid her this much Roshen. If you don't want her please go and tell her that. Don't keep on delaying this. She just wants to talk you once. She is still waiting for that opportunity. And every day she asks us whether you will call her or not. Don't ignore her this much dude. Even I feel pity of her."

This message was the only reason why I am calling her now. Still I haven't told Jessie about this.

'Hello' said the voice from the other end.

I was not sure that she herself was on the line. Sometimes her mother used to take the call. I even forgot how her voice was in the phone.

'Is it Manju?' I asked.

'Yes,' she said.

'Emm… I am-' I couldn't complete.

'Roshen.' She said before I could.

'Ow, you got it. Huh.' I wondered how she got my voice.

'Hmm how are you?' she said.

'I am fine.' I said 'How is your boyfriend?'

'Still you want to tease me?' she said

'Why you want to talk to me?' I asked

'Can we meet?' She said

'Hm, tell the place' I said.

'Tomorrow morning come to McDonalds'. The usual place.' She said.

'Don't you have any other place to tell?' I said

'Please.' She said

'And it's not a date.' I said

'Agreed.' She said. 'Do you still have that white shirt?'

'Why?' I asked. I could guess what she was about to.

'If you could please wear it.'

'No'

'I said, if you could.'

'See you tomorrow.' I said and disconnected the phone quickly.

I wanted this should be just a nightmare, but unfortunately, it was all for real. Wanted to call Jessie and talk to her, but my mind resisted from telling her about this, always. I didn't knew what to do. So I did, like usual and I called Kishore. His phone was been switched off. Then I called Roopa and her father picked up the call. He said she went out and forgot to take her phone. I got irritated and doesn't know what to do. I ended up calling Jessie.

'Hey!' She said.

'What were you doing?' I asked. I had nothing much to talk with her, but was trying to make some conversation.

'Reading. And you?' she said.

'Guess.' I said

'Emm…' She hummed 'Watching porn?' She mocked

'Nope'

'Drinking?'

'Can't you think some good thing?'

'Drinking is not bad! I finished drinking tea just now.' she said innocently.

'I thought you are just making fun of me.' I said.

'Not really. Then I asked you about porn…because I am not with you these days.'

'Any idea of having fun with me?' I asked

'Not now. I will surely call you at night. Don't you have anything else to think of?' She said

'Not much…um…Do you miss me?' I said

'Sometimes.' She said

'Why sometimes? I am missing you every time I think of you.' I said

'When I miss you, I feel to call you. And that's why I am talking to you now.' She said

'Wow. Is it.' I said

'Hm' She stressed.

'Come online?' I asked

'Um…five minutes.' She said

'Ok, see you there.' I said and she disconnected the call.

I switched on my laptop and came on line within the moment. Like always, she was punctual in whatever she said. She came in five minutes.

"I have to tell you something." - Roshen Samuel

"I am hear ☺" - Jessie J

"I want to see your face" – Roshen Samuel

Soon she accepted my video call. She looks beautiful, like always. And her black cute eyes were the same. Her lips has the same appearance and I just felt to kiss it again. Her innocent pretty face doesn't allows me to hide anything. But at the same time, my mind doesn't agrees to introduce Manju as my previous girlfriend. She kept on looking at me without uttering a word.

'What you feel now?' She asked

'I fell so comfortable that you are mine.' I said

She said nothing, but smiled.

'What' I asked feebly

'Mmhm nothing.' She said

'I have to tell you something.' I said

'Then tell' Again she smiled

Her smile was what driving me to tell her everything.

'It's something deep about me.' I introduced

'I know' she said

I wondered if she came to know about Manju from Joyal through Kishore. I had a habit of weaving such thoughts.

'That you drink alcohol, you watch porn.' She continued 'Isn't it what you was about to tell? You had told me about this Roshen? It's ok.

'I should have told you about this long before.'

'It's ok. And you don't need all this now. I am with you no.' She said and winked at me.

'It's not that Jessie. This is about my past.' I said and her face became more serious.

'What happened?' She asked as I looked down. 'Don't be sad. I am with you no'

'I am not sad. It's just that I fell so restless without telling this to you.' I said.

'Everything will be alright. I am there to console you always.' She said

I felt a little relieved by now. I felt like, how we feel after changing wet cloths. I felt like, how we feel after dropping down heavy bags that we hold.

'Tell me, whatever it is.' She said tilting her head sideways.

'I have a past. It's a bad past.' I said

'I too had a bad past. Everyone has,' she said

'This is bad for you to hear.' I said

'There is no good and bad to hear, Roshen. It's only that we don't like to accept certain things. But if something like that already happened in our past life, then we must learn to forget it. If you can't I can help you. I am there with you dear.' She said

I just looked at her. She started convincing me even before I tell her what I want to say. Now I was scared that she might feel bad about having a deep relationship with me. I was afraid that she might change her mind. I was afraid that she might avoid me completely.

'Say whatever it is Roshen. Don't you feel to tell me?' she said

'That's why I asked you to come on video call. I want to see your face.' I said something.

'You see me clearly, and I too see you.' She smiled

I took a deep breath.

'When I was in school, I had a relationship with a classmate of mine.' I didn't look at me.

'Look at me.' She said and I looked at her. 'Now you will feel better.' She winked at me.

'It only lasted for one year and three months.' I said and she was listening carefully.

'What was her name?' she asked.

'Manju.' I said

'Full name? She asked.

'What?' I asked

'Is it Manju Millen' she said

'How do you know?' I felt like my head was heating up and I got more tensed.

'I searched on FB.' She winked at me.

I revived seeing her cool face. She can't never fake her expressions. Though she is smart in that while texting or while on the phone call. That's why I always preferred video call, to see her face directly to confirm whether she was fine or became sad. I had already decided to go to Thrissur to meet her up if she became distressed after hearing about this affair. She was too sensitive about her dear ones. She had once told me. And I was pretty clear about, her that nature, whenever she talked about her mother.

'Smart' I said

'I am always.' She said raising her chin.

'Hm' I smiled

'Then...' she said

'Then what, we broke up.' I said.

'That's all?' She said

'Seeing your tension on your face, I thought you are still dating her paralleled me.' She said

'No dear. That was already over. I just wanted to mention about her to you.' I said

'How do you feel now?' She asked

'I feel better doctor.' I mocked

'Fine,' she chuckled

'What's that meddle for?' I asked her seeing the golden meddle hanging on the wall in her background.

'I will tell you about that later. Just one more thing about your Manju' She said

'She is not mine any more' I blushed

'I was just kidding' she said

'It's not a matter for that.' I snapped

'Ok, I am sorry, but tell me one thing.' She said

'What?' I asked softly.

'Do you still feel anything about her?' she asked

'Oh my God! I told you already. *She. Is. No. More. Mine!*' I said

'I trust you' she smiled 'Do you saw her?'

'Why?' I asked

'Nothing, I asked simply.' She said.

'Should I?' I asked.

'Why?' she asked

'Because she asked me to' I said.

'That's why you told me about her?' she said

'Hm' I said

'If you had nothing in between you, then what's there in meeting?' she said

'I don't have anything in my mind.' I made it clear.

'I know. That's why you told me about her.' She said and I smiled

'Should I see her?' I asked her again.

'If you think she is not clear what's there in your mind, then you should definitely meet her. It will help in avoiding misunderstanding.' She said

'Between' I asked

'I know you well Roshen. Thus, I don't have to misunderstand you. Instead I only want to trust you.' She smiled.

'You look more beautiful when you smile.' I said

'What you like the most in me?' she said

'Your eyes.' I said

'What's special about my eyes?' she asked.

'I don't know. Go look into the mirror.' I said

She smiled.

'So what you want me to do?' I asked to make things more clear.

"Today I have someone to ask suggestions and to discuss with and to trust." She had once told me. Now I too felt the same.

'I was referring Manju. Just go and sort out everything pending between you. Because now it's only you and me.' She said

'As you say.' I said

'Roshen?' she called me

'Hm.' I heard her.

'These days I feel more possessive of you.' She said

'You are all mine, and I will be always with you. Forever.' I said

'So…can we think of our marriage when it's time?' she asked.

This time her question doesn't confuses me. I can't imagine a moment. without her.

'We still have time.' I said.

'Shall I dream about it?' she said.

'Dreams are all ill. Let's believe in our destiny.' I said

'Like we believe in each other?' she said

'The same.' I said

'I love you.' She said

'It's only you whom I can love.' I said. 'Ah tell about that meddle hanging there.' I pointed towards her back.

'It's something that I got for becoming first in academics, when I was in my tenth grade.' She smiled.

'Wow!' I said

'What will you do for your entrance now?' she asked.

'Hey! Your sister.' I said as I saw her entering to the bathroom in her room.

She immediately shut the lid of her laptop as I said that. I waited for some seconds and she was back.

'Bye' She said and waved her hand to me on the screen.

'Bye.' I too did the same.

She logged out. I sent a message to Manju before I logged out.

"Bye"

Again McDonalds'
but It's Not a Date

I took my car. I drove all the way to McDonalds' through the roads of Palakkad. As I reached there, I steered my car into the parking lot. There, nearby the entrance I spotted her, Manju. It's months I have seen her. She had no difference. Only that her hair was been cut shot from the usual length. Now it ends just above her shoulders. Most of our fights were on bobbing her hair short. So she never did that. Hence, this was the first time I am seeing her like this. Still she looked somewhat ok.

'Hey. It's been so long.' She said.

'Doesn't seem to be.' I said to make her know that I never missed her.

I don't know whether she understood that or not. But still she was smiling. So I too complimented one.

'It's hot. Let's go in?' She said.

'Yeah it is.' I said and walked ahead of her.

I pushed open the door and stepped in. One of the staff smiled. Maybe, seeing her tailing me. I wanted to shout at him that she is no one to me. I took bigger steps and sat at a place of my choice. She stood near me.

'Do you want to have something?' She asked.

'No' I chuckled and she left.

It resembled like a bearer who came to take orders from me.

I had made a mental note that I will only reply to whatever she ask, but not to everything and anything, she asks. I don't know how far that would be possible. She came back with a glass in her hand and sat near me. She was facing to me. I could see her face, which once I had loved to see the most. Those cheeks were once I had rubbed the most. And those lips are once I kissed many times, whenever she comes to my home. But, those lips were the only reason to make me hate her a lot. Those are the lips, which someone had kissed her in front of me. She was no more mine. Who know whose all houses she had went like she came to mine. I hate her the more I see her. Every moment she was not with me after that incident was so glad. Now each passing second was killing me and feels to run away from hear. Why I am here was only to make this end forever.

'You are admiring me a lot. I feel like you missed me.' She said.

'Never' I said and looked away from her.

'When you became so much reserved? You used to talk too much, and now you changed a lot.' She said

'Manju. Let us end this.' I snapped.

'What? But why?' she said. 'I asked you to meet because; so that we can talk and I thought we could continue our relationship in a... good way?'

'It's not possible.' I said

'But why? Can't we talk and settle down everything?' she said.

'I am already regretting for being with you once.' I taunted

'You hate me that much!' she said softly and held my palm.

'Stop this. Don't be seductive. Anything won't change.' I blushed.

'If you still feel that I am seducing you, then I have no hope in this.' Her voice fainted.

I felt that she was being so dramatic. Or else she had changed a lot and became much more matured than how I saw her in our school days. Now, I was being so stubborn, as how far I tried, I was not able to forget what I saw. My mind was still nagging on the past life.

'Why you want to end this?' she said.

'I have my own reasons for that.' I said. I don't want her to curse Jessie for entering into my life.

'Can't you tell me that?' She said 'please'

'Manju, I just came here to let you know that I am no more interested in a relationship with you. And you very well know why it is so. So there is no need for explaining it to you. Now, please stay out of my life. Let's break-up.' I said and walked out.

She came behind and held my hand once I reached near my car. I looked at her and she released her grip on my hand.

'Sorry.' She said. 'I don't want to end this. Please?'

'Manju, I,' I understood that there was no more use in hiding it. She was looking at me constantly 'Things changed a lot around me.' I said and got in my car. I started and drove my car out of that place. I saw her standing there itself. I don't want to know whether she left, or whether she was waiting for someone to come and pick her up. I hate her as much as I feel to ignore her completely.

I reached home. As I entered in, I saw my father watching TV news. That was something she used to do most of the time. His favorite was either the news or the share market. Mother may be in the kitchen. That was my guess, as I could smell the usual fragrance-of-the-kitchen. It made me feel hunger, which gave an urge in me to go and ask what was she preparing for lunch. But I stepped back from that idea. I already skipped the breakfast in the morning. So the firing from my mother for leaving out the breakfast was still in pending.

I directly entered into my room and just sat on my bed. My phone beeped in my pocket. I flopped on where I sat, reading the name on the screen. Jessie used to sent me that separated the feeling of missing each other.

"Read the message I sent you on FB and call me after having lunch" That was her message.

I immediately logged on into my FB account and looked her message. It was not like a usual one. And I felt this message sounds too crazy because it was some stuff like horoscope that she might have checked. I don't believe in such things. But still, like something that has being sent be my girl, I certainly have to have a look at it.

"I took our horoscope with our date of births ;) - Your compatibility is good so there are no reasons not to start a good relationship! All you need to do is let things happen on their own without forcing events. Some misunderstandings are perfectly normal and can be overcome. If you know how to listen to one another, nothing and nobody can get in your way."

I was expecting her to be there online, but she was not. I don't understood why she wanted to take our horoscope. By now, she very well knows what I like and I do not. This was one among in what I do not like.

Immediately after having my food, I called Jessie. But the line was engaged. I felt disappointed and tried again. Still it had the same result. I felt miserable and from there I kept on trying her continuously. Each time I call her, I hear – "The number you are calling is speaking to someone else. Please call after sometime". Who would be the "someone" she would be calling? Or was someone calling her. It's been more than half an hour I kept on trying to get her on the phone. But every time it fails and get paranoid.

I seriously wanted to talk to her regarding nothing. I just felt to talk with her. Day by day I was getting more obsessed to hear her voice or to feel her presence by a message or a phone call. It was our rule that we would talk to each other at least once. After receiving her message, I was feeling more tempted for speaking something with her. Each time I feel that I miss her, a possessiveness was growing in me. Now I could feel that more.

I felt lost, as she did not picked up any of my calls, yet. I got faded and lied on my bed being depressed. As I closed my eyes, the door of my room was been pushed open suddenly. It was my father. I sat on the bed at once.

'Why were you sleeping at this time? I told you many times, not to sleep just after taking food.' He said standing in front of me.

'I was not sleeping. I was just stretching out on the bed. That's it.' I said merely staring on to the floor. I know he was here in front of me to say something stern to me, which either I have to obey or I have to answer perfectly.

'I want to know something seriously.' He said.

Yes, he wants *answer*. I prayed silently in my mind for having a good luck for me in this moment. If Jessie sees my missed call, then the very next moment she would call me for sure. If my mobile rings when my father is present near me, he would ask me to attend the call and finish of talking to that person. I know this well. And I made up my mind for anything that was going to happen.

'What's your plan?' he asked.

'What,' I asked doubtfully.

'I am asking that, are you planning to write the entrance exam.' He asked

'Yes,' I said clearly

'How?' he asked.

'Huh?' I uttered

'You have not got enough of coaching. Then how are you planning to write it?' he asked

'Em…' I thought for a while and kept quiet.

I was not thinking about how will I write the entrance. Instead, I thought "should I really write this entrance". Or else should I try for something else.

'Or, do you have any idea of dropping it?' he broken up my thoughts.

I shook my head. 'No' I said.

My phone rang. It was not in silent. My ringtone was echoing in the room in between my father and me. Without looking into the screen, I very well know who was calling me. It would be no one else other than my sweet. But, there would be time, we have to avoid sweets. So I tried not to pick up the call. My dad got annoyed by hearing the continues ring and asked me to pick up the call.

If I pick up the call I definitely have to talk to her, in front of him. If I didn't pick up this call she would send some text message. And that is certainly dangerous at this moment. I was afraid that my dad would pick up the phone and read it out. He does it at times, to check my "way of contacts". I never save any messages from Jessie. Either I never let Manju to message me. Instead she use to call me always.

But between me and Jessie, we haven't kept *any* kind of barriers. We were each other's personal diaries and none of us had become any kind of threat against our relationship. Our bond was very hard and tight with a simple trust that we had to each other.

So I was very much in panic, thinking about the incoming message from her. Right then, I held my phone in my hand for the table. Unfortunately, the call was been ended. I know she would call me once again instantly.

'See. I told you to pick it up. Now it will keep on ringing like this. I have to talk-' he stopped whatever he was about to say as my phone rang.

I took the call as soon as the light flashed on my screen before the ring.

'Hello' I said. I wanted to go out of the room. But, my father would get that I was hiding something from him. So I stuck to where I sat.

'Hey! Were you busy?' she asked.' She said

'Em, yes. I am. Call me after sometime' I said

'I see…' she said 'um your mother is there around you?' she asked

'No, the other' I said. I was not able to say anything clearly.

'Is it Dad?' she said.

'Hm.' I said

'Red the message I sent you?' she said

'Hmm' I stressed

'It's the horoscope of ours. Felt interesting to take it.' She said

'Luckily it's good.' I said.

'Why luckily?' she asked

'Afterward' I said

'Will you call me once he leaves?' she asked

'Of course' I said.

'Bye. Fathers' kid' she mocked.

'Will catch you in a while. Bye.' I said and disconnected.

I sighed as I kept the phone down on the bed.

'Who was it?' he asked immediately.

'Kishore' I said without thinking

'So tell me. What have you planned to do with your entrance exam?' he continued.

'I will prepare and write it?' I said

'Will you be able to clear the exam that way?' he asked.

I nodded

'Say yes or no' he said.

'Yes.' I said in a vague.

'Ok, let us see' he said and left.

I collapsed on the bed.

KISHORE, IN BETWEEN ROOPA AND ME

Next day I was with Kishore forcing him to join at the coaching center along with me. I was on the way to the institute. If he would be coming with me, I can easily escape from Roopa's advice in everything I do. She would always consider about Kishore and me. But I was the one who becomes the culprit in front of her. If Kishore would be there, then he would act like a shield on me, like a protection from advising-Roopa.

Dad arranged another couching center, which was near to my home. Roopa talked to my mother in phone, informing a new tuition center that was been started, a few months before. The information landed in my father's ears from my mother. She wanted him to make me join there.

'Please…' This was the seventh time I am pleading to him.

'Roshen, but, you know what. I am not sure I can come always.' He said

'It's ok, just join there with me.' I said

'Who all are there?' he asked

'Roopa is there.' I said

'Owww… now I got why you want me to come along with you.' He said

'Please…so you know it. Common, let's go.' I said

'Ok let me see.' He said

'What's there to see? Just come along with me.' I said. 'I will take care of the rest.'

'What about Roopa then,' he said

'She! She is the only reason why we have to join there.' I said and narrated the whole thing about Roopa informing about this center at my home.

He laughed hearing all that. 'Ok, let's go then.'

He started his bike and climbed on it.

'I haven't taken any books with me now.' He said, turning around his head as much as he can and bend his upper body a little forward.

'Wow, perfect. I too have not taken. Roopa called home and said that it is almost time. Let's go.'

He accelerated the bike through the traffic. It didn't took much time for us to reach there. He parked the bike in front of the institute, were many other bikes were been parked. Some bicycles were also there. A small building that had a blue board hung in front was my mother's last resort for clearing my entrance. The name of the institute was been written on it, in bold and italic with white color. It was, "CPIEM Entrance". Underneath it was written elaborated as; "Cracking-Pont Institute of Engineering & Medical Entrance." And the other details like time and a pair of e-mail ID was written along with a set of three phone numbers were written on it.

'I think, it is not that beautiful board to admire at.' Kishore said walking to me.

'Yes I agree. They could use some other font. Then it would be at least fine. I said.

'Now what?' he asked

'What? Let's get in.' I blushed

'Engineering or medicine?' he asked

'Why?' I looked at him.

'If it is engineering we have to enter from the left side of the building. It is medicine, then we have to step in from the right.' He explained.

'So you know this place earlier?' I asked

'I asked to the students standing there.' He pointed to a corner outside.

'I see, look bro. We are here for engineering entrance!' I said

'How do I know? You grabbed me just like grabbing a book from the library.' He said.

'Take it easy man,' I smiled at him

'HEY!' Roopa came and stood in front of us. 'Why you are standing here? Come in.' She said and turned around. We followed her.

'See. She is calling us as if we are invited for her sister's wedding.' I murmured to him.

'Sh…' she said to me.

'This is not a church.' I said to her.

'Whatever, come.' She said and we moved in.

We selected the very last bench in our classroom. I made Kishore to sit in between us. Roopa sat to his left and I sat to his right. The class was gradually filling up by students sitting at different places of their choice. The teacher had not come yet to the class and the best part was that the classroom does not have a CC TV camera.

'Like the class?' Roopa asked Kishore.

'Hm, not bad.' He said

'What about you Roshen?' she asked me, leaning backward in her place.

'If I don't like, can you give a better option.' I said

'I know what you are referring to. You just want to enjoy the holydays. Isn't it?' she said seriously.

'Roopa, I have the materials already. I can easily manage with that.' I said

'Then why you came?' she asked as if she doesn't know the reason.

'You don't know?' I asked 'Who asked you to call my mother?'

'I thought it will help you.' She said

'Yeah someway it helps.' I said 'I could escape from home for some time.'

'Why that?' Kishore asked.

'The hostel-issue triggered my father a lot. And he is very much angry with me for that. I am not able to remain at home peacefully. Every time I see my father I fell he would say something to me regarding that again.' I said

'Now you are here. We are there no.' Kishore said.

'Hm…On the other hand, I am really have no idea about what to do with Jessie.' I said

'Planning to have a break-up again.' Kishore said.

'Hey sh.' Roopa slapped Kishore's hand. 'He is serious about her.' She said to him

'Really' Kishore said. I nodded silently.

'What's the matter? Tell us no' she said

'Have you called Manju?' Kishore interrupted.

'Yes I did. Yesterday itself, we met and sorted out everything. Here after don't even tell her name to me.' I said dejectedly.

'Leave it guys, tell about that.' Manju shook my hand and asked excitedly.

'What?' I said

'What were you about to tell before? About Jessie I mean,' she said

'Ow yeah. That!' I said

'Hm' she said

'The main problem is that…you know we are quiet serious about our relationship. And it won't work out if she goes to U.S.

'Where? EU…YES…' Kishore pronounced dramatically.

'United States' I informed.

'So…Is she a foreigner?' he asked

'No, Indian. And her native is at thrissur.' I said

'And she is a Malayali too.' Roopa added.

'Have *you* seen her?' Kishore asked Roopa.

'Ah yes!' She shook her head enthusiastically. 'In facebook' she added.

'She is there in facebook!' He exclaimed. He took his phone and started searching. 'What's her second name?'

'Jessie Joseph.' I said.

'Unbelievable' he shrieked.

'What?' Roopa asked

'She is beautiful,' he said and turned to me. 'Does *she* love you?'

'Then what?' I snapped.

'I thought you are just tailing behind her without having any idea about how to propose. I guessed you wanted our help to propose her and all that. It's quiet unbelievable that you got her.' He said and Roopa chuckled.

'What the fuck!' I blushed

'Really. How come she could accept your proposal? When Roopa and Joyal told me about this I didn't expected she would be this beautiful!' He said admiring her profile photo.

'What you mean' I said

'Now I got the exact reason for why you broke-up with Manju.' He teased

'Manju is just a piece of shit! She kissed someone in front of me you moron! Now don't blame me for what I did.'

'Yeah yeah! Whoever sees Jessie will accept that Manju is just a piece of shit as you said.' He giggled.

'And for your information I broke-up with Manju long before I met Jessie.' I said.

'But you said that to her only yesterday!' he said 'And you never un-friend from your facebook account too.'

'That doesn't count and we never chatted after that. It's over.' I said

'Ok guys, leave it.' She said and I sighed. 'Now what are you going to do about her?' Roopa interfered our serious argument.

'Don't know,' I said mournfully.

The teacher came in finally and started giving her class. I remained quiet. Kishore put his hand around my shoulder and said. 'We are there with you.' He smiled.

'We can't do anything about it. She should do.' I said.

'She should do what?' he asked

'She should talk to her father. Because it is his decision to settle there for rest of their life.' I said

'Shhh...' Roopa hissed into Kishore's ears, which reached mine too.

'This is not a church.' I warned her peeping across Kishore to see her face. She stared me at once and I ignored as usual.

This was the only reason why I do not like to come to any classes with Roopa. Earlier I used to go to the maths tuition class near to Manju's home. Kishore, Roopa and Manju accompanied me there. We four were in one tight company in our school days. Roopa was a disturbing housefly between Manju and I; telling that we never concentrated on the class and me. Once I kissed Manju on her cheek while we were talking much intimately at the time when tuition teacher came too late. From the next day, Roopa sat in between us only during the class hours. Manju fought with her for sitting in between. I was not able to do anything about that. A slight enmity started between Manju and Roopa. It was too late when we understood that. It took days for us to make the girls be compromised. But Manju agreed to compromise with Roopa with one condition. And that was; Roopa should never interfere in anything about Manju and me. However, Roopa agreed to it, and that brought a slight spark within our friendship. Manju started showing disinterest in our friendship.

Whatever it was, we all loved Roopa because we can understand that Roopa was too caring about her friends. Manju was the only one who never realized that. Thereafter, she could never see Roopa as her dearest friend any longer.

Now the whole thing has changed and I was in a new phase of life, which has a whole lot of happiness in it. And the reason was Jessie.

Bunging CPIEM & Waiting Jessie

I went to CPIEM Entrance classes for the past four days regularly. Saying that "Roopa dragged me there" would be more apt. Naturally; I have to pull Kishore out of his bed early in the morning; according to him, that was at 8PM. Today was so special. Jessie called me and told that she would come home by today evening. So I took leave from the institute and Roopa and Kishore too took leave with me. They all wanted to meet her. Moreover, that if they are at home, and then it will be easy for us to talk privately. In addition, the happiest thing was that my dad went to a study tour with his students in Navy Tutorial Collage. So, he would be out of home for three days. I am sure that Jessie won't be disappointed at any cost.

That day was as if it's all mine. I was overreacting to everything, out of happiness. Kishore and Roopa came home after having their dinner. I already had told Jessie that she would be meeting some of my best friends and she became excited to meet them.

I sent messages to Jessie asking where she reached. This was thirteenth message I am sending her since she told she left from her flat. I started becoming restless and shifted from one place to another in my house. I wanted to go to the railway station right now, and wait there until she comes. The last time when I called her, she informed me that she boarded her train. I took my phone and called her. It tells that the number was out of coverage area. Again I sent the message.

"Where have you reached?"

I hit send button.

'She will call you, when she reaches hear.' Roopa came near me. She took my phone and kept it in my room.

Kishore switched on the TV and put a sports channel on. I sat in front of it but my ears were towards my phone, to know whether it was ringing. It has been so long, that my mobile did not make any noise. I stood up to leave to my room, but Roopa pulled me and to make me sit down.

'She will call. You sent the message only a minute ago no.' she said

I did not say anything to her. Instead, I looked on to the television waiting for a call. Finally, my phone rang. I jumped from the sofa and sprinted to my room.

I took the phone.

'Hey! Reached?' I asked excitedly.

'I will reach there in half an hour.' She said sweetly. 'What are you doing?'

'Waiting for you! What else' I said

'I will come soon.' She said

'I have arranged everything for your stay.' I said

'I won't be able to stay Roshen' she said

'Why?' I asked

'I will ell you.' She said

'huh?' I said.

'I will tell you once I am' she said.

I wasn't able to hear anything she says, completely. The voice cracked regularly.

'Hm...come soon.' I said and she disconnected the phone.

I walked to the living room. The television was off. Fan too was been switched off. Kishore was reading a magazine. I couldn't see Roopa, anywhere in that room.

'Where is Roopa?' I asked Kishore.

'Outside,' he said looking into the magazine.

'What she doing there' I went out and spotted her. She was standing nearby the boundary wall speaking to someone on the phone. I turned around to come back to the living room.

'Roshen' She called me from behind.

'What' I said

'Em...don't shout at me. I think this is the best thing you have to do in order to be settled with your problems.' She said

'What problems?' I asked being confused.

'The problem with Manju' she said

'It's over, already. Everything was been sorted out' I said

'Yeah, for you everything was already resolved. But Manju haven't believed that you have another girlfriend.' she said.

'She is not another girlfriend. She is mine. The only girlfriend I have.' I snapped.

'Ok, I know that.' She said

'Then what you mean?' I asked

'Don't keep anything on pending Roshen.' She kept her hand on my shoulder.

'You all made me to speak to her and tell her everything directly. So I did. Still' I said dejected.

'Manju was on the phone, just now. I was talking to her. However I tried I cannot convince her that you have a girlfriend.' She said

'So?' I said

'She is saying that you are just trying to avoid her. The "girlfriend" I am telling to her is just a fake to evade her.' She said

'It's ok Roopa, let her say whatever she wants to. Just ignore her.'

'How can I? or why should *I* do that?' she said

'Do whatever you want.' I said and moved into the living room.

I sat on the sofa.

'Have any idea when the current comes?' Kishore asked me

'Huh? No, I don't know.' I said

Roopa came in.

'Manju will be hear soon.' She said

'For WHAT!' I shocked

'WOW! That's wonderful.' Kishore raised his chin to look at standing Roopa.

'Why she wants to come? I asked

'I called her. This will solve things.' She said convincingly.

'Why the hell you want to do that? I have told you many times, not to interfere in any of my things without asking me.' I shouted.

'But-' she said

'What's going on? What happened?' Kishore asked.

'I asked Manju to come here, so that we all could solve this. He does not understand what's going on with Manju.' Roopa told to Kishore and sat on a chair facing us.

'Roshen, Roopa has a point. You don't know how she is behind you. Even after you met her.' Kishore said

'And she calls me three times a day asking about you.' Roopa said

'I thought if you talk to her and finishes everything directly would solve everything. But it didn't work out.' He said. 'Let she come.'

'And if your Jessie misunderstood something we are here to solve immediately. That's why I bunged my class and came here. Not just to meet her.' She said

'Jessie won't misunderstand. She knows me well.' I said.

'Then' what's the matter?' He said

'I don't want to see her any more. That's it.' I said

'For that, she should come today, when Jessie is here with you. Otherwise Manju would be behind you always, considering your relationship with Jessie, just as a fake story that you have created.' He said

'Hm' I said but still I was not comfortable with it.

We have not had much to talk about and nothing to do too; because of the power cut. The

'Will she reach before lunch?' my mother came to us and asked.

'Yes mom, I called her. She will be here within half an hour.' I said and she smiled.

She was referring to Jessie's arrival. I have told my mother that today some of my friends would be coming home. She already knows Roopa and Kishore, because they have visited before. Roopa was my mother's companion and like always, she went to the kitchen to be with my mother.

Kishore and I sat and talked about the upcoming cricket matches under various local clubs. He used to participate for his club and he was a star in between the other players. Kishore has various fans among girls too, which made other guys jealous. I was the one among those guys. But, apart from those guys, I was evidently different. I had a girlfriend; Manju. School matches was so awesome that we entered none of the class hours, except the lunch break. That also includes most of the girls. That certainly helped boys. If girls get punishment, boys will have company for standing outside their respective classes, after the sports. Manju and I enjoyed that a lot.

Punishment and lunchtime in our school was our favorite. Manju would be standing so close to me, and her skin would be touching mine. That itself throw a spark on to my spine and to other's eyes. Unfortunately, rust of the boy's girlfriends would be in other classrooms. So they won't be sharing the same punishment. That's why I loved the punishments a lot.

And the lunch our would be heaven. Most of the days there would be probability for getting a kiss at least on the cheek. We don't like kissing after having food. So we would have food when everyone finishes it. During lunch break, both of us will be using the extreme right corner bench at the end of the classroom. Because the door was located at, the right side and anyone, who passes through the corridor outside the classroom would not notices us easily. If at all someone comes at the door, there are more than five close friends to give us signals.

During holydays other than Sundays, we would adjust our interactions and fun time at the tuition center. On every Sunday our mobile phone would heat up to the maximum that we can no more keep it on our ears. As both of our mobiles were of Nokia, it was pretty much easier to get another battery. Still we had never felt any pity for our own mobile phones.

'Let's go up to the terrace?' Kishore asked me.

'Yeah' I said and we left to the terrace through the stairs located outside.

A Guava tree situated at the right side of my house was now had had grown for long heights that one could pluck its fruit from the terrace only. Whenever my friends come here, they would pluck as much as they can. We had fun too. It's been so long since we had enjoyed much. It's all entrance, entrance & entrance. Parents haven't let us bother about anything else, so no enjoyment too.

'Roshen' he called me and thrown two guavas to me instantly. I missed. One fell down next to my foot and one slipped down the stairs.

I looked at him and he shrugged his shoulders and carried on plucking the rest. I ate the one in my hand, simply looking at him plucking briskly. This time, I did not felt to do anything. So I simply sat on the hedge of the terrace.

Kishore's phone ringed. He had kept his phone on the lid of the water tank, when he went to pull all those guavas left on the tree. I picked up the phone. It was Manju, and I picked up the call. She disconnected it immediately. She meant to give a missed call, but it didn't worked. I understood that she wants us to come down. I called Kishore and we went down.

I followed him, as he stepped into my house first. When I was about to get it, I found a footwear lying beside the steps, in front of the entrance door. I know that scandals well. It was Manju's and I figured out that she came already.

I would never be able to forget the day I went for shopping with her. We entered into every footwear shop in the town. She started her journey from the evening of a Sunday and it only ended at night, at 7'o clock. I too had to tag along with her for all the time. Because we met in town for a treat offered by her as a result of failing a bet I kept with her. And the bet was a simple thing. During her dance rehearsal of Onam competition in our school, she looked so beautiful in the white Sari. That too after the practice was after the school hours. That day she asked me stay with her for two reasons. One was to hold her specs and the other was to give her a company until the practice was over.

When I saw her all the time during her dance practice, I suddenly had an urge to grab her and kiss her. They got a break in between their dance practice. As her water bottle got empted while continues practice, she asked me to come along with her to fill it up. We went to the cooler at the other end of the building. She filled the water, and drunk some from it immediately. I saw her neck so close and her sweating forehead, and the beautiful hair. Suddenly the reality strike my mind that she was my girlfriend.

"What if I kiss you Manju?" I asked her.

"Not now, later. Someone would see." She replied seriously taking deep breaths every time.

"You look sexy" I complimented

"Whatever you say now, no kissing" She said and held my hand *"Let's go. They might have started without me."* she said

"No one will see. I bet." I said

"Why now?" she came closer.

"I told you already. You look stunning today." I smiled

"Umhm" she said and came much closer.

She raised herself on her toe and touched her lips on mine. I gripped her naked hips through the Sari. We kissed, hugging tightly. She pulled her face an inch back from mine and looked into my eyes. "Rest, at home" she said and winked at me

"Don't forget the bet."

"Umm my treat. Let us go to the town tomorrow. It's a half day no," she said

"Ok."

"Wait here, I will adjust my sari and will come soon" she gave me a peck on my right cheek and ran to the toilet.

IT WAS NOT A NIGHT MARE

I saw Manju sitting on the sofa, with my mother and Roopa sat next to Manju. They were busy talking about something that doesn't bother me. Like usual, my mother talked about her only son and the whole thing happened in the hostel. She says that she was not sure about; weather I would clear my entrance exam. Even I am not, but had a faith in God like the same faith I had, while proposing such a girl like Jessie.

'Don't worry aunty, he will clear it anyway. He is smart.' I heard her saying it to my mother.

'But, not as smart as you, Manju. Kissing some bitch and coming to boyfriend's home shamelessly.' I said in my mind.

I was standing there like a pillar without talking to anyone, even to Roopa and Kishore. I doesn't even feel to care about Manju. I seem too been changed a lot.

At present, my desire was only to receive Jessie, as soon as possible. I looked at the time and it shows that five minutes more was there to go for completing half an hour after I talked to Jessie at last in the phone. As she told me, she would reach here in half an hour. I wish I could see her this moment, so that I could avoid the eye contact with Manju and teasing eyes of my friends. Every expression on Manju's face irritates me.

Manju was busy in talking to Roopa and Kishore about her whereabouts of new places that she had gone these days. It touches almost all the places in the North India and certainly, she was traveling around all the places with her family. I already got to know that through her facebook account.

'That was the only solution I found, when I felt so sick without you Roshen.' She looked at me and said after covering all the details about all the places she had visited.

'What?' I asked.

I know what she meant, but I wanted to let her know that I was not interested in her being here in my home today. If her character had not changed, then she should have left the place as soon as possible when she found that I am not interested in what she does or speaks. That was how she used to show her anger. And this time I wanted that to happen, but nothing happened like I wished.

When someone wants something so badly, then it will never take place. And whenever someone doesn't want something to occur, it certainly happens as soon as possible and in the best way it screws the situation. This was something that was usual in my life.

She was still looking at me, when Kishore switched on the TV again as the power came back and Roopa went to the kitchen. When Roopa called her, she shyly hesitated to go and stayed there itself looking at me feebly.

'You don't want to meet my mother?' I asked seriously.

'We met already and also talked for some time. You were on the terrace at that time.' She smiled, I didn't.

She got up from the sofa and came near me. I remained standing at where I stood. Kishore turned his face to look at us and gave a fake smile to me. Everything that was been happening at that moment where ironical to my mind's desire. I never wanted to be in this situation and that's why I hesitated to them when Roopa said in advance that Manju would be coming home. However, I tried to make them understand, they remained stubborn and wants Manju to join us. As a result, I became a victim to what all was happening now.

Manju was standing right in front of me, in half a foot distance. My body trembled at once, thinking what will happen if Jessie comes right now and sees the way we were standing. Anyway, I was not responsible to the close distance we kept between us. Manju was the one who came and stood near me. I could easily convince Jessie on whatever happens, but she definitely gets hurt and I would not be able to afford that.

I felt like the bottom-tip of her Salwar was touching my body, but it wasn't when I looked down. If she raised her hand an inch, she could touch me. What if she grabs my face and kisses me? I was afraid that I might not be able to resist it. According to her boldness, being Kishore sitting at the background will never bother her. But, what bothers me was when thinking about what would happen if Jessie sees these things happening.

Due to the anxiety I had for meeting Jessie, I forgot to mention that Kishore and Roopa would also be present in my house. Moreover that Manju was also there. Jessie won't be having any problem on seeing Kishore and Roopa here, but knowing that my ex-girlfriend too shares the happy moments with me…it sounds odd. I still remember her telling me that she doesn't want anyone to be there around us when it's a date. I was been tensed about Jessie freaking out on this. I can't imagine about what will happen if my mother sees Jessie shouting at me for this. What if my mother figures out about her sons' past and present relationship? According to some parents, it's a crime to have a girlfriend or by knowing that their son or daughter is in love with someone whom they feel wanted. And of course, a blast would happen when it reaches my dad's notice.

'Can't you just talk to me?' she broke all my scary thoughts.

'Manju, I told you that it's already over between us.' I said simply.

'Doesn't Roopa and Kishore talks to you?' she asked.

'But they are my friends.' I justified

'Can't we be just friends?' she said and held my hand.

'And not standing so close to me like this.' I said

'Don't worry. I won't have babies by just standing close to you.' She said.

'You won't change. Being seductive will not bring change to anything.' I said.

'You are badly mistaken me Roshen,' she chucked.

I pushed her a little away and sat on the sofa.

'What's the score?' I asked Kishore who was watching cricket dramatically. I know that he was listening to our conversation.

'This is not a match.' He said

'Kishore, switch to some music channel please' she said

'Yes of course.' He said and stared changing one by one.

'I want some movie channel. Put *Star Movies*' I just wanted to oppose her.

'But I asked first' she snapped

I looked at her. 'This is my house, my TV, and my remote.' I said

'But I am operating!' Kishore winked at her.

I stared at him but he ignored and continued changing channels in the sequence. No music channel came yet. I looked at the channels that came in order while changing. *CNBC. F TV. Assianet. Discovery. Movies Now.* I stopped him there.

'Yeah, this is perfect! That's enough.' I said.

'But you said Star movies.' He ignored me and continued changing.

Star Sports.

'Yeah! Star movies,' I shouted with joy 'no it's star sports huh,' I said lowering my voice with guilt.

'Hey hey it's not Star movies...' Manju teased and I gave her a deadly look.

Next came *Star Movies* and I snatched the remote from him.

'I want to see this movie. "Abduction"' I said

'How many times would you see this?' Manju asked me

'That's up to me.' I snapped.

'There was "Eagle Eye" in Movies Now. That's better.' Kishore said.

'Who asked you to keep changing?' I blushed.

'Yeah he told you to put Movies Now,' She tried to be supportive.

I didn't felt much better. I ignored her and took my mobile as it ringed. The screen showed *JESSIE CALLING*.

'Hey!' I answered the call.

'Where are you?' she asked

'Home' I said 'Have you reached the station?'

'Yep, just now' She said. 'I am starving,'

'Do one thing. Go to the tea stall and have a cup of hot tea. By the time you finish it, I will reach there.' I said

'Hm' she said. 'Will you become late?'

She knows me well by now. I should say, more than Manju knows me. More that Manju understood me. Jessie was a very much special person in my life.

'No baby, I will be there in fifteen minutes.' I said

'Great! Give me a call when you reach at the Railway Station. Then I will come to the stare case at platform No. 3. Ok?' She said

'Yeah that's fine. I will call you then.' I said.

'And Roshen!' she yelled

'What!' I asked

'I have a bag with me. You must hold that ok?' she said.

'Ok, whatever. Let me come there first. See you then,' I said

'So…sweet. Come fast,' she said and ended the call.

I went to the kitchen excitedly to tell my mother that I was leaving to pick up Jessie from the station. Roopa who stood there in the kitchen with my mother, smiled at me and I too smiled.

'I will come now,' I said to Kishore and took the car key which hung on the wall.

Shortly, I started my car and left to the railway station. I felt like I was again going to have the pleasure. It all had happened when I was in Thrissur. Everything was in order until I was been fired from my hostel.

LET KNOW IN ADVANCE

Jessie has not yet talked to me since we entered into the car. I was afraid that she felt bad by knowing that my friends also were there in my house. I know that she was expecting privacy, but I could not help it, because it would be safer to invite her to my home with their presence. Their presence would help to introduce Jessie as my old friend.

'Are you angry?' I asked to know her present state of mind. She was not even smiling.

'No' she said looking outside.

'Then?' I said

'Then. What?' she said.

'You are not talking to me,' I said

'I am not angry with you and talking while driving is not good.' she said and remained silent 'I was just thinking something else. That's all.' She said after sometime.

'But, what I am going to tell will certainly make you angry.' I said

She looked at me while, I was looking at the vehicle moving ahead us. She then turned the other side.

'Can we talk about it?' later she asked softly.

'Jessie, I called my friends so that I could at least convince my mother that you are my friend. If you came home, all of a sudden she may think something else.' I said

'Why?' She said

'To them, I am a bad boy, due to many reasons. One such reason is the hostel incident. And many such things have happened before. If my friends are there along with me, then everything would be fine. Moreover that, my mother knows my friends intimately and hence, the chemistry works.' I said.

'What chemistry?' she said

'My mother trusts my friends more than me, because she knows that when I am out of home with them, like tuitions, they really do care me a lot. So she trust what my friends would agree about my outdoor connections like friends I make randomly apart from those you are just going to see.' I explained 'And the best part is that, my friends support me a lot at the same time.' I winked at her.

She smiled for the first time, after entering into the car. I discovered something new that her eyes were always more beautiful when she smiles. I felt myself completely happy by Jessie being beside me. I wanted her to be there by my side throughout my life. Without her was so painful. Though we contacted each other, I still fells wanted when she was not around. I feel to feel her presence; I feel to hear her voice all the time, to admire her cute and beautiful eyes every time, and to kiss her at every moment I feel to get her lips close to mine. I always wanted to pull her hips and to feel her warmth on my body. Above all these I wanted to own her completely as mine.

'Crooked fox' she teased.

'Then what! One thing is that I need you always, and the other thing is that I can't marry you at this age.' I said

'So?' she tilted her head to a side.

'So, we certainly have to play some tricks.' I winked at her.

'You said that you have to tell me something that makes me angry,' she said and took her purse.

I remembered the first time I met her! And I thought what I thought at that time and how I admired her completely lost in her beauty. Now I feel the pleasure of being intimate with her and in love with her.

'Um…Jessie, don't make your face dull and don't spoil your mood too.' I warned.

'Why?' she blushed

'Hm…' I drove my car into the McDonalds' Drive Thru.

'Wow, so are we not going home?' she asked me innocently.

'I want to talk to you.' I said and parked the car in the parking lot.

I got down and went to her door. By the time, she opened it, and I held it until she got down. After she stepped out of the car, I shut the door and locked it. She was standing a foot away from the car looking at me. I moved towards her and held her hand.

'Is this place near to your locality?' She asked as we moved ahead hand in hand.

'Here there is no one to judge us.' I assured her and she smiled.

'By the way, why are we here?' she asked.

'I want to talk to you something very seriously.' I said

I pushed opened the door and we took a seat at the far end. I made her sit there comfortably, and went to take something to eat lightly, just to make her all right. She told me that she was hungry, and if I buy her something heavily, she will not take food from home. She eats less. So I carefully took what will make her just alright, for temporarily.

I went and kept everything on the table and sat beside her.

'Have this, and we can fill the rest of yours hunger from home.' I said.

She started eating soon, and in between, she fed me too.

'So, tell me,' she said 'but say it casually. Don't be serious.'

'Why?' I asked moving her strands of hair fell on her face.

'If you become serious,' She puffed her mouth with a hand full of snack 'you look funny.'

She fed me too. But when it's my turn, the quantity will reduce. And she will feed me only what would occupy in between her three finger tips. (The thumb, pointer & middle figure. She folds her other fingers while bringing near my mouth.) In this way she fills my mouth only once and tree times hers' at the same time.

'Hm, yeah I will tell, but by hearing what I have to say, don't slap me with the same hand you fed me.' I said

'Huh?' she said

'Just kidding' I said

I was feeling a starting trouble to tell her about Roopa's presence in home. She held my palm with her left hand and kept on her lap.

'What happen?' She asked sweetly and put a small piece in mouth.

'Um…Do you want to have one more plate?' I asked as our plate became clean and empty.

'No,' she shook her head. 'You tell what the matter that you have to say. Soon after that, let's go home quick. I feel to see your mother.' She said innocently.

Hearing that, I thought after knowing that my ex-girlfriend was in my home, at present; Jessie may decide to return her home now and then. Anyway, she will know when we reach home. So, it's better to reveal it as early as possible. So that it would be possible to convince her and that, she would not blame me saying that I hid her about this.

'Um…you know Manju, right?' I said

'Yes,' she said wiping her hands with a piece of tissue paper.

'And…I also told you that I joined in CPIEM,' I said

'Ah! I forgot to ask about it. How are your classes going?' she said.

'It's all going well' I said irritatingly. 'First, hear what I have to say, please…'

'Ok, ok. Tell.' She rested her chin on her arms supporting her elbows on the surface of the table in front. She was looking at me cutely like a kid.

'So Kishore and I were planning to bung the class,' I said

'Wow' she mocked. 'So teachers there won't say anything?' she asked and I gave her a stare. Then she covered her mouth and carefully listened the rest.

'When I told that you are coming here to Palakkad, they all decided to come, all of a sudden. I couldn't say "no". I know you wanted us to be alone. But, don't worry. Let's find a solution.' I said

'It's ok.' She said

'That is not the actual trouble here.' I said 'Roopa and Kishore planned to have a get-together with the old friends and Roopa wants to add you too into our company. So, eventually Roopa called Manju for the get-together, saying that she is not at all believing when she said about our relationship. And she wanted to sort out everything between me and Manju in your presence.' I took a deep breath. 'Jessie, it's all Roopa's plan. I have no involvement in this, and even know about this only after Roopa arranged everything already. At last, I became a victim of the whole play and so you.'

'That's all. Why you are so tensed about this?' she asked.

'I want you to take this easy. Don't get hurt due to her presence. I love you. Only you' I said

'I have faith in you and your words. I know everything about you from what all you said to me all these days. So I believe in you and I have the hope in you that you won't ditch me soon.' She said and smiled

'I will never do that. I want you throughout my life.' I said 'It's just the matter that, I thought you would get the wrong idea that I am still dating Manju, by seeing her there in my house. That's why.' I winked at her and she caressed my hair.

'Nothing would go in wrong way between us Roshen,' she said. 'Let's go?' she asked

'Hm, come.' I said and picked up her bag.

HOW SAFE IS TWO GIRLS IN ONE HOUSE

Jessie removed her scandal, stood on the step, and looked at me. I smiled at her. At the same time, Roopa came and pulled her hand taking her in. I removed my slippers and kept aside. I noticed something very interesting and fascinating. Jessie's scandal was between Manju's and mine. I pushed away Manju's scandal from ours with my leg and entered into my house.

Though Roopa was meeting Jessie for the first time, she was introducing her to my mother as a long lost friend of hers. While Manju stood aside at my mother's background staring at what was going on. Surely, she was not able to remain comfortably with Jessie being here. She was very much disturbed by her presence and even more frustrated by watching me, always looking at Jessie with love in my eyes. Occasionally, Jessie smiles at me too and Manju stares at her. I was worried whether Jessie would notice Manju staring at her. (Apart from all these; my mother and Roopa was talking more and more with Jessie, as they were talking for the first time.) I moved ahead and stood behind Jessie. Not only for protecting her from *staring-eagle-eyes*; but also that I don't wanted to keep any distance between us when she was around.

Jessie sensed me behind and she turned and looked me at once. I smiled and she winked. Then she went back to their conversation. The three of them was literally busy with their talk. I saw my mother was holding both her hands and they stood too close to each other. I was happy that my mother became happy about talking to Jessie and I can feel that from the way she talks.

I wanted her to finish off the conversation soon and take her to somewhere, were there would be no one to disturb. I twitched her softly behind her hips without my mother noticing. And she shrugged simultaneously. I understood Jessie would have recognized why I did that. Roopa notice that as she was standing at the sides of both of them. I hope, Manju also have noticed that as she was shifting from one leg to another.

Kishore came near me and put his hand around my shoulder. He made me moved a step aback.

'How are you going to manage this situation?' he whispered in my ears.

'Mr. Bastard, you only put me in this junk.' I grinned.

'Me!' he exclaimed as if he was not aware of anything happening here. 'Roopa only prepared everything telling that this should have an end. She asked me to support her in this, so I did.' He said.

Yes, I too want to end Manju's nuisance. But not by hurting Jessie. I know Roopa had invited Manju too, because she wanted to show her that what she told about Jessie and me was all for real. For that, this was not to be the appropriate time. Today is the first day my Jessie was visiting my home. It's only to see me; and not for being an evident to Manju.

'End, what? If Manju acts something odd in front of Jessie, then I will definitely kill you both.' I murmured.

'Nothing will happen dude,' he said 'Let's see.'

I wanted Manju to leave the house and never come back. I was afraid that she would say something nasty to Jessie, when no one would be around her. Like, what if she tells Jessie that I was her boyfriend and warns her not to interfere in the relationship and that definitely would hurt Jessie. I would absolutely lose my tolerance and may react to Manju so badly in front of everyone. I may not be able to care my mother's presence in the house. Because, I won't be able to withstand Jessie getting hurt. (Not even seeing her cry for her own reasons.) She too knows that, and sometime even hides many of her sadness from me. She even lies to me earlier but nowadays she knows that I can easily find out whether she was lying or not, so she simply tells me that she don't want to share it. But, gradually she tells me everything she hid from me.

'Aunty, something smells bad in the kitchen.' Roopa said to my mother and she ran towards the kitchen. Roopa followed her.

When Jessie too went behind, I pulled her hand holding her elbow. Seeing Jessie near me, Manju came near us. Kishore too stood there beside us. Seeing Manju in front, Jessie didn't shown any dejection towards her. She simply smiled and said 'hi'

'Hi' Manju replied but she never smiled or even didn't showed a pleasant face to her.

Jessie stood close to me. When our hands touched each other, she gripped my palm tight. It was sweating inside her palm. I could feel it wet and cold. Her inner palm was a little slippery and I clutched it supporting her upper arm with my thumb. I know that she too missed me a lot, like how I did and I wanted to get rid of everyone around us as soon as possible.

'So…' Manju looked at me. 'This is the girl they were telling was your girlfriend.' She said

'What you mean by *was*? She still is my girlfriend and always would be.' I said.

'Really' she giggled 'How long?'

I wanted to slap her at once. 'What you mean?' I asked instead.

'You won't be together for much longer time.' She said. She looked at her and continued. 'Why you want to keep on dating someone who just walked into your life, in between?'

'In between what?' I was getting more irritated.

I expected such things and hence I was prepared.

'Roshen, we were in a relationship. I want you back. I didn't had a break-up with you! Let's still talk and sort out everything.' She said.

I could feel her loosening her grip from my hand, but still I clutched it tighter and never allowed her to withdraw. I want her to be with me and never want to be apart, in any situation. She already became a part of my life. Now, for me it's better to have her beside me when there would no more food for me to eat throughout my life. I could at least exist smiling until I starve and die. That much I feel wanted these days.

'Nothing to sort out. It's over. And never meet me again,' I said.

'I will. The time when you become apart.' She said 'How long can you stay with a girl you met in a short time? Roshen, we were dating almost for a year! I love you so much. Understand that. I told you that I already regret for what I did. It's my mistake. I promise that I won't repeat such things in our life.' She said.

'Manju. I understand that you won't be repeating what you did. As like that, I also don't want to repeat *my* mistake. And that's *you*.' I said

'Huh?' she miffed.

'Yes, you are the greatest mistake I am regretting now. And I don't want you to be any were around me. And also that I want this to be our last meeting.' I said

'Are you sure?' she asked

'Not much,' I said

'Why?' She smiled.

'You want to see how long will I stay with Jessie no? Bet that I would call you for our marriage' I snapped.

'If, that doesn't happen?' she asked.

'Will do whatever you say' I chided

'Marry me' she said without a second thought.

'Hm,' I said 'then it's mandatory for you to start learning to forget me. That will help on the day you see the wordings *"Roshen weds Jessie"*.' I giggled

'Kishore, I am leaving.' She said immediately to him and took her handbag, which she had kept on the sofa 'Tell Roopa that I left already.'

Jessie has not said anything yet, until now. She silently stood beside me, like a kid, as I held her close to me.

'I am going' she said to me, finally.

'I haven't asked you to come here. You came on behalf of someone else. No need to tell me then.' I said

'Bye' she mumbled without looking to anyone of us and left. I sighed watching her going out of the house.

'Thank God!' I said to myself and looked Kishore.

'What?' he asked

'Don't repeat this.' I said 'Tell this to Roopa.'

Roopa was busy in the kitchen, helping my mom. This was regular practice and whenever my they comes home Roopa sticks to my mother in the kitchen. Roopa loves cooking.

'Now, where are *you* going?' he asked

'Up stairs' I said and turned around. 'Give me a call when they finish their cooking. Please.' I said

I know that he would get bored. But what to do! I feel so much wanted to be with my Jessie alone.

'I will leave soon after the lunch.' He said

'For the time being the lunch gets ready, the TV would help.' I smiled

'Hm, whatever' he said

WE MADE OUT
IN MY ROOM

She sat on my bed as soon as we entered to my room. She was looking at me when I stood still, leaning on the wall behind me. She looked strikingly gorgeous in her neatly worn peacock-blue Salwar kameez. Maybe because she was sitting in front me in my room or may be because she was looking deeply into my eyes with her *bizarre-black-cute-eyes,* which made me, fell in love with her again and again instantly. Whatever maybe her expression, weather angry, sad, happy; those eyes of hers' compliments the beauty on her face. But there was something else that supports her beauty which I haven't yet identified, because she even looks beautiful when she sleeps. So certainly, there was something apart from her beautiful eyes that made her like an angel.

'I feel too lucky to have you' I drooled in front of her.

I missed something then. Yeah! Got it, it was her smile.

'Can't you give a smile for your boy?' I asked smiling at her.

I kept on wagging the upper part of my body, back and forth on the wall were I was leaning.

'I am trying,' she said and got up from the bed.

'Huh?' my jaws plunked.

I stood straight as she came looking at me. By reaching near me, she leaned forward and hugged me. I too hugged her and she moved little more ahead, squeezing me as much as she could. She was a beautiful and the lightest feather to me. I felt her breathe so close to my neck, below the chin as she had kept her face on my chest raising it a little upward.

'What happened baby?' I muttered as silence filled up the room.

'I didn't like the way she talked.' She said softly

'I too' I said

'I smiled, but she didn't,' she said

'Ignore her like I did,' I said and caressed her hair slowly.

'Do you talk to her frequently?' She raised her head and faced me.

'What do you think?' I asked simply

'No way, but-' she said

'Then don't ask such blunders.' I snapped.

'Sorry,' her lips curved down she said and again she lied on my chest.

I felt her like a kid like any other kid, but much more beautiful than any other kids. She was my baby. She was more than a girlfriend to me. She was even something more than that for me. She always made me feel happy and cheerful. She was the only one I always feel wanted. Wanted her to be beside me and always feels to hold her closer and never let her go. Everything would become still around me whenever I missed her before. I don't feel alive when I won't able to see her, or at least talk to her.

'Sit here.' I made her sit on my bed and I sat nearby.

She looked at me. 'Is it over for real?' she asked.

'What,' I said

'Will you have to meet Manju again?' she asked

'Why?'I asked

'Because, you said that you are not sure about this would be the last time you would meet each other.' She said

'I want to invite her for our marriage.' I said promisingly and she smiled.

'That's fine... but, are you sure that our relationship would lead to our wedding?' she said.

'Why should I not be sure about it?' I asked

'What if my father takes me to States?' she asked. 'And what will happen to us if he never let me come back?'

'Can't you not stay here? Forever?' I put my hand around her shoulder and she lied down her head on my shoulder. She tugged the hair that fell over her face behind her ears. Then she held my hand and started playing with the ring on my finger.

'I want to but...' she frail.

'After you reach home, call your father and tell him that; by the way when are you going back to Thrissur?' I asked

'Does not feel to go' she hugged me.

'I too don't feel to leave you. If possible I would have made you stay here, with me for a life time.' I said 'But now I am asking something practical to do. So, first of all tell me when are you planning to go back home?' I asked.

'I am not going now' she said

'Then?' I asked 'Do you want to stay with Roopa this night?'

'No' she shook her head.

'Why not? I will pick you from there tomorrow early in the morning.' I said

'Not that, I am leaving to Hyderabad.' She said and looked at me.

'To meet your friend there?' I said

'Hm,' She said

'Have you told anyone that you would come to my house?' I asked and she shook her head.

'You should have at least informed Joyal about this.' I said

'I don't trust him' she said. 'I have already talked to my dad about going to Hyderabad.

'So you can talk to him about this, except about our plans. Huh?' I asked.

I have been asking her to talk to her father about let her stay here itself and complete her studies. But she always tells that she doesn't have enough courage to speak to him about this. This was our main topics of our fights. I don't want to have a fight now, and spoil the mood. So I decided not to ask about it much.

'I used to go to Hyderabad occasionally. And by reaching there, her father will come and picks me up. That's how I visited her place every time.'

'When will you come back then?' I asked

'Soon' she winked 'Are you coming?'

'Me! No, I can't' I said 'Then?' I said

'Then. Then what?' she said. 'You should also have come.'

'what about your father. Will talk to him?' I said

'I am afraid.' She said

'For what?' I said

'I don't have a reason first of all!' she said

'So you will go with him?' I said

'You have Manju here.' She mocked

'WHAT?' I blushed

'Mmhm, nothing. I was just kidding with you.' She said 'Leave it.'

'Are you still thinking that something is wrong between Manju and me?' I asked

'No Roshen. I am not. I was just trying to make you angry.' She said softly

'Why?' I asked

'Have you red our horoscope that I send you?' she said

I wanted to talk about her future plans on leaving or staying here. I wanted to talk to her about it patiently and convince her to talk to her father soon. But I know definitely this would end up in a fight. So I didn't bothered on how quick she changed the topic.

'Yes, but I don't remember what exactly it was.' I replied

I smelled the next fight ahead. She used to feel bad about me forgetting anything about *us*. But she would never have any problem if I forget her on personal matters.

'There would be misunderstanding in between us.' She said without making a face to me for forgetting the horoscope.

'So?' I asked 'Ow...so you mean that you think I am still dating Manju apart from you? That I am cheating you?' I asked, as I got paranoid.

'Have I said any of that?' she asked

'Then what you mean by saying all these?' I said

'I think, Manju would be behind you always and moreover that I am sure that I may not even stay here in India for long. Any time my father would take us back. He told that he want to make things ready there. And so-' she said

'So what? If you want to be with me forever, then you can very well can talk to your father, and also that you can easily find out a reason too.' I chided

She didn't speak then. She just sat there holding my hands, keeping it on her lap. She was looking down and I felt like she was sobbing slightly. I made her look at me, by supporting her chin with my fingers. I saw her eyes were wet.

'What's wrong with you Jessie?' I held her upper arm tightly and asked softly. I could feel her shaking all over the body. She started crying. It hurts a lot.

'What's wrong with *you*' she snapped suddenly asking the same thing to me.

She started weeping more.

'What did I do?' I asked confused. 'What happened?' I asked again as she did not spoke.

'I feel so insecure' she said

'My God! Please stop crying Jessie. Let me explain to you.' I said and held wiped her tears.

She lifted my hands and immersed her face in my palms. She cried for some time. I let her cry, though I trembled seeing her cry. I wanted her to stop crying own her own. It took a little time for her to stop her tears. At last, she looked at me. The black in her wet eyes where now shinier than usual.

'You still look prettier.' I pulled her cheeks and she pushed my hands away.

'Um? Still sad?' I mocked

'ER….' She pinched me with her nails *'Don't. Irritate. Me.'* she yelled.

'Ew…Ok, ok…' I said and forcefully withdrawn her immersing fingers with nails. 'It pains!' I said

'I know. I was not tickling you.' She was extremely angry with me.

I know she got annoyed because of three reasons. (I was already expecting these to happen and that's why I wanted to evade Manju as soon as possible) The very first reason was that she didn't liked the way Manju behaved; secondly she didn't liked me talking to Manju, that too in her presence and finally apart from the first two reasons, she didn't even liked Manju's presence in my house.

'I am sorry for what all happened, but realize that I never invited Manju.' I said.

'But you agreed no? That's why your friends called her.' She said.

'Jessie! I never agreed to anyone!' I was been fumed at once, but consoled myself. 'They called her in advance and afterwards they let me know it. Then how can I say a "no" to them?' I explained calmly.

'You must have told her, then' she said

'I don't even want to talk to her!' I said

'But you talked well when she was with you.' She said

'Jessie you heard what I talked about.' I said

'Sorry,' she said feebly 'I know you didn't mean anything by calling her, but-'

'Jessie, they wanted to end the problem that they wanted to finish. By telling Manju that I have you in my life, she told them that we all are faking a story to her, just to avoid her. She was not able to contact me and I was not even responding for any of her messages in face book. So she constantly asks them about everything about me. Even Roopa asked me weather she could give my new number to Manju. I didn't allowed her to give. Day's before I met Manju and talked and finished everything. Still that idiot things what all I said to her are just lies. She even told Roopa that *I made a fake FB account in your name, just to make her believe.* So I also thought when Manju comes here she would be able to meet you in person and everything would be solved at once. But, still. I. Have not. Invited. Manju. Don't misunderstand.' I sighed after explaining everything so patiently.

'I am not misunderstanding you. It's just that I can't endure by loosing you. I felt so sick by seeing you talking to her. I controlled and tried not to show any agitation towards you as much as possible. But I couldn't resist myself. I am sorry. It may be because I love you so much and I can't bear up any more seeing her around. That's why,' she said

'And I already gave you my FB account password. So don't talk such things to me again. I only wants you, and I have nothing to hide from you. Understand that.' I said

'I never lost the trust in you. I love you. I am sorry.'

'It's ok, now leave it.' I said.

She whipped her eyes to clear out the tears that remained in her eyes.

'I would never make a chance for you to meet her up again.' I said leaning back supporting my hands on the bed.

'So it means you both will meet up. Huh!' she shrieked and stood up from the bed facing towards me.

'No! I didn't mean that!' I smirked

'Stupid Bitch!' she said and kneeled on the bed keeping her knees beside my thighs respectively. She grabbed my neck and pushed me. I flopped flat on the bed. She snuggled over to me and we cuddled up once more.

'One sec.!' I pushed her aside and rush towards the door

I peeped out. No one was around and changed my mobile phone's profile from *silent* to *general*. I shut my door and bolted it.

'Everything fine?' she asked as I crawled on to the bed and laid beside her.

'Yes! But one thing.' I slid my hand underneath her head and she rested on my hand. She then turned to my side and wrapped her legs on mine 'Remember not to moan heavily.' I said and kissed her. In between, she pushed my face and sniffed.

'Um…not now.' I mocked.

'Yuck,' she said.

She put her fingers on my lips when I was about to kiss her again.

'What!' I asked.

She lay on my chest, holding my hand. I wrapped up my arms around her and made her comfortable.

'How will we know if your mother would be searching us there?' she asked

'Don't worry. Kishore would give me a ring once everything gets ready down there.' I said and kissed her forehead softly.

I checked my mobile, to make sure that it was been kept underneath the pillow safely.

She hugged me tightly and kissed all the way from my chest, then neck, chin, cheeks and finally stopped at my lips. She lifted her head and looked at me.

'Don't stop,' I raised a little trying to reach her lips. She still moved back and keeping her fingers on my lips. 'What?' I moaned.

'I had put lipstick, today' she said moving her fingers of the other hand in between my hair.

'Still it's your lips. So it doesn't matter' I winked

'Naughty boy friend,' she said and wooed over me. Still her fingers covered my lips. So, I held it to move it aside. But she didn't allowed and continued smooching me on my neck.

'I want your lips,' I whispered in her ears.

'Ok, but don't go erotic like last time.' She smiled,

'Sure baby....' I drooled.

Once she set my lips, *finger-free-lips*, I kissed her and started making out more passionately. Every time, it's the same. She herself makes the rules on every dates and I agrees to everything. And each time we break those rules enthusiastically and thrillingly. For us, nowadays, rules were been meant to be broken.

We cuddled and rolled all over the bed, leaving different marks and stains on my light colored bed sheet. Earlier we made out relaxingly in her house and finally there was a great trouble for me after words. (I still remember the way I had the terror in my mind after coming back to the hostel). But today, there was no responsibility for me and I don't want to get into any trouble. Or her being in some troublesome. So I did what I could do to resist anything that could happen like before. I don't want anything to happen to us that would put us again in problem. I prayed to Jesses, like usual and had a word with him silently in my mind. Then we made out passionately peacefully.

HEADING TO RAILWAY STATION

I took the car for drooping her at the Railway Station. She was sitting beside me and as before. She never talked much while I drove, instead, she listened to music silently sitting beside me.

I didn't had a problem in leaving her to Hyderabad. It's only that, Hyderabad is too far from my home town as compared to Thrissur. It's not that I feel insecure. As a matter of fact, there was no need to feel so, because we both know very well that we can't stay away from each other for too long. Then, what the problem was with me was that, somewhere in my mind, I felt sick in leaving her alone. But unfortunately that's what she was doing.

I relaxed myself by consoling me on realizing that Hyderabad is not as far as United States. I can't neither use sea root nor air root due to the lack of money in my hands. (There was no way, that my father would give enough money for me to go and see my girlfriend. And, sadly, there are no scholarships available for meeting one's love.) As I can afford train tickets, Hyderabad was good. So I let her go there happily.

'Jessie,' I called her softly as I stopped at the traffic signal.

'Um,' she looked at me.

'You must think well and promise me something before you go. Then only I let you leave this car' I said seriously

'What happen' she asked curving her eyebrows.

'Tell me. Will you promise?' I asked

'Say whatever it,' she smiled. 'I will see to give you the promise' she winked.

I muted the stereo in my car.

'I have asked this a lot many times. By now, both of us know what we want to do about this. But, this time I want you to do something for sure.' I looked at the signal as I heard the vehicle behind was blowing hone twice. The signal was still red. I grinned looking at the rear view mirror, watching the stupid guy sitting on the motorbike. 'What I was about to say is that,' I looked at her and she was still looking at me without taking her eyes away, even for a moment. 'Before you come back from Hyderabad, talk to your father that you want to stay here, as before. Then call me and let me know what the final decision is. You understood?' I asked.

She looked forward and thought for a while.

'You don't need to be afraid of talking to your father, Jessie. It's ok if he won't permit you to stay here; but don't lose the chance of getting the permission if he is willing to.' I said. 'For that, at least you must talk to him dear.'

'Hm. I will, but,' she said

'But what? Jessie, if you too want to be with me forever; then be bold and talk to him.' I said

From the last month itself I have been telling her to talk to her dad saying she wants to stay here itself for completing her studies. It's not only for us to be with each other, moreover she never wanted to go and settle abroad.

'Yes, I will. I will let you know what he says.' She shook her head and kept her hand on mine.

'Seriously?' I asked.

Because she always used to divert the topic whenever I asked her to talk to her father about this. One thing was that she was afraid to talk to her father, as he remains stubborn to his decisions. And the other cause was that she herself assumes that he won't allow her wish to stay here; so I always insist her by asking her to try the opportunity to talk with him and if he permits, then everything becomes fine as usual. However, she won't agree to ask him. She always remained on her believes that he will not allow her to stay. (Fathers' daughter, I once murmured and she had not talked to me for a whole day. Still I don't know the reason for why she got angry.) Now, I was happy for her agreeing to talk to her sweet dad. I wish her dad to remain sweet for letting her to stay here for the rest of her life.

Soon the traffic light turned to green making the vehicles move. For me, it symbolized like a green light blown for a *life-time-happiness* with Jessie. I peddled the car forward thinking that her father would take only her sister, but not Jessie. I felt like, soon everything would turn positive. I can see that all unwanted things that made me rustles was moving away from my life, one by one.

When I was fired from the hostel, it was in a state of mind, as if I don't know what to do and what not to do. The only thing that I could sense and feel was that; I missed Jessie a lot. I even feared weather I would lose her due to this, because I was leaving Thrissur. I haven't thought that I would be able to see her this soon.

Similarly, I meant Manju would be remaining as a threat for our relationship. Somehow, that too was been solved immediately. I had a shiver on my spine throughout till, Manju left my home. I expected either Manju would shout or create some problem against Jessie. Instead, she just ignored her. That itself was a great relief then. I too had a fear that Manju would mention to my mother who Jessie was to me. For god's grace, without doing such stupidities she just left out.

Likewise, one by one, all the problems that I faced faded away from me one by one. Now the only sadness remained was the fear of losing Jessie. Though we love each other and we feel like we need each other, I was partially sure that her father won't leave her to India, once they settles there. I don't want that. Now I believe that, likewise how the other problems calmed and how I became happy again; I wish this also would settle soon.

Minding these thoughts, we reached the station. I parked at the parking lot and opened the back door to take her bag. It doesn't had much wait and I carried all the way to the ticket counter. She walked beside me. She didn't said a word yet. It hurts, but if he talks that too hurts, as I would think of missing her soon. If she goes back to Thrissur, then also I would miss her. As Hyderabad is comparatively far away, I feel sick.

'Wait here.' I gave her the bag 'I will take the ticket for you.' I said

As she took her bag from me, I left to the ticket counter. There was a *Indian-queue* that slid towards the left of the counter whole. I also joined them and did what all did in front of me. I too moved each inch forward after every two-minute.

I kept on looking at her. She was sitting on a bench outside the ticket counter, facing me. I could see the wind taking her hair over to her face, and she moved it aside, simultaneously. Meanwhile the same thing happens. Being busy on adjusting her hair, she forgot to mind that I was looking at her. I wanted to call her name allowed, but I did not do it as she was sitting a little distance away and I was not sure the she could here if at all I called her name. I took my mobile and gave her a missed-call. It worked. She looked at me. I smiled. She too smiled and winked at me. We kept on looking at her. At the same time, she too did the same. We played exchanging gestures with our eyes and eyebrows. But both of us didn't understood what we said to each other.

Someone patted on my shoulder from behind. I turned head facing to my left. It was perfectly a stranger. He was beard and was looking; no staring at me, without having any expression on his face. I gestured "what" to him. He too did the same. I shrugged my shoulder.

'If you could see, please step forward. The line is moving!' he informed.

'Ow!' I looked forward. 'I am sorry' I whispered to him.

I moved behind the queue, which was moving towards the right. I reached very near to the counter whole and after the person ahead was me. I looked at where she sat. She was not there! Her bag too was missing. I looked around. The person in front of me left after receiving his ticket. Now it's my turn. I too took a ticket for her.

I moved out of the ticket counter and spotted her near the tea stall. She was standing there keeping her bag near to her leg and sipping her tea slowly and carefully. Both are hot! I walked to her. She saw me coming and I saw the stall-keeper giving her one more glass of tea.

'I thought you left,' I mocked approaching her.

'Huh?' she looked at me and gave her tea glass for me. She took the other one, she had ordered.

'Wow,' I drooled 'I think, you don't want to go?' I asked

'It's not that.' She took a sip of tea. 'I felt alone when you left to the counter.'

'That's because, you don't want to leave me.' I said

'May be,' she said forwarded her glass towards my mouth. 'Have a sip from this.' She said I drank from it. Now she started drinking from that glass. I know she wants me always, and if she leaves to Hyderabad, I definitely can't head there. If she returns to Thrissur, then at least I can jump from my house in the name of meeting some friends of P.C.Thomas Collage.

'That's why I told you not to go there for now.' I said

'Please, I have to.' She said. 'I will call you daily...' she said

'I will miss you.' I said

'Me too...' she said 'Let's have phone sex at night!'

'Hm...' I groaned.

It's not sex that I miss from her. It's her absence. That was what bothering me whenever she leaves to any place other than Thrissur. I want to stop her from going, but at the same time I don't want to hurt her too. I know how much she feel wanted to meet her friend. Like me, friendship means a lot to her too. By now, I learned that, there were a lot many things that remain common in us. And one such thing was friendship.

'We can come on Skype...' she said

'Hm...' I groaned.

I didn't felt to reply anything. Instead, I kept on groaning. I wasn't able to speak. If I speak, my voice may jerk. My heart was already aching. It was like someone wrapping arms tightly over my chest that made me feel difficulty in breathing. It was like, I was not able to inhale but I was breathing. As I look at her, I felt like hugging her and kissing her, without bothering the public around us. I wanted to grab her hand and take her to somewhere less public and make out one more time before she leave. I want to take her for shopping for the last time before her train comes. I wanted to take her to some good restaurant that gives a romantic moment to share with her. I wanted to take as many photos; standing with her, hugging her, kissing her, cuddling over the bed, rapping my arms around her.

'We can come online in facebook…' she said

'Hm…' I groaned again without looking at her.

'Always…' she said

'Hm…' I groaned.

'Stop it Roshen, talk something. Do you want me to stay?' she said

I felt like saying *yes* that could definitely make me happy. If I ask her to stay she will and once, I could make happen everything that I just dreamt. I would become more than happy, but she would only act joyful around me. I know if I won't leave her now, she gets hurt, and so I.

'You must go' I fondled her hair and looked to her eyes.

'Should I?' she asked

I withdrawn my hand from her hair and stepped back to throw my emptied tea glass.

'You should.' I said

'Then why you are dull?' she asked

'Um…nothing.' I took her bag in my hand.

'Is it because I am leaving too far away from you? I told I will call you.'

'I would be having the same feeling if you return to your home. So it's not that. Go and enjoy as usual. And don't forget to talk to your father.'

'Sure,' she said and out her tea glass too in the *"Use Me"*.

We walked to the platform and sat on an empty bench and kept her bag beside..

'I think your train has delayed for twenty minutes.' I said

'Doesn't matter. You know something?' she said and wrapped her hand around mine. 'I can't be comfortable without talking to you. So be available when I call you. Charge your phone regularly. Don't go off-line. And eat properly and go for your classes.'

'Yeah. Ok,' I said 'Is this the only baggage you have?' I asked.

'Can't you see?' she snapped

'What?' I prodded

'Do you hear what I say? If I couldn't talk to you, I won't be having food. That's all.'

'Oh my God! Jessie, don't be a kid. I hear everything you say. My phone would be there always with me. And if for any reason I couldn't attend your call, don't think that I am doing it purposefully. And for that, don't starve yourself.' I said

'But-'

'Jessie, if I found out you skipped your food, then I won't be eating for two days. Mind it.'

'Ok, compromise. I thought you were not listening to what I was talking to you.'

'I am sorry.' I said. 'I will call you sweetheart.'

She smiled and laid her head on my shoulder. We didn't talked much till her train came. Time rushed to bring her train to the station. All rushed to the compartments and I took her to hers. Usually the A/c compartments won't be having any kind of rushing like the other compartments.

We reached her seat and I put her bag under her seat. There was no one in that berth. She sat down. She pulled my hand and made me sit beside her. She looked at me.

'I will come back within a week. Promise.' She said and kissed me.

She stretched forward her hands, and hugged me tightly. She kissed my neck.

'Awch!' I exclaimed as she bit my ears.

'Kid' she giggled

I caressed her hair lying on her shoulder.

'I wish you could also have come with me.' She whispered in my ears.

'At last, you will make me come with you.' I said

'Let's elope?' she jumped excitedly and looked at me. Her eyed twinkled as usual.

'Later,' I said 'If your dad decides to take you to U.S.'

She laughed. 'He won't. I won't go.' She said

I heard the train whistling aloud. The time for her to leave me was too short.

'Come here.' I said. She came closer.

'The train leaves the station in a minute.' I said

She looked down. I raised her chin and made her look at me.

'Jessie,'

'Um.'
The train Whistles again.
'I want to kiss you,' I said.
'I need a long one' she smiled.
I held her cheeks as she closed her eyes.
We kissed.

SIX MONTHS FELT
LIKE A DECADE

This time, I cracked my engineering entrance examination. My mother became happy. My father became proud. But, the person whom I felt to be wanted the most was not anywhere near me. She talked and encouraged me a lot when my parents was scolding me for losing the opportunity to study from a good and reputed institute like P.C.Thomas Institute.

It's been one month, three weeks and four days, since she left me. I still felt alone without her. What surrounded me were just her facebook messages, text-messages that flashed on my old Sony Ericson and her sweet and melodious voice through phone/Skype daily.

The day she reached Hyderabad, I got her phone call saying she talked to her father. When her father did not allow her to stay back in India, she behaved in a hostile manner to him. After narrating everything, she immediately disconnected the call without allowing me to say a word. She did not even let me talk. She wailed throughout the phone call. I know she would be crying and shredding all her available tears. I called her back. Though she attended, she was not able to talk to me on the phone. I only could hear her weeping.

She shouldn't have talked to her father in that way. Otherwise, slowly and steadily, things might have got better. Now it's all became more worse. I came online in facebook. She was not there. I waited. Still she was offline.

"Come online baby" I texted her and started waiting with a hope that she would come online, in the very next moment.

Meanwhile, I started replying to random friends when they started chatting with me. Kishore came online and quickly went offline messaging a "hi".

I kept quiet for the recent messages I was getting. I didn't replied. It was no one else, other than Manju. I don't understand why she want to mingle with me even after showing who I am dating with. I wanted to chat with her, when I thought of flirting with her. But there was no time I didn't thought of Jessie. And Jessie and her memories stopped me from flirting with my ex-girlfriend. Still I used to keep her as a fiend on facebook. And for me, there was no reason for that. I just didn't felt to un-friend or block her. So she remained in my facebook-friend-list.

Manju sent me seven messages. It red;

"I am sorry for coming to your house that day"

"Sorry for talking with you in that way in front of that girl"

"Sorry for being a disturbance for you"

"Don't you feel to reply me? At least once?"

"I soooo sorry for creating all the problems if I caused you any troubles"

"I said enough sorry"

"Please give at least one reply!!! I won't come to see you again"

Reading all of those messages, I felt that I am becoming too stubborn with her. What if she might have understood everything and she herself might have changed. Any way once, she was the one who cared me a lot and she was the one whom I loved for the first time. If not rejoining the relationship, at least I could forgive her.

"It's ok" I typed in her chat box. I hit send.

"Thank you for replying" Manju replied

This way we started chatting.

"You are welcome." – Roshen Samuel

"It's not nice to see you becoming so formal" – Manju M

"☺" – Roshen Samuel

"Hope you don't hate me now" – Manju M

"Not much" – Roshen Samuel

"☺☺ So chweeet…" - Manju M

"Not much" – Roshen Samuel

"Yes. You are" – Manju M

"If you say so ;)" – Roshen Samuel

"So you don't hate me no?" – Manju

"No manju…." – Roshen Samuel

"☺ So you see me like the same old Manju" – Manju M

"Means?" – Roshen Samuel

"Like….without hating…" – Manju M

"☺ Sure" – Roshen Samuel

"I love you Roshen. I want you in my life like the olden days. Lets' together make the coming days golden days. I am missing you soo…much. Please take me back.

Please don't misunderstand me for what I said now. Don't think that I was miss using the opportunity. But this was something that I have to say for a long time, but you were not even allowing me to smile at you relaxingly. So I don't get enough courage to say this. And this was my last resort to tell what's going on in my mind. Still I love you. I love you so much…." – Manju M

I didn't replied further.

This. This was the only reason I don't want to talk with her. Seeing all type of sorry, I thought she might have changed.

I admired at the chat box for sometime without typing anything. I was thinking what to tell her now, or just to end this conversation without replying. I had no idea about what to do with this. I got irritated and went off line.

I dialed Jessie's number again and the ring went. But she disconnected the call immediately. I thought, she could be still crying. I don't feel good whenever she cried. When she did, I wanted her to be beside me.

Again, I signed-in into my FB account. As usual, this time also there was unread messages. One was from Rihash. It red - "Why you logged-out so quickly bro?". And I replied – "Long story bro"

The other unread message was the most tempting. It was from Manju. I thought it would be the continuation of the previous. I felt the urge to read it. I opened her chat box and it was so unusual that it almost shocked me.

There was a message send to Manju from my account, as a reply to hers. It red strange.

"Fuck off Manju. Don't be an ass here. Why you want to talk to me again and again when I hate that? One more time, if you repeat this, I am going to make you cry. Mind it."

Ow shit! It may be Jessie. Yes. It's her. She only could open my account other than me. She was the only one who had my password. I never thought giving my password would create this impact on the incoming hot messages.

Finally, Manju replied:

"What"

"Why"

I think she only knows two question words in English language. It's time for her to learn more. She should have asked me with "Who", then I could at least tell her that Jessie sent that message.

Anyway now everything got settled and I was happy that Manju blocked me on facebook in the name of that message. I feel quiet relaxed now. I wish Jessie could come online. But still there was no green beside her name. She has not come online yet. I took my phone to call her again. As I took the phone in my hand it's screen flashed with her name. It was a message from Jessie. I opened the message and red it.

"Come on Skype, you Horny bastard"

I turned my laptop on and got myself ready for Skype. I was not sure what she was about to. But she was angry with me. May be because of the frustration she was having because of her father not allowing her to stay. Moreover, when she saw the conversation between Manju and I, she couldn't may able to tolerate. I can understand her well. Now I want to make her understand what had happened. As she trusts me so much, I believe, making her understand would be quiet easy.

I accepted for her video call on Skype. Everything was much clear on the camera. In her background, I could see the television, and the Hindi movie *"Ashique 2"* was been played at the channel Sony max. On the wall behind her, someone's shadow was moving back and forth. It was becoming larger and smaller instantly.

Jessie has not started speaking yet. Instead, she was just staring at me without even blinking her eyes even at once. Her hair was a mess and the stain of tears on her face was clearly visible on my screen. I know she was crying throughout for a longer time, but apart from that, her mood at present was not that good. Because being sad and getting angry at the same time was not a good combination. That too, her angry would be for the reason that I talked to Manju.

I smiled looking at her. 'Hi' I said, after some time when her reaction doesn't changed.

'I don't feel to smile.' She said sternly.

'Still you look cute.' I said, still smiling

'Why you did chatting with Manju?' she asked

'Is that the reason, why you are angry?' I asked

'I asked you first.' She snapped

'Oh God! She said a lot of sorry and apologized to me. So-' I said

'Saying bloody "I love you" to you is not the way to apologize. YOU ARE MINE.' She said

'But I didn't replied anything to that no,' I said

'But I did.' She said

'Good. I don't have any complaints for that baby,' I said

'No need to show any over affection towards me.' She said

'Why? You are my baby. I love you.' I drooled. That was what I do with her always, despite caring her mood.

'You call me baby, and then go and chat with her.' She said

'No dear. You are mistaken. I only need you.' I said smiling. But she haven't yet smiled.

'Why you need me? Any way I would be going to U.S. You happily go, fuck her and make babies.' She chided.

'Don't say that. You know me. I kept smiling until now. Now don't make me angry.' I said

'Are you still at your friend's house?' I asked to divert from the topic because I know this will only end up in a quarrel. I noticed her eyes becoming wet.

'Then, where else?' she said in a yank.

'Can you smile? Please.' I muttered.

Finally she did. I became happy. She too became happy. That's how it happens nowadays. We would start to quarrel and finally we solve it by ourselves as quick as possible.

VANISHED FROM HYDERABAD

Days after she reached at her friend's house at Hyderabad, her father came and the stayed at a hotel room for two days. Within the second day her sister went there with the luggage and her uncle too escorted her sister from Thrissur. As she ones said, no one could change her father's plans. He always used to stick to what he decides. Soon they left to Indiana, North America and she called me for the last time from the airport, before she boarded the plane. I sensed that she was weeping silently from the other end of the phone, while narrating everything about her father's quick plan. I couldn't console her. It was too hard for me to settle myself after hearing that.

I was having the frustration of not been able to bring things in our favor. I was not angry with her, because it was not her fault. I know that. Then earlier I got angry with her was because she was not ready to talk to her father regarding this. Yes. She know what will happen. And she had mentioned that to me a several hundred times. But I was never ready to accept that. May be because I love her more than the realities I have to accept in life.

I wanted to hold her back. I never thought the kiss we had in the train would become our last real kiss and the freaking out make outs would never happen again. The hardest thing was to accept that I was not able to see her at least once, before she left with her father. I felt so alone without her.

The next day, she send me a text message from a new number. It red;

"I know you loved me. I too love you more than you did. I cut my vain. – Your Jessie"

I became restless as I read her message. I called her immediately, from my landline phone, without bothering to where I am calling. But I very well know, that the call I am doing now was an ISD and definitely I was not going to put the receiver down unless my ear starts to pain. It's the same always.

It rings and someone picks up the call. 'Hello'

'Um...is Jessie there? I am-' I tried to introduce myself but the one at the other end didn't mind to know who was calling. Instead, she called out her name aloud.

'Who is it?' I could hear the footsteps louder. Hope that was hers.

'Hello' she said.

'What you did to yourself Jessie? Are you insane?' I blushed as soon as I heard her voice on my receiver.

'Roshen!' She yelled

'Yeah it's me.' I said 'Hope I can still be concerned of you,'

'Why are you talking like this? If not who else would be there to be concerned?' she mocked

'Stop kidding Jessie! And who asked you to cut your arm?' I shouted

'Listen…' she said

'I am not the one who should listen. It's you! It's you, who have gone mad already. So you want to listen. Listen to me first, you ass hole.' I quivered on the phone

'Roshen, let me explain,' She said

'Have you thought of me you idiot?' I asked 'What would have happened if something had happened to you?'

'That's why this happened' she said

'What!' I said

'I was just kidding' she said

'Huh? So nothing happened? You didn't cut your hand?'

'Let me speak. Please…' She said

'Tell.' I sighed

'I was pealing apple and accidently I cut my wrist. Before that, I was arguing with my father telling him about what all reasons I could justify to make a change in his decision. In that talk my wrist got cut accidently. But my father and sister thought that I did it out of anger in not allowing me to stay with my grandparents. Seeing this, my sister was got panicked. She told that she would convince my father and make him change his decision.'

'Are you hurt a lot?' I spoke gently

'Not as much as I got hurt when I saw you talking to her.' She said

'Who?' I asked

'I am talking about Manju' she said

'Jessie, I have already told you many times what's happening between us.' I said

'Yeah, I understand. But still it hurts when I know you still keep in touch with each other.' She said

'Just trust me. We are not keeping in touch. She even sent me messages in facebook and I never replied. The previous time I thought she was talking just as a friend, so I too mingled with her friendly. I never thought she would take it in the other way.' I said

'I do trust you, but-' she said

'Moreover, I never hide anything from you. So why you are having this insecurity?' I interrupted her.

'No, I am not having any insecurity feeling. I am fine.' She said

'What are you doing?' I asked

'I am tying a bandage over my wrist.' she said

'Is it still paining?' I asked

'A little' she said.

'But, how come your wrist got cut while pealing? According to what you said, it should be your fingers no?' I asked.

'I told you, I didn't do it purposefully! Why you are haunting on that?' she said. I felt her getting irritated.

'What happened?' I asked as I felt the change in her tone.

'Mmhm nothing. When you repeatedly ask the same thing, somehow I am getting irritated.' She said

'Is it?' I said 'The same thing is with me Jessie. When you frequently talks about Manju connecting to me I too feel annoyed. Also that I am getting angry out of frustration. Am I showing my anger towards you?'

'But that is different! That's because I see her getting involved in your life! Therefore, there is a reason for me to get unsecured with you.'

'So, it's the same with me too. As I came to know your hand got cut I became more concerned of it. Because you are that important for me. So I feel to know your condition and hence, I become concerned of you. You got it?'

'I told you, that my hand got cut just because of my carelessness. It was an accident and I didn't really did it purposefully like I said to my dad. And I also told the reason why I lied to my father.'

'Ok, I know. But when I felt a little strangeness in your talk… that's why I behaved that way. It's because you are the only person I think about, all day and night.' I said 'And when I ask why you want to get irritated?'

'Because you are asking and I am telling the same thing again and again. That's why I got irritated.'

'If you are feeling so, then just imagine how I will feel when you talk about someone whom I never care anymore.'

'Ok….Sorry.'

'I know you will say this stupid word after all these mess. I called you to talk and you are the only one who spoiled my mood now.'

'I will change your mood then. Let's talk about anything?'

'Means'

'Our…future…about our life…and of course our usual phone sex too. I miss it a lot nowadays.'

'Then, let's start with the last one.'

'No. Let's talk something else first.'

'Sex first.' I chided.

'Last!' She blushed

'Why Jessie? You made me disappointed and now you are responsible to make me on' I argued.

'I didn't say "no" to that! I just said that; now let us talk about anything else. Otherwise I know you will sleep-off even after phone sex.' She snapped

'You also used to drift-off' I protested

'Then what! If you dozes-off then what else should I do alone?'

'Ok, I won't sleep.' I tried to convince her.

'Whatever, but I want to talk to you about-' she said

'But we did enough of talking Jessie. If you start talking then you will say something that I don't like. So, let's have change,' I interfered.

I feared that she might again talk about Manju. This feeling was not unusual for me. Every time she talks about Manju, it made my mind weaker to response to her questions about her. Though she says that she trusts me, I know how she feels with the presence of Manju. But unfortunately, however I tried to avoid her from my life, somehow she appears. It brought the usual terror in my mind that made me panic, thinking she may slip away from me in the name of Manju. I don't want that. I can't bear it either.

'Nothing like that. I just want to talk about....um... about, I mean...' Her voice faded and she paused. 'Oh my God!'

'What happened?' I asked realizing something was wrong there.

'My dad came, will call you later. Bye.' She said after a moment.

'So what! Spare some time na!' I shrieked out.

'Next time for sure I will spare my time for you. Promise.' She snapped

'This is the reason why I told you not to make any kind of useless argument with me.' I said 'As if we always tug together and have enough time to spare together. Shouldn't we have talked about something that was pleasant?' I murmured.

'Next time I will accompany you with pleasant things *only*. But this time, you jerk-off alone. But don't think anyone else other than me. Mind it. Will call you later. Bye.' She quivered.

Though she disconnected soon, she called me after some time and it continued until late night. We talked about nothing, but certainly regarding everything that made us happy. And of course every call after a fight would turn romantic.

The way we talked gave us the hope that we would meet again. We started discussing our life, and it started mattering to me more than my present life. She already became a part of my life and I became serious about it. However, nothing would happen any soon, when we talk about the way of our living in the future; it sounds promising. It holds the depth of our relationship and love, strong and bonded forever.

FORTUNATELY OR UNFORTUNATELY

'Seems like everything is changing bit by bit' I muted.

'Why so?' he asked

'I felt so.' I said

'Is it about Jessie?' he asked

'Yes.' I said. 'It's been months since she had called me, talked to me, and even no messages from her. I feel lost Joyal.' I said.

I thought telling everything to someone about what hurts me will reduce the pain in me. So I decided to talk about it to Joyal, because he was the one how know everything about us; expect our make-outs. Unfortunately, it didn't worked. Nothing changed in me by talking to Joyal. I was still ailing. The more I tell about the way I get hurt when I miss her, the more I get upset. Still, what I only feel wanted. I feel to meet her, hug her and never leave her. Or at least I may feel better by talking to her.

Because of not been able to get what I want the most, I was not able to care eat food at time. I was not able to watch television. I just got paranoid and continuously started flicking channels without stopping anywhere. I didn't even give a pause at Fashion TV. Even the 16 GB pen-drive that was been filled up with new movies, songs, and HD pornographies are lying simply inside the draw of my table. I have not touched it at least once, since I took it from one of my old classmate. (I collected that from him while coming back from McDonalds' after meeting Manju.)

I started sitting simply at home. Though it made me feel more alone, I began to love loneliness. Or through that, somehow I was learning to live without her. But never was able to forget her. Not even a single moment. Every time her memories haunts me.

'Hm…I didn't know that part.' He said.

'What you knew then?' I asked.

'Em… I thought you people are still in touch. By the way, I forgot to mention something to you. Jessie send me a letter' he said

'See…that's what I said. It's changing. She is changing drastically.' I blushed 'She send letter to you, but not me! I think it's getting over.'

'Man! Don't over react. First, let me complete what I have tell you. It's true that she sent it to me but, actually what's inside it was not for me. It's for you. She called me days before and told; she was not sure that your address that she knows was correct. So she sent it to me instead of sending to a wrong address. She asked me to hand over the letter to you safely.' he explained.

I was relieved immediately after knowing that it was all my assumptions on our relationship. I misunderstood that I lost her. Eventually, I have something from her! Moreover, it's a letter.

I was imagining certain situations on my own. That made me obsessed. Now I am all right. Perfectly all right. I know that she is mine. Like always and always forever.

'So,' I gushed. 'Where is the letter?' I asked.

'I sent it to you already. It might have reached you.' He said

'Ok, let me see. Bye, will call you later.' I said and stepped out of the room for the first time in the day. Because I never came out of the room for any purpose other than for having food. I went to the kitchen in search of my mother. Where else I could found her. She was there. Peeling oranges. If I wait in my room for some more time, probably those oranges would have been delivered into my room. These days my mother takes extra care for me. May be because I cleared entrance this time, or may be because I look like someone who really starves.

But now, I am out of my room in search of the letter. I want it. I don't know what's happening around me and my room for days. So I have to ask someone whether the postman came any of these days. Asking my mother would be more apt than asking for it to my father. Although he doesn't like me sitting inside the room all the time. "No one here has considered you as a prisoner." He used to say.

'Mom, do I have any letter?' I asked casually, as if I used to get letters regularly.

'What letter?' she asked pleasantly.

'Um… I mean…did post man give any letters.' I asked

'Ah, yes. It's there in the living room I think.' She said and within no time, I was in the living room.

The teapoy was the only place where I could get the letter. But I really have to take strain to fetch it from there. There was a pool of newspapers on it. And fishing out the letter from those was really a tough job.

I don't want the letter to get misplaced. Either I don't want it to be lost. As she wished, I want to get it in my hands safely and perfectly. Hence, it is in my hand now. I entered my room with it and bolted the door. I sat on the bed and sighed out.

I held her letter in my hand happily as it was the only message from her that I got after months. I got hope. I know she can't stay too long without talking to me. And I believed that she know that I too can't stay too long without getting her presence. Finally, this letter was a relief from the suffocations I was suffering.

I opened the envelope and took the folded piece of ruled paper from it. We never had a practice of sending letters to each other. I never had experienced it yet. This is the first time I am reading a letter in my life. So far, it was only facebook messages, Skype, phone calls and text messages. Moreover, we never had a situation of being away from each other for this long. Unfortunately, we couldn't use any of the source of communication, which we were using to keep in touch.

The taste of reading letter was so different that I was able to feel her presence, as if I could feel that she was there somewhere too close to me. Unfolding the letter, I saw her handwriting. It was much better than mine. The content was too short. I started reading it anxiously.

Dear Roshen,

This is the hardest letter I have ever had to write, but it is necessary that I let you know. I tell you that I have met so many friends, but you will always have a special place in my life and in my memory.

I am sorry.

Jessie

P.S. Please read my e-mail.

I loved her blindly. Realizing it came to an end for real hurts me more than before. She shouldn't have sent this to me. If she ends this without letting me know, I would have still think that she was quiet unable to contact me because of the restrictions of her father. I would have believed that way. So that I can always remain, believing that she always loves me. She herself mentioned a break-up though it's been said indirectly. Now I understood why she was not calling me. This would be the reason why she was avoiding me by not taking any of my calls or not by coming online on facebook.

Now, it's not just that I miss her. It was as if I lost something from my life. I partially started fiddling between Manju and Jessie. When I tried to forget Jessie, I feel like betraying our relationship. Maybe because, still I love her just like I did always. I still feel wanted.

Every time I cursed myself so much for mingling with Manju. Even after knowing that Jessie doesn't like me talking to Manju. It's the only mistake I have done. I started to think the reason why she wrote this letter. I still can't believe that she decided for a break-up. I know that she decided to stay with her father because of witnessing me interacting with Manju. Whatever I said to Jessie about everything happened between Manju and me; I felt that Jessie still feels that I always kept a relationship with Manju. Likewise, I started realizing that she lost all the trust in the relationship with me. I started to imagine all kinds of ways that was probable for Jessie to think about me and on those terms, I started cursing myself for doing what she does not liked. Our relationship had became a past tense now.

In my life, everything was happening all of a sudden even without giving me a chance to regain. Everything from falling in love for the first time in my life with a girl (Manju), all the happy and sad moments in that relationship and eventually I took a back from our relationship as she broke my heart. Flowingly I lost my entrance exam and for repeating it and to run away from Manju's presence I decided to join P.C. Thomas Entrance Couching classes at Thrissur. When I started enjoying life again, I became happy once more. The only reason for that was Jessie. Though she was just a girlfriend who made me happy, eventually she became my soul mate for me, in all the sense. She was the only reason why I forgot all my past and started a new life. Still my faith never allowed me to be happy. She too left. But, this time somehow I passed the entrance exam.

Thinking all these, I found my eyes been filled-up. Yes. Tough I never cried in my life, now I felt lost. It ached a lot. I felt my hart getting shrunk as time passes. I realized my life sucks and it never gives happiness all the time. But loosing Jessie was not the case of being sad; rather it was like been unstable and breathless. I would have felt better if someone would have took my life at the same time when I lost her completely. I never was this sad and hurt while I left Manju. Jessie knew how important she was in my life. Still she did this. Instead of sending this letter, she would have stayed there itself and I could have waited until we could meet each other in any of the coming days.

Who Else Will I Wait For

This is the seventh time I was reading her letter. Every time I felt lost as I read her name at the end. What's the use of having me in her memory instead of having me in her life. I would always think, each time as I finish reading it. As I read the letter again; this time I noticed "P.S.". I always left it carelessly. I was not able withstand after reading her name at the end. It flashes all the pleasant memories of her at once. I opened my e-mail and checked my index. There were 104 e-mails and all of them were notifications from facebook. I searched for her mail eagerly. I sighed out of relief as I got it. It showed *loading* as I clicked on it. Thus, I waited until the mail was got opened.

It's subject red: "*I have not changed yet Roshen.☺*"

I continued reading further.

> *I miss you a lot Roshen. Maybe a lot more than you miss me.*
>
> *I know that I did hurt you a lot through the letter. Forgive me. This would be the first and the last time I am hurting you. I am sorry.*
>
> *But Roshen, I feel like it's time for us to break-up. You know I never had dated anyone before, other than*

you. Then why I loved you more, even after knowing that you had a past life is because I realized how much you loved me. And why I do this now is because I came to know how much Manju haunts in your life. You may have any kind of feelings towards Manju. But the very first love in one's life can't be forgotten so easily? Right? (Maybe that would be the reason why you still keep Manju as your friend. You also chat with her.)

Though you had told me several times that you never loved Manju anymore...not that I didn't trusted you. I do. But, I feel that something is wrong in what we are doing to her. Because, she needs you and that's why she was stalking you all the time; even after knowing you are in a relationship with me. The more you avoid her the more she may be cursing you and me. And maybe that's why our relationship has got this faith. See, you there and me here. I think it won't work as long as Manju moves away completely from your life. It's you, who had moved out of the affair with Manju. So there is a reason why she is behind you.

I won't blame her Roshen. Roopa told the whole thing about you people to me. She also told that, after all still Manju is behind you, with a hope that you will come back to her soon.(If that has to happen, I won't be in between) Roopa also told me that Manju always says her that she will get you again. (Don't get angry with Roopa for revealing everything to me.)

Don't worry... here, I am fine though not perfectly happy. I already talked to my father about a college in India. It's in Hyderabad. I would be joining there for MA English. So, definitely I would be would be coming there after three years. And these three years, I will be here with my father. If you want to be with Manju again, I wish you a happy life with her. (I won't say no if you decide so) or else wait till I come there and we can... If you don't want to leave Manju forever, then please keep my letter safely forever with you.

And Roshen! One more thing. I didn't mean to have a break-up as such and I never wanted that to happen. (As you know, I will never think about it.) Neither, I meant to leave me. (A part of me tells that I need you baby & so I can't live without you☹.)

Still I love you Roshen. I never did hate you. (It hurts to hurt you, but this is the right thing to do)

If you want to be with Manju, then keep that letter as a gift from your long lost friend. Or if you want me, I need to let you know that I will be back. So I sent this mail.

I will come...

(I want to complete that wish. Remember? We planned for a date at the City Center that day, but you left leaving me behind. This time hope we could have a date there again and definitely I need to kiss you in the escalator.)

I don't know what I am doing is right for you, but
I just felt to let you know what's there in my mind.
(Because I don't have anything to hide from you.)
Bye,
Your own Jessie…

Days Passed…

I started waiting for her with a hope that she would definitely call me as soon as she lands back here in India. It was just her insecurity about Manju, which made her do all these. I was not angry with Jessie for reacting this way. As a girl she has to do atleast this. Though I was sad about this, I can't be mad at her. Because Jessie was still far more better than Manju. I was happy to wait for Jessie, even throughout my entire life.

I never wanted to think about compromising with Manju even for a moment. It was just that I reply to her non-problematic messages in facebook. But, if that makes her insecure, I know to find a solution.

I opened my laptop and connected to the internet. Immediately, I took the facebook and typed my user ID: roshen$samuel's@gmail.com

Then the password: transcription MANjuJESSIE

The home page appeared and the first thing I noticed was the notifications. There was one friend request and nine messages.

I accepted the friend request and eagerly took the unread messages. Surprisingly all the nine messages where from Jessie Joseph. I became so happy and thrilled. Quickly I opened it and red it.

1) "Hi Roshen. Hope you are fine. I have sent you a letter. Contact Joyal.
2) "Where are you? I always wait for you to come online. But you never come online these days"
3) "Are you angry for not been able to contact me?"
4) "Is it the reason why you are not bothering me anymore?"
5) "No facebook nowadays?"
6) "Entered which college?"
7) "I learned to settle up without you"
8) "hmf! I just wanted to inform you, before doing it. That's why I waited for you hoping someday you will come online. Now I will leave this message, so that you will let know that I AM GOING TO DEACTIVATE MY FACEBOOK ACCOUNT.
9) Bye… my sweet friend…

I searched for Jessie Joseph. Five-six similar names appeared in the result, but none was my girl's profile.

As these messages was been sent before she sent her e-mail, I believed that she would come back as mentioned in her mail. I was happy for that atleast. I was happy for giving me a hope. I was happy for assuring me that she would come back. I was just sad about deactivating her facebook account.

Quickly I did un-friend Manju. I also search Jessie almost all the time in a day, expecting her to re-activate her account again. There were no signs of her profile and no messages from her. I even feared that she might have got a new boyfriend there and might also created a new account by deactivating the current one. But I just considered this thought of mine, as a worst night mare. Instead, I just did what we do always in this kind of situations. I trusted her. I never again allowed such bad thoughts to haunt me.

I tried many thing to not to get such evil thoughts about her. That was the time when the college admission came through allotment. It helped. Certainly it was a distraction for me. Only from such evil thoughts. Still my dreams were all about her. Not even felt to flirt with someone. The first days of colleges itself was good because Kishore and Roopa was with me in the same department.

Imagine childhood friends tugging together in tuition classes, entrance- couching classes, and even in the allotted college. It's was a very good luck for me to get them in the same class. Kishore and I sat in the same bench and Roopa occupied at front. Just in front of us. The days… weeks… months…and years… went just as in the calendar. In between, the examinations accompanied; which Roopa was always a last resort for me to pass those exams. As always, she was my teaching-machine!

Apart from college, my life was been just balanced by enjoying with friends. I bought a new bike. I bought a new mobile phone. I started partying. I started smoking less and stopped watching porn. (That happened long before itself. Jessie was the reason behind it.) Likewise, three long years have passed by shortly celebrating new-year and Christmas with scotch, whisky, vodka and of course beer and wine too as the beginners.

I gradually started taking care of things at home. "I became smart." My father rarely says. Yes, maybe because I am going to get a job after this final year of college life, or may be because the three years that Jessie mentioned was getting over.

Epilogue

After, three long years …

This is the day; I was waiting for so long. Jessie called me in the morning from her old flat where she lived with her grandparents at Thrissur. We talked like the kindergarten kids; who talks for the first time after a long time. (She has not dated anyone else there!) Though I told that I would come over there the next day, she didn't wants that. Instead, we decided to meet up after she gets settled there with all her belongings. She also told me that she had to arrange everything for me at her flat, so that we could remain there calm and quiet for sometime after a long time.

I always wanted the same. Jessie. Still I haven't understood what she mean to say through the letter. When asked to Jessie she told me to tear it away and she told me what had really happened to her. She had beautifully misunderstood that I am still having an relationship with Manju. And that was because I still keep her as a friend in facebook; I guessed that already. Moreover, the misunderstanding came after Jessie saw the message in Manju's chat box from my account. However it is, now everything was back on the track. Therefore, both of us are happy than usual.

Hence, I am here at the same City Center waiting for her. When she called me in the morning, she had asked me to come here. She wanted to start our settled relationship peacefully and happily ever after, from where we used to date before we parted. It was here; The City Center. After, completing our wish and spending time outside; we would return to her flat. Then my night stay had arranged at Joyal's house. (I will only go to Joyal's house only at late night, after spending enough time with her.)

"Where are you?" She texted me when I kept waiting for her at the City Center mall. I rushed to the entrance. Yes there she was. Though she went abroad; she hasn't changed. Still she looks the same, with her untied silky hair, shiny black cute eyes, the charming smile on her face are all the same. As I kept drooling at her, she came near to me and held my hand. I could feel the similar warmth I felt the last time she touched me.

'Seeing me for the first time?' she asked

'Better than first time.' I said without blinking my eyes, at least once.

'Come! Let's ramp up' she yanked my hand.

'Awch!' I shrieked as her nails pierced into my skin.

'Sorry, sorry, sorry,' she chanted

'It's ok. When you started growing this much long nails?' I asked and she simply winked.

'This is long enough to cut some ones neck.' I mocked holding her hands and looked at her nails.

'It's for you.' She said bring it in front of my eyes and I looked at her. 'I would have cut both of your neck if I have seen you with Manju.' She smirked

'Will you stop that?' I said miffed dejectedly.

'I am sorry.' She smiled 'come, let's go…' she put her hand around my waist and I held her closer to me keeping my hand around her shoulder. 'I love you Roshen…' she muttered

'Then next time, ask your father to come here if he wants to see you' I mocked and she punched me playfully.

I was happy to regain back what I thought that I was lost. We are here, not to purchase anything. The escalator. That was our aim. The kiss in the escalator… then dinner at her home…then makes out…and the scenario continues…

Joyal became happy with his girlfriend, Arini. Yeah, it's new. He understood how Avita was. They broke-up within months and Arini came into his life. She is his classmate in his new college.

Suresh had never turned up again to Thrissur. We never came to know anything about him. He just left to Coimbatore, after his course and no more contacts with him.

In my college, the rumors that "Kishore and Roopa are in love" spread like a forest fire. But who cares. We are what we are. Good and thick friends. Jessie is now in our gang. Whenever Joyal comes to Palakkad, Jessie too comes along with him.